Willy Vlautin is the prize
The Motel Life (2005), whic
Northline (2007), *Lean on Pe*
IMPAC Prize, and *The Free* (2014). He is also the frontman of the
band Richmond Fontaine, whose albums include *Post to Wire* and
Thirteen Cities, and guitarist and songwriter in the band The Delines,
whose debut album, *Colfax Avenue*, was released in 2014. Originally
from Reno, he now lives in Portland, Oregon.

www.willyvlautin.com

Further praise for *The Free:*

'Original and compelling.' *Guardian*

'Excellent . . . Vlautin's great achievements are the moments of in-
tense light he blends into this brave, dark story.' *Metro*

'This beautifully, leisurely paced work subsequently unfolds around
three major narrative strands, interwoven like a fugue . . . Vlautin
has produced perhaps his finest work to date.' *Irish Independent*

'Beautiful and haunting . . . Whatever Vlautin breaks down in you,
he builds back up. Walking away from *The Free*, I felt a renewed
sense of humanity and hope . . . In my estimation, no writer is doing
more important work.' *Los Angeles Review of Books*

'Willy Vlautin demonstrates an impressive ability . . . [His] characters face their burdens with unwavering dignity, and Vlautin's
affection for them is evident at every turn . . . Vlautin's unadorned
narrative is affecting; these unassuming characters bore into us in
surprising ways.' *New York Times*

'Vlautin's prose is influenced by what's often called the "kitchen
sink reali . . . By

the end, the book has achieved a kind of bleak grace, and with it something rare in fiction: an unsentimental realisation of goodness.' *Prospect*

'A masterful cry from the heart.' *Catholic Herald*

'Already on many "book of the year" lists, Vlautin's fourth novel takes you deep . . . [his] skill lies in making you root for all involved.' *ShortList*

'There are similarities to both Steinbeck and Haruf, but Vlautin has something all of his own, something that lurks in the interstices of his simple, undeclarative sentences, a pragmatic kindness, a knowledge that his people may not make it out the other side in one piece and yet for all that life goes on . . . You come away from Vlautin painfully aware of the blessings of your life, cherishing what you have and maybe others don't.' *Bookmunch*

'There is the rare blending of intelligence, lightness and seriousness that only the greatest art evokes.' *Caught by the River*

'Another outstanding book from one of America's most underappreciated artists.' George Pelecanos

'I couldn't recommend it more highly.' Ann Patchett

'Brilliant and beautiful . . . what a gorgeous book. There are so few writers out there with such ambitious humility.' Sarah Hall

'Vlautin is one of the bravest novelists writing . . . It takes real courage to write about ordinary people . . . Willy Vlautin tells us who really lives now in our America, our city in ruins.' Ursula K Le Guin

'It is a dazzling original novel, profound and full of hope. And it will stay with you long after you finish reading it.' *Bite the Book*

---

by the same author

THE MOTEL LIFE
NORTHLINE
LEAN ON PETE

The Free

Willy Vlautin

ff

FABER & FABER

First published in 2014
by Faber and Faber Limited
Bloomsbury House,
74–77 Great Russell Street,
London WC1B 3DA

Typeset by Faber and Faber Limited
Printed and bound by CPI Group (UK) Ltd, Croydon CR0 4YY

A CIP record for this book
is available from the British Library

ISBN 978–0–571–30030–3

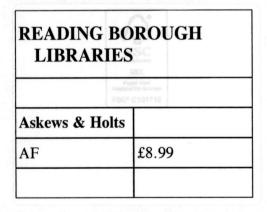

2 4 6 8 10 9 7 5 3 1

For the Patron Saint of Nurses,
Camillus de Lellis

Leroy Kervin opened his eyes to see a woman in a blue-and-white-starred bikini holding a pneumatic drill. He could see her blond hair and high heels and thin, long legs. For the first time in seven years he could see her without blurred vision. He could see her clearly from the glow of a small colored nightlight.

He lay in a twin bed and looked at the girl. He could read the company name below her on the calendar: Jackson's Tool Supply. He remembered that his cousin worked there. Suddenly he could think things through, he could put things together, where in the past years he'd been unable to. It was like his mind had suddenly walked out of a never-ending snowstorm. Tears dripped down the side of his face in relief. Was he finally free? Was he really himself again?

*

Leroy Kervin had been twenty-four years old when his National Guard brigade was sent to Iraq. Six months into the deployment a roadside bomb had destroyed the vehicle he was in. One soldier had been killed, two others severely injured, and he'd woken up in a hospital in Germany with major brain trauma and two broken arms. He couldn't speak and he couldn't walk. The life he'd known before the bomb no longer existed. That Leroy Kervin had vanished.

The new Leroy Kervin couldn't recognize people he had just met. He would become instantly agitated and just as quickly depressed. He'd throw things in frustration one minute and sob the next. It took him months to re-learn to walk, months before he could again hold a fork, and always he struggled with his speech and with his emotions. There was no miraculous recovery for the new Leroy Kervin. Rehabilitation turned into caregiving, and eventually led him to a second-rate group home for disabled men in a town in Washington State.

*

But that night, for the first time since the explosion, he woke with clarity. Memories flooded into him. He could recall his routines, the week's menu, what time he went to bed and which days he took a shower. He could remember his mother bringing him takeout food and sitting next to him while they watched TV. He could remember his girlfriend, her eyes and face, and the birthmark on her calf and her walking around in her underwear. He could suddenly recall the way she laughed, the sound of her voice when she was upset, the way she sneezed, and the way she sighed sadly when the alarm went off in the morning.

What was happening to him?

Time passed and he didn't know what to do. He grew tired. He could hear the kid Rolly in the next room jacking off, and the old man Hal, snoring faintly in the room across the hall. Farther down he could hear Donald having a coughing attack. Donald, who would run around the place naked, who would come into Leroy's room, shake him

2

awake, and spit unintelligible words all over his face. If he fell asleep would he wake up lost and in the fog again? Would the clarity be gone? Would he have to spend the rest of his life there?

He remembered suddenly the long months when every time he closed his eyes it felt like he was drowning in mud. And then there were periods when his thoughts fell into nothing but frustration and violence. How days would pass when every time he heard a door shut or open he felt certain someone was coming to kill him. The fear of that would engulf him and when the fear passed, the fog would again come and he wouldn't be able to remember anything. It would just start over. Was this all his life was? Was this clarity just another illusion, a trick? He knew that most likely he would close his eyes and sleep would come and the clarity would disappear and the frustration, the bleak thoughts, and the fog would return. But at that moment, on that night, he had a window and he decided to escape through it.

He decided he would kill himself.

He got out of the bed in such hysterical panic that he began hyperventilating. He shuffled to the kitchen trying to catch his breath. He tried to open the silverware drawer to find a knife but it was locked. He checked the meds cabinet, but it was also locked. He went to the door leading to the garage and opened it. He found the light switch and turned it on. The space was empty except for a barren work bench on the far side of the room and an old four-foot picket-fence gate leaning against the back wall. There were no tools; there was nothing of use but old paint cans. He stared at the wooden gate, and then went to it and put his hands between the stakes. He dragged it from the garage to the living room and set it next to a childproof gate that blocked the stairs to the second floor. His legs began to shake from the effort and he sat down on the living room couch and rested.

He needed rope but there was none. He lumbered back to his room. He took the one dress shirt his mother kept for him in the closet and walked back to the childproof gate and opened it. He climbed the first step and turned around. He shut the plastic gate and dragged the wooden one in front of it and leaned it against it. The old pointed wooden stakes faced toward the stairs. He used a shirt sleeve as a rope and tied the gates together and sat down.

He was overcome with exhaustion. He closed his eyes and leaned against the wall and waited. When he stood again, he was shaky, but he plodded up the stairs. As he neared the top he could hear the sound of Freddie McCall, the night man, snoring. He took the last few steps and then reached the second floor. A lamp on the office desk shone. He could see Freddie lying on his stomach, fully clothed, asleep.

He walked to the back of the room, the farthest he could from the stairs and turned around. He was out of breath and dizzy. He thought again of his girlfriend, Jeanette. He remembered their house together, her lying in bed next to him asleep, how in the end she secretly put a note in every pocket of every shirt, of every pair of pants, and inside each sock of his travel bag. How she drove him in tears to the base. How she would break down on the phone from halfway around the world and then spend the rest of the conversation trying to make him laugh. Where was she now?

And was he making the right decision? Maybe the clarity wasn't just a brief illusion; maybe suddenly his brain had somehow fixed itself? But that couldn't be, could it? Those sorts of things didn't happen, did they? Tears fell from his eyes and he tried to run.

He asked his legs to move faster than they had in seven years and he flew down the stairs with his arms stretched out. He landed on top of the old wooden stakes and they plunged into him as he crashed to the ground and lay unconscious and bloody on the floor.

Freddie McCall woke from the noise and reached for his glasses. He turned on the lights and ran down the stairs to find Leroy unconscious with a piece of wood sticking out of his chest. There was blood everywhere. He ran to the phone and called 911.

When he hung up, he held two kitchen towels over the main wound and stared at Leroy's face. There was a two-inch cut on his cheek leaking blood and a growing welt on his forehead. Freddie wanted to say something to comfort him, but every time he tried to speak he began to cry.

He'd always liked Leroy. For a man who couldn't speak, whose brain had been caved in by war, he had personality. He liked Cap'n Crunch and would watch the science fiction channel for days on end. He had never picked a fight or become violent toward the other residents. He would fall into fits of despair when he refused to leave his bed, but who wouldn't? And there were times, dozens of them, in the two years that Freddie had been there, when Leroy would wake him in the middle of the night. He would pull Freddie to the back door and knock on it. Freddie would find the key, unlock it, and they would go outside and look at the stars. Leroy would move around the small lawn like an old man, his head back, staring at the faraway galaxies.

He'd heard that Leroy's mother would visit him after she got off work. She would watch *Star Trek* reruns with him and help him eat dinner. When she was leaving Leroy would hug her so tight she could hardly breathe. "Don't worry. He did that before he got hurt too," she would always say. She was usually gone by the time Freddie started his overnight shift, but there were times when he would run into her and he always felt for her when he did. She worked at Safeway. She lived alone in a small house in a failing neighborhood, and drove a twenty-year-old car.

*

The sound of a siren was heard and then an ambulance parked in the drive. Two EMTs ran in and began working on Leroy at the foot of the stairs. While they did so, Freddie went to the kitchen and called the manager of the group home and then left a message for Leroy's mother. The residents came slowly from their rooms. Hal, the forty-six-year-old, stood next to Freddie. The kid, Rolly, was behind him, crying, and Donald, the thirty-five-year-old Indian, was nearly catatonic staring at the TV.

"It's alright, guys," Freddie told them. "There isn't much we can do to help, so let's try and get back to bed. Leroy's going to be fine. These guys know what they're doing." But none of them moved, not even Freddie. They all just stood there watching the EMTs put Leroy on a stretcher and take him outside to the ambulance. They watched him being loaded into the back and driven away.

*

The group home's manager, Julie Norris, arrived. With her help he put the residents back to bed, picked up the broken gates, and tried to clean the blood-stained carpets. It was four am when she left. Freddie was so worried and upset that all he could do was drink coffee and wait for his shift to end. When the day man, Dale Riley, arrived fifteen minutes late at quarter after six, Freddie realized he'd only slept an hour.

He got into a battered 1965 Mercury Comet and started it. He turned the heater on full, got out again and scraped the windows, then drove home. He could see his breath as he walked inside. The kitchen timer sat on the counter and he took it and set it for six minutes. Inside the bathroom he turned on a small box heater, put his work uniform next to it, and got in the shower.

Thirteen minutes later he was back in his car. He drove to the industrial section of town and parked in front of Heaven's Door Donuts, a small, white cinderblock building that had once been a walk-up hamburger stand. A sign hung from the roof spelling out its name in pink cursive neon. It was a donut shop he had frequented at least five times a week for the last fourteen years. The owner, a sixty-year-old Vietnamese man named Pham, made the donuts in the back room. The counter was run by a middle-aged obese woman with dyed-blond hair named Mora. When he pulled up in front he flashed his lights twice and she hurried outside with three dozen assorted in two pink boxes.

"Jesus you're late today," she said. Her hair was pulled back with a bright orange head band and she wore red sweats and a white apron. She handed the boxes to him.

Freddie set them on the seat beside him. "Dale was late again."

"They should really fire old Dale."

8

"I wish they would."

"You look tired."

"I am a little," he said.

Mora leaned down and placed her arms on the door. Her lips were blue from the cold and her breath came out like smoke and trailed off.

"You know your boss hasn't paid the donut bill."

"I'll get him to."

"He's getting on my nerves just like Dale is," Mora said and smiled.

"Me too."

"Did you hear the game last night?"

"I meant to. I had the radio on but I fell asleep in the first period, and then I had to go to work."

"You didn't miss much. They got crushed by Moose Jaw. Are you sure you're alright, Freddie? Your eyes are all red. Even in this light I can see that."

"I'm just a little worn out, Mora. It was a long night but I'm alright."

She stood up and began walking back toward the donut shop. "I put in an extra twist and a handful of donut holes for you," she yelled. "See you tomorrow, Freddie. And get some sleep."

He yelled good-bye and pulled out of the lot and drove to Logan's Paint Store and parked. Inside, he turned on the lights and the computer. He set the donuts on the counter, made coffee, and unlocked the front doors.

It took him four cups of coffee to stay awake through the morning rush. When the store finally cleared it was eleven am. He made another pot of coffee and began sweeping the retail floor. At eleven-forty the owner of the store, Pat

Logan, parked a year-old Ford F-250 pickup in the front lot. He was a tall man and overweight by two hundred pounds. He had bad knees and brown teeth and was going bald.

His father, Enoch Logan, had opened the store in 1970. On his death bed Mr. Logan told his wife he wanted Freddie to run the store. He wanted to give him part ownership to guarantee the business would survive her lifetime. But his wife disagreed and thought Pat, their only son, should run and own it. Their son, who had been in and out of work most of his adult life, had three small children to support. They argued about it for a long time, for weeks, but she finally convinced Enoch to leave the business in the family. So Mr. Logan brought in his lawyer and locked Freddie's wages to a three percent annual wage increase. He made Pat sign an agreement to it, and gave him the business. A month later Enoch Logan was dead, and six years after that all five employees had been laid off. The store was behind on payables, and Freddie was left to work the counter of Logan's Paint alone six days a week.

"How was it this morning?" Pat asked and set a frozen Salisbury steak dinner and a liter bottle of Dr Pepper on the counter.

"Jenson bought thirty gallons of primer," Freddie said. "And Lawson's crew came in for top coat on that apartment complex, maybe twelve hundred dollars so far."

Pat shook his head and looked out to the empty parking lot. He put the frozen dinner in the refrigerator and went to his office and shut the door. At five minutes to noon he came out again, heated the dinner in the microwave, and went back in his office. He turned on the radio to *Family Talk*, the evangelical radio program hosted by Dr. James Dobson, and called his wife. He put her on speaker phone and they listened to it together while he ate his lunch. At one pm he came out of the office again, dumped the tray in the retail trash can, and looked at the still empty parking lot. He walked back to the warehouse where Freddie was unloading a pallet of paint.

"Well, it looks like it's going to snow now," he said.

"January and snowing," Freddie said.

"It's going to be deader than dead this afternoon."

"You might be right."

"I have to run some errands. I might come back but I might not."

"Okay, Pat," he said as his boss left.

Freddie closed the store at five-thirty and went home. He lay on the couch, put a sleeping bag over himself, and slept until seven. When he woke he drank an energy drink, moved the box heater from the bathroom to the kitchen, and fried two eggs. He changed his clothes, sat down on the couch, and called his daughters in Las Vegas. He spoke to each girl for five minutes, but at the end of both conversations they had run out of things to say to each other.

He looked at his watch. He had an hour and a half until his shift at the home began. He lay back down on the couch. From the kitchen light he could see the mantel and the dining room. He could see the hallway leading to his daughters' old rooms, and the stairs leading up to the master bedroom. His grandfather had built the house, and now Freddie was failing it. He was given it free and clear, and now it was mortgaged twice. There was no heat and no garbage service and he was behind on the electric bill. In the end he knew he was going to lose it all.

He drove the Comet through downtown and through the suburbs, and in the distance he could see the county hospital set on a hill. He parked in the visitors' lot and got out. At the front desk he asked for Leroy Kervin, and a woman gave him directions. Five minutes later he found Leroy in a room by himself on the sixth floor in a post-surgery ward.

There was a tube running down his throat and tubes running in and out of his chest. He was unconscious and there was a film of sweat covering his swollen face. His lips were chapped and part of his bottom lip was cut and swollen. The cut on his cheek was now stitched and the deep bruise on his forehead was turning yellow and purple. Freddie took off his coat and sat down in the chair facing the bed.

A nurse came in the room.

"Is Leroy going to be alright?" Freddie asked.

"He's got a long way to go, I'm afraid," was all the nurse said. Her name tag read Pauline. She was a thick-set woman of mid-height in her thirties with dark brown hair and brown eyes. She smelled of shampoo and cigarettes. From a distance she had a pretty face. It was only close up that the lines around her eyes and lips and the scars from acne appeared. She looked tired.

"Are you his family?" she asked.

"I work at the group home where he's been living. He fell down the stairs last night and I found him."

"The good news is they say the surgery went well," she said and checked the ventilator, the chest tubes, and the canister at the side of the bed. She looked at his med chart and made a series of notes on a computer in the corner of the room and left.

He looked at his watch and got up and went to the win-

12

dow that overlooked the hospital parking lot. There were over a hundred cars below and he couldn't believe there were so many for such a small town. He went back to Leroy and put on his coat. He leaned over him and put his hand gently on his arm. He felt the warmth and the softness of Leroy's skin. "I'm sorry you didn't make it, Leroy. I know that's not the right thing to say, but I'm sorry you didn't."

3

The nurse looked at her wristwatch. She had forty minutes
left in her shift. She was nearly done charting and the night
meds were taken care of. She kneeled down and re-tied her
shoes and then walked down the hall to her last patient, Mr.
Flory. He was a thin, weathered old man with stage IV stomach cancer. He lay on his side staring out the door into the
hallway. He smiled when he saw her come in the room.

"You haven't gone home yet?" he asked.

"Almost," she said. "I'm at the finish line. You're my last,
Mr. Flory. I save my best for last."

Even though it hurt him to do so, he moved on his back
so he could see her better.

"How's the pain?"

"Well . . ." he said.

"Well what, Mr. Flory?"

"I hate to ask, but is it time yet?"

"You're in a lot of pain?"

He nodded.

"If you were going to rate it from one to ten, what would
it be?"

"I'd say about an eight."

"You always say eight."

"It always seems about the same," he said.

"I'll see what I can do. I'll call the doctor again, okay?"

"Okay."

"Where's your wife?"

"She had to go home and take care of some things." He tried to stay on his back, but the pain was too much. He moved to his side and cried out in pain.

"That bad, huh?"

"I just get tired of lying on my side, but I guess I have to." With his left hand he tried to comb back his thin, gray hair. "Is your shift almost over?"

"In thirty minutes," she said.

"What are you doing tonight?"

"I have a big date."

"Who's taking you out?"

"Donna. But we're staying in and watching TV."

The old man laughed. "Donna's your rabbit, correct?"

The nurse nodded.

"Did I tell you that my sister had a rabbit when we were kids? She used to bring it to the dinner table."

"I bet your parents didn't like that."

"My mother didn't like it, but if my dad had his way we'd eat every meal with the animals. What color's Donna?"

"Black and white."

"A Dutch rabbit."

"I think so."

"You had her a long time?"

"Maybe a year," she said and went to the computer and looked at his chart. "My neighbors moved out of their apartment one night. They skipped out and left most of their stuff including Donna. She'd been alone in her cage for two weeks when the landlord went in. They'd left a big bowl of water in the cage but I don't know how long she'd gone without food. She was in rough shape. The landlord brought her to me 'cause he knows I'm a sucker."

15

"Maybe he just thought you were kind."

"Maybe."

"I never got used to people mistreating animals."

"It makes me mad. That's for sure," she said as she charted.

"If I saw a guy mistreat his dog or a horse, I never hired him again. When you see that you know what's in his heart. You know that's the way he sees the world. And I never liked seeing it that way."

"You're pretty smart for a guy living out in the sticks with a bunch of cows, Mr. Flory. Alright, buster, down to business. Are you thirsty?"

"I'm never thirsty anymore."

"You should try to drink more water."

"It just never sounds good anymore."

"I bet if I had an ice-cold beer you'd drink that."

"I quit drinking years ago."

"Good for you."

"I wasn't the best drunk," he said.

"Most people aren't."

"But I liked it."

"Well, you can always imagine."

"Maybe . . ." He looked at her and then closed his eyes. "I wish I could get out of here."

"I know the doctors want to get you home. It won't be long. Are you getting tired?"

"Guess all this talking is doing me in."

"You'll be asleep soon. When you wake up Rhonda will be here with new instructions from the doctor. I'm sure they'll be able to increase your pain meds and you'll be able to get some real rest."

"Alright," he said.

"Good-night, Mr. Flory," she said.

"Good-night, Pauline."

*

She clocked out at eleven pm and walked down to the parking lot and got into a dented, green four-door Honda. She started the engine and scraped the windows and left. She drove to a grocery store and bought twenty-four cans of chicken noodle soup on special, a pint of chocolate ice cream, a container of fat-free coffee creamer, and two glazed donuts.

She left the soup in the trunk of her car and walked up the stairs to her apartment with the rest. Inside she turned on the TV, let the rabbit out of its cage, and sat down on the couch. She put the rabbit on her lap and gave it small bites of donut. She opened the ice cream and watched TV until she fell asleep.

The next morning she drove to a rundown suburb on the opposite side of town, to the small tract home she had grown up in. She parked in the driveway, took a laundry basket full of clean clothes from the trunk, and set the case of soup on top of it. She carried the basket to the front door and knocked on it with her foot.

"Come on," she yelled. "It's me. Hurry up."

She could hear rustling from inside but there was no answer.

"Come on. It's heavy!"

She kicked three more times and then set the basket on the ground and looked through her purse and found the keys. She unlocked the door and went inside to see her father lying on the old military cot in the living room. He was underneath an electric blanket and in a sleeping bag and was watching TV.

"Didn't you hear me?"

He lifted his head. "I wasn't sure who it was."

"Who else would it be?"

"I don't know."

"Why is it so cold in here?"

"They shut off the goddamn gas."

"Who did?"

"The gas company."

"Don't lie to me, buster. I paid the bill and you know it. Anyway, all your mail comes to my house, and you never check your messages so you'd have no idea." She went to the thermostat and turned it to seventy. There was a click, a hum, and then warm air began coming through the floor vents. "You can lower it when I leave but I'm not going to freeze just to cook you lunch . . . I did your laundry so I want you to take a shower and change your clothes. It's cold in here but I can still smell you."

"The hot water heater's broken," he said half-heartedly with his eyes still on the TV.

"You're getting on my nerves already." She took the case of soup into the kitchen and set it on the counter. She turned on the water and put her hand under it. "Don't burn yourself in the shower. I'm gonna do the dishes and you're going to wash your body and hair with lots of soap. Then you're going to get dressed in clean clothes. I'm not going to argue. You either get up and get ready or I'm going to call Uncle Jeff again."

18

The old man sprang from the cot. He was dressed in a sweatshirt and urine-stained long underwear. The electric blanket and sleeping bag fell to the floor as he stood. He was a bony man in his mid-sixties with thick gray hair and six-day-old stubble. His eyes were small and brown and sunk back in his head.

"Why do you always got to call him?" he yelled. He picked up the basket of clothes and began walking toward his bedroom.

"I call him because you won't listen to me, and because he's your brother and he'll put you in your place. He'll come down here and kick your ass."

"Goddamn it, don't call him."

"Then do what I say." Pauline came from the kitchen. "Stop right there."

"What now?" he said and turned around.

"I want you to shave, too. And I'll be listening for the shower. If you don't smell like shampoo when you come to lunch, I'm dialing his number."

"This is bullshit."

"And when you get done, you'll eat lunch and we'll go for a walk."

"I don't want to go for a walk."

"You need to and I need to. I've gained six pounds since November and I don't like walking alone. It wouldn't kill you to leave the house once in a while."

He went to his bedroom and slammed the door behind him. Pauline washed a sink full of dishes and opened a can of soup and turned on the stove. In the cupboard were three boxes of saltines. She found one open, took out ten crackers and put them on a plate. She chopped iceberg lettuce into

19

bite-size pieces, put the salad in a bowl, and went into the living room and watched TV and waited.

He came out twenty minutes later. His hair was combed back and wet. Bits of toilet paper covered a series of shaving cuts on his neck and chin. He wore brown pants and a flannel shirt.

He pointed to the cuts. "Are you happy?"

"If you'd use the electric razor I bought you then you'd never cut yourself. Then you wouldn't hate shaving so much," she said.

"I don't trust electric razors." He went into the kitchen and sat. She poured the soup into a bowl and set it in front of him.

"It looks like you keep losing weight."

"Don't be a nurse," he said and began eating. "I don't like it when you talk like a nurse."

"Alright," she said. "Fair enough. What do you want to talk about?"

He looked up from his soup. "What?"

"What's going on with you?"

The old man slurped the soup into his mouth and stared at the table. Broth leaked out his lips and dribbled down his chin.

"What are you going to do this weekend?"

He took two saltines and put them in his mouth and began chewing.

"What are you going to do this weekend?" she asked again.

"What do you think?" he said and put his face back down to the soup. He held the spoon like a knife and began shoveling it in and again broth fell to the table.

In a man's voice she said, "What about you, Pauline? What are you going to do this weekend?"

"I don't know really," she answered in her own voice. "Maybe I'll go to New York and become a prostitute."

"Isn't New York cold this time of year?" she said in the low voice. "Maybe you should wait until it's spring."

"Spring, you think?"

"Yeah, spring's a good time to walk the streets."

"Thanks for the advice, Dad. You really are something. You're always such a help."

"That's why I'm here," she said in the man's voice and hit the table.

Her father stopped eating and looked at her. "Okay, I'm sorry."

"You're an asshole."

"I didn't mean to be an asshole."

"When you're an asshole, you're an asshole. It doesn't matter if you want to be or not. You just are. The trick is not to be."

He pushed the bowl away. "Alright, I'm sorry."

"It's alright," she said and sighed. "I guess I'm just in a bad mood. You done?"

"I'll finish the rest later."

"What about the lettuce? You've only had one bite."

"I hate vegetables."

"I don't think you can consider iceberg lettuce much of a vegetable."

"You know what I mean."

"So you're finished?"

He nodded and she took the dishes from the table and set them in the sink. "Now put on your shoes and let's go for a walk. I only have an hour before I have to go to work."

"Can I bring my cigarettes?"

"Yeah," she said. "I started again, so you're off the hook."

4

Leroy Kervin woke up to the sound of the TV. There was a Western on; a kid was AWOL from the cavalry and was killing Indians. A man with one leg was trying to stop him, but he was having a hard time. He watched the show for a moment then fell back to sleep. The next time he woke it was to the sound of crying. He opened his eyes to see a brown-haired nurse in the corner of the room. She stared out the window into the parking lot. It was night and the main room lights were off. He could hear her sobs and could see her wiping her tears while she looked at her wristwatch. He heard a voice from the hallway call, "Pauline." The brown-haired nursed replied that she would just be a minute and again looked at her watch. He tried to keep his eyes open, but couldn't.

When he opened them the next time it was daylight. He could see the sun from the window and could hear people talking. He saw an old man using a walker go down the hallway and nurses walking past. He could remember that a nurse named Pauline had been in the room crying the last time he was awake. He could remember that a Western was on TV. He still had his memory; he still had clarity. Nothing made sense anymore. He tried to move his hand to hit the call button to let them know the pain he was in, but his fingers wouldn't move. Everything felt as heavy as concrete. And then the pain worsened. He tried to speak, to scream for help but nothing would come out. His mind became hysterical while his body lay lifeless.

His thoughts grew darker. It would be more hospitals, and this time it was his fault. He'd failed, he was to blame. It would be this room and then another and then another and then finally, if he were lucky, he'd be back where he started: at the group home in the suburbs, stuck away forever.

The pain seemed to stop time. Had he been waiting like this for minutes or hours or days or weeks? It was too much to take and he was so tired of being in pain. He decided then that he would give up, that he would run his mind as far away as he could. He would lose himself inside himself. He would disappear from the world.

*

It was early morning as he walked down the crowded city street. It was cold and most of the people wore green-and-gray military uniforms. There were hundreds of them passing by in all directions. Leroy looked out to the sea and military ships filled the bay, and on the streets black-and-green military vehicles lined the curbs. He was dressed in his uncle's Pendleton wool coat as he walked to the National Guard recruiting office. As he drew closer, he saw a woman in a blue parka knocking on the front door. She was slender, in her twenties with black hair.

"Do you know why they aren't open?" she asked. Her pale face was red from crying.

"No," he told her. "They're supposed to be. They're always open."

"Oh, I hate this place."

"What's wrong?" he asked her.

24

"My friend's disappeared," she cried. "I begged him not to join but I think he did. I used to see him every day but now I can't find him. I'm hoping they'll tell me where he is. Why are you here?"

"I'm joining," he told her.

"You're joining?" she said in horror.

"Yes."

"But why?"

"My boss wants me to. He's a captain in the Guard. It sounds crazy, but I know I won't get laid off if I join. He's let half of the crew go already, but he likes me. I'm an electrician. Jobs are hard to find where I live. No one's building anymore. There's two guys that have more seniority than me, but I know he won't lay me off if I join. He thinks of me as a son. Someone to carry on the business when he gets old. I don't mind. I just want to keep my job. Anyway, he said I can be an electrician for the National Guard so I won't have to go overseas. I won't have to be in the wars."

"I think they'll send you wherever they want to send you," the woman said. "That's how it works. It has nothing to do with what you want or what you think."

"They won't send me to the wars," he said.

"You're wrong," she said and wiped her eyes with a Kleenex. They waited for nearly twenty minutes, staring at the closed brick building. It began raining and grew colder. Wind began howling against them.

"I'm starting to get hungry," Leroy said and turned to her. "Are you hungry?"

"Me?" she said as she leaned against the glass door.

"Yeah, you."

"Worrying always makes me hungry."

25

"There's a restaurant up the street. I think it's called Paul's Place."

"That's the last place I want to go," she said.

"Why?"

"I work there, but you should go. The food's pretty good." For the first time she looked at him. She had green eyes and a small face with freckles and a nose that sloped upward. He thought she was about to smile when across the street a group of twenty soldiers walked past them. They were dressed in new uniforms. One of the soldiers at the back of the pack, a haggard man of forty, noticed her and stopped. He walked across the street toward them and lit a cigarette. When she saw him coming, tears filled her eyes and she moved closer to Leroy. "If you walk me home, I'll make you breakfast."

He looked at the soldier. "He makes you nervous?"

"Of course."

"Then let's go," Leroy said and put his arm around her. When the soldier saw this and that she was crying he turned around and jogged back to his group.

"Everything is falling apart. So now it seems like all I do is fall apart."

"It's alright," he said. "You should see what I've been like. You should see where I've been living."

"My name is Jeanette."

"I'm Leroy."

"Please don't join the guard, Leroy," she said. "I know I don't know you, but I'm begging you not to."

"But I've already committed," he whispered to her.

*

26

They walked through hundreds of passing soldiers to her apartment, men and women, young and old. A sea of soldiers next to the sea. The uniforms were new, as were the packs on their backs and the boots on their feet. They spoke loudly and freely among themselves, and all of them stared as the two civilians walked by. Then Jeanette took Leroy's hand and led him off the main road and down a side street. They walked up a long hill to where she lived, a brick building from the 1930s that sat alone overlooking the bay.

The main entrance door was broken down, as were the windows around it. They stepped over shattered glass and splintered boards and passed busted furniture and bags of trash to get to the stairwell. She led him up six flights until they came to the door of her apartment. She took a key from her coat and opened three bolt locks. Inside, the walls and ceiling of her apartment were ragged, the plaster falling down in patches from water damage. Her front room was simple, just a couch, two wooden chairs, and a bookcase lined with novels and comic books. There was a balcony with a view of the harbor, which held a long row of warships. The walls had old water-stained floral wallpaper and nothing hung from them except a single framed picture of the Portuguese singer Amália Rodrigues.

"How do you know Amália Rodrigues?" Leroy asked. "I love Amália Rodrigues."

Jeanette went to the picture. It was an old black and white press photo. She took it from the wall and handed it to him.

"You'll think I'm crazy, but one time I had a dream that I was in a trailer. It was like an Airstream trailer but it wasn't as nice. Inside there was music playing and I was in love. The boy in the dream held me. He was very corny. He would

27

whisper in my ear that he loved me more than anything. He'd say things like, 'I love you more than a thousand planets. I love you more than all the oceans in the universe and more than all the candy bars ever made . . .' You should have heard him. He was very funny. So that day we danced while Amália Rodrigues sang to us. There was a record player on a table and he would play her albums for me over and over. He said he would take me to Portugal: he said he'd find her for me even if he had to spend his whole life looking. He would kiss my neck as he told me these things. I had never heard of her before that. I barely knew where Portugal was, but in my dream we fell asleep together in the trailer. He held me on a fold-out bed. While I was sleeping I dreamt that she came to me and told me to find her. When I woke up, I remembered her name, and began looking for her records. It took me a year to find one."

"She just came to you in a dream like that?"

"Yes," Jeanette said.

"That's the strangest thing I've ever heard. My uncle had a trailer once, and we would sit in it and listen to Amália Rodrigues records every Friday after he got off work . . . See, years before that, after he'd gotten out of high school, there were no jobs. He wasn't really worried at first, but then everything he applied for he didn't get. He was going to have to move to a different city to find work, but then he got drafted. The Vietnam War was going full blast by then. In a way he was relieved. At least he'd have money, at least in a way he would have a job. The notice he received said he had three months until he had to report. So his father took him aside and told him he should see something of the world in case he got killed. He gave my uncle his life savings of two thousand dollars and a plane ticket to Europe.

"My uncle landed in Madrid, Spain. He worked his way to Portugal and one night in a club in Lisbon he heard Amália Rodrigues sing. He said she sang the most heartbreaking songs and had the most beautiful voice he'd ever heard. He stayed in Portugal until his time ran out. He saw her night after night after night.

"Years later he lived with my mom and me in the backyard of our house. He lived in a trailer, a trailer that looked like an Airstream but wasn't as nice. On Fridays when the work-week was done, he'd sit down with a twelve-pack of beer and listen to her music. My mom would sometimes yell at him for playing the records so loud, but my mom liked her too, and she liked that there was something her brother still loved. Sometimes you'd go into his trailer and Amália Rodrigues would be singing and he'd be sitting at his table smoking ci-garettes and drinking beer, smiling and crying at the same time."

"I can't believe in my dream there was a trailer, and in reality your uncle listened to her in a trailer. That doesn't make any sense. How would we both like Amália Rodrig-ues?"

"I don't know," Leroy said.

Jeanette took off her coat, turned on a portable heater, and went to the kitchen. She came back with two bottles of Rain-ier beer.

Leroy took a bottle and drank from it. "You know what else? This beer is the same beer my uncle used to drink."

"I've always liked Rainier," Jeanette said.

"Me too."

"Is your uncle still alive?"

"No, not anymore," Leroy said.

"What was he like?"

"My uncle was like my father and my brother, except he never gave me a hard time. I think really, he was always just glad to see me. It's lucky when you know someone and you can tell they're glad to see you, almost relieved to see you. It doesn't happen very often, but it sure makes you feel good. My mom says my uncle was one person when he went into the army and another person when he came out. Before he went in, my mother said he was the funniest person she knew, and she's his sister. She's supposed to be annoyed by him. But it wasn't like that. She loved him but she liked him, too. He was a clown and very goofy. But when he came home from the war it was like that part of him was gone. There was no silliness left, the lightness he'd always had had disappeared."

As they spoke, they heard a loud siren coming from below. It was followed by the distant sound of sledgehammers breaking down doors. Then came the sounds of yelling and boots running up the stairwell.

"It's them," she cried.

"Do you have any neighbors who they could be coming for?"

"I'm the only one left in the building."

"Are you sure?"

"Yes," she said. She lifted her leg and pulled down her sock. Her skin had the mark, the blue-and-red-and-green mark that looked like a deep bruise.

"Do you have any place to hide?"

"No," she cried and began to hyperventilate.

"Are you sure there's nowhere?"

She shook her head in panic.

There were fists beating on the door and then a sledge-

hammer breaking it. They rushed into her apartment. There were three of them in military uniforms. Two men and a woman. They carried rifles and wore bulletproof vests and helmets with spotlights on them.

"Take her pants off," the leader of them yelled. He was a young soldier, not even twenty years old.

"No," Jeanette cried. "Please don't."

Leroy ran to stop them, but the woman soldier hit him in the chest with the sledgehammer. The pain exploded inside him. He fell to the ground. He couldn't breathe. It felt like his chest had been ripped open and was being pulled apart. He was unable to move or speak. A fat, middle-aged male soldier, out of breath and sweating, dragged Jeanette to the living room. Leroy could see her from where he lay. The soldier began taking off her clothes. She screamed and kicked at him but he wouldn't stop. The female soldier went to Jeanette and hit her in the face and then held her down while the other soldier finished stripping her. They left her naked and crying on the floor.

"She's got it," the woman soldier yelled and pointed to her foot. The young commander got on the radio and called it in. He took a pistol from his holster and pointed it at her head. Leroy tried to scream for them to stop but nothing came out. He couldn't move and the pain in his chest swelled.

5

Freddie McCall left the sixth-floor elevator and walked down the long hospital hall to room nine. He found Leroy alone and slowly moving his hands to the tube running down his throat, his eyes wide open in panic. Freddie ran to the nurses' station where a middle-aged Filipino nurse sat working on a computer.

"I think something's wrong with Leroy," he said.

The nurse followed him in. She pulled Leroy's hands down and used restraints to keep them at his sides. She looked at the chest tubes to make sure there were no blockages and that the fluid level was right. She looked at his medication record and left the room. She came back a minute later and increased the morphine amount on the drip.

"I know he's in a lot of pain," she said as she held Leroy's head still. "But with a flail chest we have to be careful about the pain meds. I had to confirm it with his doctor. If we give him too much he won't breathe deeply and we need him to breathe as deep as he can. The mechanical ventilation only assists his breathing right now; he still needs to do some work himself."

"What's a flail chest?" Freddie asked.

"The fall he took was so severe that part of his chest wall separated. Three of his ribs were fractured in multiple places due to the blunt trauma of his injury. They became displaced and were moving independently of the chest wall.

This also caused three lacerations in one lung and the other collapsed. The mechanical ventilation helps him breathe, it makes sure he breathes enough per minute and that his lung volume isn't too shallow. That's why he's intubated. We have the chest tubes to help push out air, blood, and fluids. He'll settle down soon."

*

"Don't shoot her," Leroy cried, and this time his voice was heard. He was shaky but he had the strength to stand. He staggered to the living room to see the young commander pushing his pistol into Jeanette's forehead. He pulled the trigger but the gun didn't fire.

"Christ!" he yelled. "It jammed again."

"Please let her go," Leroy begged.

"Use mine," offered the woman soldier. As she handed him her pistol, Leroy went for the gun. The middle-aged soldier saw what was happening and hit him in the chest and again he fell to the ground in breathless agony.

"Hurry up," the woman soldier said. "Finish it and then check him."

The young commander put the new gun to her head, but as he did so a woman came into the room. She had long, black hair and brown eyes. She wore the dress of a working-class woman from the 1930s.

"It's Amália Rodrigues!" Jeanette cried.

The woman began yelling at the soldiers in Portuguese. She screamed and hissed and cast spells on them, and one by one the soldiers disappeared until they were all gone. She then kneeled to the floor and held Leroy in her arms. She sang gently and softly, and a great euphoria rushed into him.

*

Leroy's eyes closed, his breathing steadied, and he quit moving. The nurse went back to her station and Freddie sat down and turned on the TV. He went through the channels until he found an episode of *Gunsmoke*. As he watched, he thought for a moment that it was his youngest daughter, Virginia, in the hospital bed again and not Leroy. Parts of him even wished it were so. That she was right there next to him and not in a different state living in a new house with a new father. He watched the show for twenty minutes as Leroy slept, and then he left for work.

A half-mile from the group home he passed a large crate full of scrap wood. Next to the crate was a handwritten sign that read free wood. He looked at his watch and turned around. He moved his car beside the box and began loading in broken pallets, scrap two-by-fours, and chunks of four-by-four. He filled the trunk until he couldn't close it, then stacked more in the backseat and in the passenger seat, and went to work.

Julie Norris was in the kitchen doing dishes when he came in. She filled him in on the day: Hal had vomited during dinner and might have the flu and Rolly and Donald got into a fight but nothing came of it. The carpet in front of the stairs had been professionally cleaned, but the blood stains, although faded, were permanent. The drain in the bathroom sink had clogged, but her boyfriend had come by earlier and fixed it. Everyone was now in bed asleep, she told him, and then she started the dishwasher, put on her coat, and left.

Freddie did the series of chores he did every night and then lay down on the couch exhausted. He woke two hours later to Donald standing over him, naked and shaking him. Freddie put on his glasses and sat up. As he did, Donald ran up and down the hallway screaming. Freddie went to the kitchen, took a cup from the cupboard, and filled it with milk. He poured chocolate syrup into it, stirred it, and put it in the microwave. He walked to the living room and waited until Donald came running back toward him.

"You're going to wake up the whole house," Freddie told him quietly. "How about you quit yelling, and I'll get you a hot chocolate?"

Donald heard the words "hot chocolate" and stopped.

"But to get the hot chocolate you have to get dressed first," he said and led him down the hall. Inside Donald's room there was a dresser, a twin bed, and four basketball posters on the wall. Freddie found his pajamas on the floor and helped him back into them. He led him to the kitchen and took the cup from the microwave and gave it to him. Donald drank it standing in front of the refrigerator. When he'd finished, Freddie put him back to bed and the house was again quiet. He went to the couch, turned on the TV, and tried to sleep.

At five-thirty am the alarm on his phone woke him. He washed his face and made a pot of coffee. Dale arrived on time at six and Freddie drove home, unloaded the wood onto his front lawn, put on his Logan's Paint Store uniform, and left. He drove the two miles to Heaven's Door Donuts and parked.

"You're doing good this morning," Mora said leaning

against the glass counter. She glanced at the clock hanging above the door. "You have seven minutes."

"I can relax," Freddie said and smiled. "How was your dentist appointment?"

"I have to get the tooth pulled."

"Jesus."

"Pham's loaning me the money. Now I just have to get my nerve up."

"At least it won't hurt anymore after that."

"Let's hope it won't. It would be a pretty mean tooth to hurt me when it's in the garbage somewhere." Mora smiled and then moved her large body backward and bent down. She set four glazed donut holes in a plastic basket and poured a cup of coffee. She set it all on the counter in front of him.

"Sorry about the game last night," he told her. "I heard part of it." He took a drink from the cup and ate a donut hole. Mora opened two pink boxes and began putting donuts inside. Behind them on a counter sat an old radio playing. He could see Pham in the backroom lowering a batch of donuts into the fryer.

"My poor boys," Mora said as she worked. "They get beaten up all series, and now Leipsic's been suspended for three games." She stopped and looked at him. "I hate saying this, but you look worse every day I see you, Freddie. It really worries me. Are you getting any sleep at all?"

"I'm sleeping some."

"How many hours?"

He ate another donut hole. "Three or four."

"That's not enough," she said.

"I know."

36

"Are you eating?"

"I have to eat better."

"That's all you're going to say about it?"

"I'll sleep more this weekend," he said and smiled.

"How are the girls?"

"They're okay. Kathleen hates the school. She's in the third grade. How can you hate the third grade?"

"School's always hard, you know that. Does Ginnie like kindergarten?"

"I think so, but Marie hasn't been taking her to physical therapy because the place is twenty miles away."

"But she's got to," Mora said and shook her head.

"I know. She promised she'd do it. We'll see. To be honest I'm just having a hard time thinking of what to say to them. My own daughters and I don't know what to say. I run out of questions. I wish I could go down there, just once even. Then I would know what to ask. But I don't know what their house looks like or their neighborhood. I don't know anything about their school or Las Vegas. When I ask them to describe it, they just quit talking. All day long I think of things to ask them but when I talk to them I don't know what to say."

"Little kids are always bad on the phone," Mora said.

"Maybe," he said.

"What else is going on?"

"I don't know," he said.

"You're a great conversationalist today. Now I know who your daughters get it from."

Freddie laughed. He put the last donut hole in his mouth and finished the coffee.

"At least get some sleep tonight, okay?"

"I will," Freddie said.

"I put an extra twist in for you."

"Thanks," Freddie said.

She handed him the boxes. "I'll see you tomorrow."

"I'll see you tomorrow, Mora."

*

He opened the store on time and drank three cups of coffee until the morning rush ended at eleven. He called Pat and told him the morning numbers, and Pat told him he wasn't coming in. Freddie hung up the phone, leaned the chair back against the wall, and fell asleep. He was startled awake twenty minutes later when two old painters came in. They saw him asleep and quietly went to the counter. They waited for a moment and then looked at each other and shouted "Freddie!" as loud as they could. Freddie yelped as he woke and fell off the chair. The two painters doubled over laughing.

"Jesus!" Freddie yelled from the ground.

"We're sorry, Freddie," they both said.

"It's alright," he said and got up.

"We didn't mean to scare you that bad," one of the men said, still laughing, and set down a piece of stained trim board.

"It's alright, Paul," Freddie said. "What do you guys need?"

"Can you match the stain on this piece by tomorrow, and we'll need twenty gallons of Super Spec, same color as this morning. Plus we're doing an old lath-and-plaster job, and Andy said you knew how to make the cracks disappear without re-texturing the whole wall."

Freddie took a drink of cold coffee and once again began working.

*

He closed the store at five-thirty and drove home. With the scrap wood from his front yard he got a fire going in the fireplace. He sat at the kitchen table, took off his coat, and opened a worn folder. He laid out his bills across the table.

Memorial/Providence Hospital total bill: $74,798

Monthly hospital payment: $575

Monthly alimony and child support: $600

Monthly mortgage payment: $692

Monthly home equity loan payment: $423

Credit Card monthly (in collection): $200 (total bill $9,000)

Natural gas: $570 past due and turned off

Cell phone: $58

Electric: $556 past due

Water and sewage: $263 past due

Garbage: $192 past due and cancelled

Car insurance: Cancelled

Health insurance: Cancelled

As he did each week, he tried to think of a way out of the mess, but in the end there was no way out. He just didn't make enough money. He should declare bankruptcy, but he didn't want to declare bankruptcy.

Why did he have to be proud about that?

He shuffled through his bills. It never made sense to him how he could have health insurance for his family, insurance that cost him seven hundred dollars a month, and still his policy didn't cover everything. For years his wife had sat at the same table arguing with the insurance company about what they would cover and what they wouldn't. Which specialists were approved and which weren't, which surgeries were covered and which weren't, which medications and which physical therapies. Even with mortgaging their house they fell behind on those payments, and then his wife had to quit working to take care of Ginnie. They began to drown. Now after four years he was left with a total bill of nearly seventy-five thousand dollars. He put the papers away and set his head down on the table and closed his eyes.

When he woke he looked at his watch and it was thirty minutes later. He put the papers back in the folder and went into the basement. He looked through a box of his father's things and found the stack of postcards he was hoping to find. He went through them until he saw a pin-up girl, a redhead in a white cowboy hat. She was leaning against a wooden rocking horse in a tight cowgirl outfit, smiling. Her large breasts, her slim waist and long legs. She held a silver pistol in each hand. He took it, put it in his coat pocket, and left.

6

Darla Kervin, a thin, middle-aged woman with brown hair, sat in a chair next to the hospital bed. A worn leather cigarette case and a red plastic lighter sat on her lap while she read, out loud, a paperback novel titled *The Burning Cliffs of Planet Ryklon.*

"They found you," Freddie said as he entered.

Darla looked up, startled. She set the novel on her lap. "Hey, Freddie . . . I was visiting my mother in California," she said.

"Are you holding up okay?"

She shrugged her shoulders and said sadly, "I'm okay . . . What happened, Freddie?"

"I don't really know," he said and leaned against the wall. "I was asleep upstairs. It was around one in the morning or so, and somehow he found an old wooden gate in the garage and tied it to the plastic gate at the bottom of the stairs. He climbed up to the second floor and threw himself down on top of the stakes. I didn't hear anything until he landed. I'm sorry, but I didn't."

Darla nodded and picked up and set down the cigarette case on her lap and tears welled in her eyes. "Thank you for coming to visit him," she whispered.

Freddie took the postcard from his coat pocket and handed it to her. "You might think this is stupid, but I thought maybe it would cheer him up somehow."

She looked at the postcard and smiled, and leaned it

against a box of Kleenex on the table next to the bed.

"What are you reading to him?"

She picked up the paperback and showed him the old weathered cover. "I used to read to him when he was in the military hospital. I figured I'd do it again. He's a science-fiction buff."

Freddie looked at his watch. "I have to go to work," he said. "But can you tell me is there any news? How is he?"

"I don't think very well," she said. "That's the general opinion anyway . . . Can I ask you a question before you go?"

Freddie nodded.

"When you found him, was he in pain?"

"He was unconscious when I got to him. I never heard him cry or moan or anything like that."

"Are you sure?"

"I'm pretty sure," Freddie said.

"Good," she said.

*

Two hours later Pauline gently shook Darla awake. She sat up in the chair, took off her reading glasses, and put them in her purse. "Was I asleep a long time?"

"An hour or so," said Pauline.

"Is anything wrong?"

"Everything's the same. I'm almost done with my shift and wanted to let you know that we increased Leroy's pain meds again. He shouldn't move around anymore."

"I guess I'm not used to staying up this late," Darla said and yawned.

"I'm sorry I had to wake you. I just wanted you to know," Pauline said, and then she charted and left the room.

She walked down the hall to room seven.

"Well, buster, you're finally up," she said.

"I am," the old man said and smiled as he lay on his side facing the door.

"All my patients have been sleeping tonight, and you've been out my whole shift. I got to say it's been lonely without you, Mr. Flory."

"I tried to wake up, but I couldn't."

"Well you're in luck now, 'cause it's that time again," she said.

"It's why I started waking up, I guess," he said. "My body could feel the pain coming on. I woke up a few times earlier, but I knew it wasn't time for my next dose. So I made myself just stay still. I was trying to hold out before I started bothering you again."

"You never bother me, Mr. Flory. And there's no use being a tough guy around me."

"I'm not tough," he said.

"You're a real cowboy. They seem pretty tough."

"Some are, most aren't, though."

"But you ride horses."

"I haven't been on a horse in a long time. I just use my four-wheeler. Anyway, anyone can ride a horse."

"Not me."

"I could have taught you," he said and winked.

"I bet you'd be a good teacher," she said, smiling. "Okay, I'll be back in a minute."

She left the room, went to the Pyxis Medstation, and entered Mr. Flory's information. The drawer opened and she

43

took his pain medication, counted the remaining, noted it, and went back. She handed him two pills and he washed them down with water.

"This should take care of you for a while," she said and began charting.

"How's your shift been tonight, Pauline?"

"Not bad."

"Did you do anything nice before you came in?"

"I watched TV and ate a half a pint of ice cream," she said while typing.

"Ice cream," the old man said.

"It's bad for you, Mr. Flory."

"My wife makes homemade ice cream."

"No wonder you married her."

"She makes peach ice cream and shortbread cookies every summer. To tell you the truth, Pauline, she makes ice cream almost every Saturday from June to August. But guess who has to turn the crank?"

"You."

"You're right."

"You seem strong enough, Mr. Flory."

"I used to be. You know I bought her an electric ice-cream maker one Christmas. One that does all the work for you, but she never even took it out of the box. That next summer comes along and it's back to rock salt and my arm busting over the crank."

"Women like watching men work."

"Maybe, or maybe she was just mad at me," he said and tried to laugh.

"I think it would be hard to be mad at you, Mr. Flory. Alright, I got to keep working but you should feel better in a

44

minute or two. Think of something nice and close your eyes. Think of the electric ice cream maker. I won't see you tomorrow but the night after I will. Okay, buster?"

"Good-night, Pauline," he whispered.

"Good-night," she said and left.

In the hallway she took a piece of gum from her pocket and glanced at her watch. One more patient. Mr. Delgado was an overweight, middle-aged alcoholic with a gastrointestinal bleed. He was ten hours out of surgery. As she entered the room she saw a short, plump woman with dyed red hair and black fingernail polish sitting in the chair next to him. She wore a pink sweat suit that read TOP SHELF across her breasts in gold lettering.

"How are you feeling, Mr. Delgado?" she said and stood at the foot of the bed. His face was bloated and red and veined. He looked at the nurse in a fog of Dilaudid, but he didn't respond.

"Mr. Delgado?" Pauline said again.

He looked at her but he didn't speak.

"The TV doesn't get cable," the woman said suddenly. "The ones in the other rooms do. I checked." She had her purse on her lap. She took a small plastic container of hand sanitizer from it and squirted it in her palms. "For the amount of money this is costing, you'd think we'd get cable."

"I'll tell maintenance," Pauline said while she checked his vital signs and made sure the drainage tubes were working properly. She looked at the staples and felt around the incision. It seemed normal. She went to the computer in the corner of the room and began charting. "I'll try one more time. How are you feeling, Mr. Delgado? I can see your eyes open. Can you understand me?"

45

"I know he's been queasy," the woman said.

"A lot of people get nauseous from anesthesia. We can give him something for it if he feels that way. Mr. Delgado, have you been feeling nauseous?"

He looked at her but again he didn't respond.

"How are you dealing with the pain, Mr. Delgado?"

"He's in a lot of pain," the woman said.

"Mr. Delgado," Pauline said and moved again in front of him. "On a scale of one to ten how much pain are you feeling?" The man's skin was gray and yellow. He looked at her but he couldn't speak. "Can you tell me how bad it hurts on a scale of one to ten? Ten being the most pain."

His eyes suddenly watered and he broke into a sweat. He moved his hands to cover his mouth and began vomiting blood. It sprayed out through his fingers, bright red and fetid, and ran down his gown and onto the floor. Pauline hit the emergency button, and the woman began screaming.

Mr. Delgado fell back into the bed. His bloody hands dropped to his side and his eyes closed. His blood pressure dropped and his heart raced. Another nurse rushed in and the rapid response team was called. The fat woman became hysterical. She moved to the back wall, pacing and crying.

The team entered the room: a doctor, a nurse, and two men to help lift him. It took all of them to get Mr. Delgado's immense body off the bed. The gurney moaned under his weight. They rolled him out of the room unconscious while they worked on him, and the frantic woman followed behind them, crying. Her shoe soles, wet with blood, left faint tracks down the glossy hall floor.

Pauline went to her locker. She changed out of her blood-stained uniform into a clean one. In the bathroom she washed her face and hands twice, made sure her shoes were clean, and looked at her watch. She had half an hour until she had a night off.

*

At a Chinese restaurant she picked up a takeout order and drove home. She ate in front of the TV and drank a bottle of wine while Donna hopped about the apartment. It wasn't until four in the morning that she fell asleep.

She woke up on the couch the next afternoon, hung-over, to her phone ringing. She reached across the coffee table, saw it was her friend Cheryl, and picked it up.

"I called you four times last night," Cheryl said. "Why wouldn't you call me back?"

"I was too tired last night," said Pauline. "I just got Bing's and came home."

"Why do you still eat there?"

"I like it."

"That was my mom's go-to barf bag."

"I know." Pauline sighed.

"What about tonight?"

"I'm staying home tonight."

"But a couple of my brother's friends are in town. We're all going out and I told them you'd come with us."

"I don't feel like it tonight."

"These guys are good-looking."

"That's what you said last time."

"We had a pretty good time last time."

"Did we?"

"At least you did," Cheryl said and laughed.

"Where are you going?"

"The Bucket."

"I hate that place."

"It'll be fun," Cheryl said.

"I don't know."

"What else are you gonna do, watch TV then cave in and make brownies?"

"I was thinking chocolate chip cookies."

"You're turning into an old lady."

"I feel like an old lady . . . Let me think it over and I'll call you back." Pauline hung up the phone. She put the blanket back over her and turned up the TV. The rabbit hopped underneath the coffee table and Pauline reached down, picked her up and set her on her stomach.

*

Six hours later she left the Bucket, drunk, and got into in a white pickup truck with a friend of Cheryl's brother, a thirty-year-old man named Ford Wrenn from Dothan, Alabama.

He was a tall and thin man with a sun-weathered face who worked on bridge construction throughout the western United States. He lived out of a suitcase ten months a year and at the time didn't have a permanent home.

"So where do you want to go?" he asked her as he started the engine. "I'd take you back to my place, but it's a Super 8 motel and I'm rooming with TC. We probably don't want to go there."

"We can't go to my place either," she said.

"You have roommates?" he asked.

"Just one, her name's Donna," she said and looked out the window.

"Would you be alright if we got a motel room?"

"The lowest I'll go is a Red Lion," she said and laughed.

"You know where one is?"

"Sure," she said and gave him directions. "Is your name really Ford? 'Cause if you haven't noticed you're driving a Chevy."

He laughed. "My daddy's daddy, he was named Ford. This was before Ford Motors really got going. That's who I'm named after. People ask me that all the time. The truth is I hate Fords. Their front ends are always loose, and their trannies are shit."

"I feel the exact same way."

"Sure you do," he said and again laughed.

They stopped at a mini-mart for a six-pack of beer and then drove the rest of the way to the Red Lion, where he got them a room. He led her to the third floor and they went inside and Pauline turned on the lights, set the thermostat to seventy-five, and took off her coat.

"Is it alright here?" he asked.

"I like it," she said and sat on the bed.

Ford opened two cans of beer, handed her one, and sat down on the bed a couple of feet from her. As he drank his beer she moved closer and closer to him until their legs were touching, and then she kissed him and he kissed her back. She began to take off his baseball cap, but as she did he stopped her.

"This is embarrassing," he said. "But I'm going bald. Do you mind that too much?"

"No," she said.

49

"I'm sorry about my hands, too," he said and showed them to her. He had the thickest fingers she'd ever seen. Two of his nails were black and the rest were chipped and cracked and ragged. The pinkie on his right hand was bent out, as was the ring finger on his left.

"Wait until you see me naked. I have my winter weight going right now." She laughed and took off his hat and began kissing him again. She took his beer from him and set both cans on the dresser. She pulled her blouse over her head and unclipped her bra, and then kicked off her shoes and her pants. She straddled him on the bed and they took up with their kissing again.

Ford Wrenn could hardly breathe as he held on to her. She took off his clothes, took a rubber from her purse, put it on him, and got back on top of him.

"Jesus, Pauline," he whispered. "I like you."

"I like you too," she said back. She kissed him as she moved back and forth. She went faster and faster until they were both finished. But as soon as she cried out she got up and went to the bathroom. When she came out she began to dress.

"Alright, buster," she said. "It's time for you to take me home."

"You want to leave?"

"If you're too tired, I can call a cab."

"I can give you a ride home," he said. But as he lay under the sheets he didn't move. He watched her dress. Her underwear was pink with black dots. She wore thick green hiking socks that she put on just after her underwear. She had to lie on the bed to pull her pants all the way up and button them.

"Talk about embarrassing," she said. Her bra was hidden

50

in the corner of the room. He knew where it was but didn't tell her and she walked around the bed, topless, looking for it.

"Shit, Pauline," he said finally. "Don't go yet. We could always get room service and watch a movie."

"I can't, but you should stay. A free night. You get laid and you get the room to yourself. I bet you TC snores like a truck."

"He does."

"Then you have a night off."

She found her bra, and put it and her blouse on.

"The truth is I don't want you to go," he said.

"I'd stay, but I have to get up early," she told him. "I'll call a cab."

"No, it's alright," he said. "I want to take you home." He got up from the bed, found his cap, and put it on. He dressed quickly and they left.

In the hotel parking lot he tried to kiss her as he unlocked the truck door, but it was short and awkward. As they left, he drove hunched over the steering wheel, trying to think of something to say.

"Maybe we could go see a movie tomorrow?" he asked.

"I had a great time tonight," Pauline said back to him. "But if I had to choose between running a marathon and having a boyfriend I'd be running right now."

Ford laughed. "If you don't want a boyfriend then I'm your man 'cause I'm only in this area for a week more. After that we're heading to Utah."

"What's in Utah?" she said.

"A bridge project in Salt Lake City."

Pauline pointed to a mini-mart coming into view. "See

51

that 7-Eleven up there?"

"Yeah," he said.

"I'll get out there."

Ford's heart sank. He didn't know what to think. He parked the truck in front of the empty store and turned the engine off. "Do you have a boyfriend? Is that why you don't want me to take you home?"

"No," she said. "I have to pick up a couple things so I figured I could just walk from here. My place is right around the corner."

"Did I do something wrong tonight?"

"No," Pauline said and put her hand on his arm. "I had a great time. I really did."

"I know I might seem lonely. I am a bit, I guess. Maybe that bothered you."

"It didn't bother me."

"Did I do something wrong while we were in the sack?"

"No," she said and smiled. "I liked that part."

"Would it be alright if I called you?"

"How about I call you? I'll get your number from Cheryl," she said and then got out of the truck and went inside the store. He watched her as she walked down an aisle, but then, not wanting to seem like he was staring, he started the truck and pulled out of the parking lot.

Pauline waited inside until he drove away. She bought an ice-cream sandwich and ate it while she walked down the sidewalk to her apartment. Part of her had wanted to stay in the room with him. To watch TV and order room service. Maybe to even sleep next to him. It had been years since she had fallen asleep next to anyone. She stopped on the sidewalk and finished the ice-cream sandwich and forced

52

herself to stop thinking about him. She cut across a lawn and kept going. Her apartment complex was two miles away.

*

When she woke the next afternoon she was still dressed in her clothes from the night before. The rabbit sat under the coffee table and the fading afternoon sun peered through her living-room window. In the kitchen she ate leftover Chinese food, took four ibuprofens, and called her father.

"What are you doing today?" she said.

"Nothing," he coughed. She could hear the sound of the TV playing in the background and him rustling around on the cot.

"I'm gonna come and get you in an hour, okay?"

"Why?" he asked.

"We're going to get pizza."

"Why?"

"'Cause I'm in a good mood."

"I don't like pizza."

"It'll be like old times."

"I don't know," he sighed wearily.

"I don't want to argue. I have to be at work in three hours. I'll come by and we'll get pizza. It'll be good for both of us to get out of the house."

"Goddamn it," he yelled suddenly and slammed down the phone.

She got up from the couch and took a shower. She cleaned the kitchen, did a load of laundry, and then drove to her father's house. As she arrived, the old man stood outside waiting on the brown, frozen grass of his front yard.

53

She pulled alongside him and stopped. "Have you been out here long?" she asked as he opened the door.

He shook his head and sat in the passenger seat. "I didn't mean to get angry," he said.

"It's alright," she said. "I should have let you know earlier. I know sometimes you're not in the mood for pizza. I should have asked and not just told."

"Pizza's alright," he replied. He wore a down coat, a ski cap, and a red scarf Pauline had knitted for him when she was in high school. She took them through side streets until they came to the half-deserted downtown and parked in front of an old pizza parlor. They ordered at the counter and then sat in a booth, in silence, until a high-school girl came to them with a pizza and a pitcher of Coke.

"I have some news," she said and took a slice, put it on a plate, and handed it to him. "I'm gonna apply for a school nursing job again. There's an opening for a nurse who handles both the elementary and middle school over on Fairview."

Her father began eating; he didn't acknowledge her. He just looked around the restaurant. She poured them both sodas from the pitcher and took a slice for herself. There was a family seated across from them who had a crying baby. Her father stopped eating and looked over at them.

"You'd think they could get it to shut up."

"They will," said Pauline.

He shook his head. "The sauce is too spicy."

"It's been the same for twenty years. That's why we always come here."

"They've changed it. I don't know why they would, but they did."

"It's the same." Pauline refilled his glass with soda and then leaned back in the booth and undid the top button of her jeans. "Tomorrow I tell you I'm really gonna start working out."

"You are getting fat," he said.

"I know," she said.

He looked at the family with the baby again. The infant had quit crying. It was sleeping in its mother's arms.

"You should have had children by now," he said and took another slice and put it on the plate in front of him and began eating it.

She didn't eat or say anything more to him after that. She just watched him take three more slices of pizza and drink two more glasses of soda. When he was finished he pushed the plate away and sat back. There was sauce and bits of crust on his face. He had spilled soda on his shirt and pants. He stared at the TV on the wall across from them.

"Are you finished?" she asked.

He nodded vaguely, still staring at the TV.

"Then listen to me, buster." She moved her hand in front of his face so he looked at her. "I'm not just threatening this, but if you say anything like that to me again you can walk home, and you can pay your own bills. You can live on the street, and I won't care. You don't tell me what to do. That's the deal. That's the only deal there will ever be for you and me. Besides telling you to take a shower and eat I leave you alone. When you start paying your own bills again you can tell me to lose weight and marry some dumb shit, but until then keep your mouth shut." She got up, put on her coat, and left.

Her father came out of the pizza parlor minutes later. He walked through the parking lot and nearly fell on a patch of ice. Her heart sank as she watched him from her car. The sky behind him grew black. It was two in the afternoon and the day seemed to be ending already. Inside the car he wouldn't even look at her. He just stared out the window in silence. She drove him home and in front of his house parked and turned off the engine.

"It sure looks like it's gonna snow," she said.

"I'm sorry," he said, and finally looked at her. He put his hand on her arm.

"It's alright," she said. "All in all I had a nice time. They have great soda. I love crushed ice. Plus it's always dark in there."

"I'll listen better."

"Don't worry about it. Just lay off my personal life. I never tell you to get a job or bring up the past, but you, you can't help telling me what to do."

"I know," he said and tears began falling down his face.

"Don't cry. Come on, I have to go to work."

"I'm sorry," he said and began sobbing. He tried to say more but couldn't.

"It's okay. I know you're sorry. Just make sure you keep the heat on in case things freeze. They say it's really gonna dip down tonight. I know you hate to use the heater but we can't have your pipes freeze. Uncle Jeff says it's a miracle they haven't already burst. Deal?"

Her father nodded and opened the door and got out. "I'm sorry," he said.

"I know."

"I love you."

"I know."

7

A girl with abscessed legs lay in a hospital bed staring at the wall. She was sixteen with short, badly cut blond hair. She was frail and underweight by twenty pounds, and it made her look much younger than she was. She had sad eyes that were set too close to her nose, and her skin was pearl white with no blemishes except for a single pimple on her chin. A teenage boy sat next to her in dirty, ripped jeans. He had on four shirts layered under a ragged black leather jacket. His hair was greasy and matted and cut crudely, and his hands were covered in scabs and homemade tattoos. His fingernails were black with grease and dirt. He looked ill under the fluorescent lights: pale and tired and his face was covered in acne.

Pauline entered the room and introduced herself to the girl and the boy sitting next to her. But the girl didn't acknowledge her, and the boy wouldn't look at her directly.

"Can you hear me, Jo?" Pauline said and moved to the side of the bed. She waved a hand in front of the girl's face. "Are you able to talk? I'm your swing shift nurse and I need to check your leg."

Pauline looked at the boy. "Has she spoken since she's been here?"

"She quit talking a month ago," he said, still looking at the ground.

"A month ago?"

"For the most part." He hunched over in the chair and

began chewing his nails and spitting them on the ground in front of him.

"What about her parents?"

"I don't know about them," he said.

"Where's she living?"

"We're all living at a house outside of town."

The boy stood up and walked over to the girl. His pants sagged down showing filthy white underwear. Pauline could smell him as he went by. "Jo?" he said and coughed. "Say something. The lady wants to talk to you." He shook her to get her attention, but the girl just stared at the wall.

"See, I told you," he said to Pauline.

"What's your name?" she asked.

"Bob," he said and sat back down.

"Does the house you're staying at have running water, Bob?"

"No," he said. "The water's shut off."

"Well, somehow you need to clean up. Your friend is really sick. You smell. Your clothes smell. You should look in the mirror. I'm afraid I'm going to have to ask you to leave and take a shower and wash your clothes before you come back and visit her. It's for her safety and really for yours, too."

The boy kept his eyes on the ground. He kept chewing on his nails, and then without saying anything more got up and left. Pauline watched him as he walked out and then looked at the girl. "Jo, I have to inspect the bandages. If you don't want to talk that's fine. If anything hurts just tap me on the arm, alright?" She waited a moment but the girl kept her eyes trained on the wall, so Pauline pulled back the bed sheet and blanket. She lifted the bandages covering the thighs of the girl's wire-thin legs.

"Does he always smell that bad?" Pauline asked.

"Yes," the girl whispered faintly. "He won't take a shower even when there is hot water."

"Ha, I knew you could talk," she said and smiled at the girl. "Your bandages look good. I'll repack them after dinner, okay?"

Jo nodded.

"Have you had them packed before?"

"No."

"How are you feeling otherwise?"

"I'm tired."

"How's your pain?"

"It's alright."

"On a scale of one to ten, ten being the worst, how do you feel?"

"About a three. I just feel like sleeping."

"Good, 'cause that's what you're supposed to be doing. But you also have to eat. They say you've haven't eaten anything since you've been here."

"I haven't been here that long."

"Is it the food?"

"It's not that. I'll start eating."

"Think about what sounds good and tell me. We'll try to get that, alright? Sometimes you just need to get your appetite started."

"Okay," Jo said.

Pauline charted on the computer in the corner of the room and left. In the hallway she looked at her watch and walked to room nine.

"Are you really awake, buster?" she said, looking at

Leroy Kervin. His eyes were open, but only half of his pupils were showing. The rest were rolled back in his head. His hair was combed away from the yellowing welt on his forehead. The cut on his lip was healing, and the swelling had gone down. She went to the computer in the corner of the room, looked at his chart, and then checked his chest tubes, the drainage canister on the floor, and his medication and IV drip. She charted her visit and left.

*

Jeanette found her clothes in the corner of the room. Leroy looked at her legs and saw the mark. Her right foot and calf were dark green and purple and black.

"Now you know," she said.

"I don't care about that," he said.

"Yeah you do. Everybody does."

"You're wrong," he wheezed.

"Are you okay?"

"I'm not sure." *He stood up slowly. He leaned against the living-room wall and watched her put on her underwear and bra, her black tights and pants and shirt.*

"I've never told anyone I had it," she said. "How would they find out?"

Leroy shook his head and tried to catch his breath.

"Maybe someone from work saw it," she said. "But how could they? I always wear tights under my pants no matter where I go. Even if I just go to the store. There's no way they could see. And I never go out anymore, never."

"Maybe they see you in here somehow?" Leroy said.

"Do you think so?"

60

"I don't know."

"Do you have it?"

"I never got the shot."

"How did you get away with that?" she said and found her shoes. She sat on a chair in the kitchen and began to put them on.

"They just screwed up. They missed me. I'm from a small town," he said and staggered to the kitchen table and sat across from her. Sweat leaked down his forehead and his breath was short and pained. "Everything's more ramshackle in a small town. Like I told you earlier, my uncle was in Vietnam, and while he was there he said he saw and did unforgivable things, and those things scarred his heart. He said his heart had so many scars on it that it was hard to breathe. That from the moment he woke he could feel the scars trying to stop the air coming in. For years he was drowning in that. When they developed the test they told us it was to weed out unfit soldiers, to save those kinds of soldiers like my uncle who were ruined by war. Not everyone was meant to be a soldier and not everyone is ruined by war. They said the test would save those people who would be forever scarred by it. They'd get the injection and if the mark appeared then they wouldn't have to go into combat. They would be free from it. But then the wars kept going and people started protesting. So they began testing more and more people, and where we lived they tested the entire town. Now we know it's a test to weed out those who think from those who are soldiers. Those who are easy to manipulate and those who aren't. A bad citizen from a good citizen. But back then we weren't sure what they were doing. We just thought they were trying to do something good."

"That's the way it was here, too," said Jeanette. "At first it was just for people joining the army and then they added all men from eighteen to fifty and then they added all women from eighteen to fifty and then it was everyone. They would give them the shot and if they got the mark they'd take them away and no one would ever see them again. Is that what happened to your uncle?"

Leroy nodded and paused for a long time. "When my uncle got back from Vietnam he worked at a lumber mill, but then they laid everyone off and closed it. The jobs dried up. They went to foreign ships off the coast that had mills on-board and they would buy our trees and sell the lumber back to us. So he came to live at our place. My mom got him a job as a stocker at the grocery store she worked at. He got on the graveyard shift, he moved out of the cabin he was living in, and he and my mom bought a camping trailer and moved it to our backyard. He lived in that. He didn't want to live in the house; he wanted to be alone. As the years passed he slowly faded away. He disappeared right in front of us and there was nothing we could really do . . . When he got the shot his foot turned instantly. I was with him. I was supposed to get the shot, too, but somehow they forgot about me. I don't know why, but they did. They'd made up a sort of clinic in the school gym. The walls of the rooms were sheets. Only white sheets separating everybody in town. A man in a doctor's coat and a soldier came in and they gave my uncle the shot in his arm. They told him to take off his shoes and socks, and then they left the room. Within a minute his left foot looked completely bruised. It looked like someone had beaten it. Then a different doctor and a different soldier came back. They told me to take off my shoes and socks and I did. They looked over

62

*my feet and gave me a pass notice. Then they told my uncle
to put on his shoes and they took him away. He was crying
in relief. He thought they were going to help him. That they
would save him. Save him from the way he was drowning.
He'd been having such a hard time. I said I would wait for
him and I sat outside in his car all night but he never came
out. The next morning I went to them and asked about my
uncle and they said they didn't have any record of him. No
record at all. He went there for help and they made him disappear."*

"I'm so sorry."

"Me too . . . How did it happen to you?"

*"My dad took the test when it first came out, when it was
voluntary. My dad is very patriotic. He believes everything
they say and above all he hates people who are weak. When
he passed, he came home and made my mother and I go.
This is before we even had to, before everyone was forced to.
So we went down there and he sat in the room with us and
didn't say a word. My mother was really scared, 'cause she'd
heard stories and I was crying, holding on to her. They had
taken over part of a community college and set up a testing
center. We both got the shot but nothing happened. It was
only later, months later, that my foot got the mark. Now it
keeps growing. Pretty soon it'll be over my whole body."*

"Maybe it won't."

"I hope not."

"Can I tell you something?"

"Sure."

"Maybe you'll think I'm crazy."

"I'll let you know if I do," she said and smiled.

"Last night I had a nightmare, and in the nightmare I

was in a foreign country and I wasn't sure why I was there. I was just there. I was in a truck with three other men and we were going along a road when a bomb went off and the truck exploded. I woke in a hospital with my head in a fog. I couldn't get my thoughts back and my body wouldn't work right. Years passed and I was stuck that way, lost in a fog with a broken body. Then one night, out of the blue, my thoughts came back to me and were clear. For whatever reason my mind was like it was before. I should have been ecstatic, but really underneath it all I knew it was just an illusion. Maybe not an illusion exactly, maybe more like a momentary reprieve. Somehow I was certain the fog would come back. So instead of being elated I was grief stricken 'cause I knew then what my life would end up being. And the worst part, the part I couldn't stop thinking about, was that I'd never get to sleep next to someone and put my arms around them. For the rest of my life I would never hold anyone. I would be in bed alone."

"That's a horrible thought," said Jeanette.

Leroy nodded. "When I woke from the nightmare it was still night. I'd only been asleep twenty minutes. It's weird how you can be asleep only a short time and have such terrible things happen in your mind." A pain suddenly spiked through Leroy's chest and he was again overcome with agony. He fell to the ground breathless, and as he did he could hear the soldiers coming up the stairs.

"They're here again," Jeanette cried and ran to Leroy and tried to lift him. "Can you stand?"

Leroy's vision began to blur. He tried to scream but he had no air.

"It's gonna be alright, buster. I'm going to take care of

you. But we have to get you through the window."

"You should go by yourself," Leroy said shakily.

"That's just the pain saying that. It'll go away. Don't give up."

The soldiers rushed into the apartment. Their faces were painted black and red. The first soldier pushed him down and pulled a knife from his belt and plunged it into his ribs.

*

Leroy Kervin lay in a cold sweat, whimpering. His eyes were now closed and he was trying to move in the bed. "It's gonna be alright, buster," Pauline said as she held him still and waited for the doctor.

8

Freddie McCall drove to the Western Spoke Tavern, a sports bar near the town's rail yard, and met a middle-aged Yakama Indian named Lowell Price. The large, nearly obese man sat at a small table in the back of the empty room with a half-finished pitcher of beer.

"Freddie," Lowell called out when he saw him enter. As he stood his sweat pants slipped down his legs. He pulled them up with his left hand and shook Freddie's hand with his right.

"I didn't mean to be late," Freddie said. "I was waiting in the parking lot 'cause I didn't see your truck. I thought maybe you hadn't shown up yet."

Lowell sat back down and laughed. "Shit man, I don't have my truck anymore." There was a scar on his forehead and a birthmark that covered half of his neck. He wore a horseshoe ring on his left hand and had three tattoos on his right. His hair was long and black and held in a ponytail.

"You want a beer, Freddie?"

"It's my only night off," he said and nodded. He pushed the empty glass toward Lowell. "So where's your truck?"

"I had to sell it. I'm driving a ten-speed now," he said and again laughed. "My nephew and me went to a Mariners game a few months ago. I got lost and drove down a one-way street and got pulled over. I blew just over the limit, but it's my third one. They took both the truck and me. I had to call my little sister, and she had to drive up and get my nephew.

Now everyone in my family has it out for me and I'm going to Coyote Ridge for a year and a half."

Freddie shook his head. "When?"

"Sixteen days."

Freddie leaned back in the chair and looked around. He couldn't remember the last time he'd been in a bar. He couldn't even remember the last time he'd had a beer. "You know I thought the reason you called was to get your job back at Logan's. But that's not the reason, is it?"

Lowell again laughed. "No, man. I'd rather go to jail than go back there."

"You know I even made you a work schedule," Freddie said. "And I was thinking about ways to get Pat to open up on Sundays again."

"He's too much of a Bible eater for that," Lowell said. "No man, I ain't going back. That's not why I called . . . You still working at the group home?"

"Yeah."

"So she hasn't married that guy, huh?"

"No."

"You should have gotten a lawyer."

"I know."

"You still got the house?"

"Sorta. It's mortgaged twice. They shut off the gas two months ago. But on paper I guess it's mine." Freddie finished the beer. He looked at Lowell and Lowell poured him another.

"You got a fireplace, right?"

"Yeah."

"You have any wood?"

"Just scrap wood. I picked some up from a warehouse the other night."

"My aunt has a couple cords you could probably have," Lowell said. "Can you get a truck?"

Freddie shook his head. "I don't have a credit card anymore and you need one to get a rental."

"I can borrow my cousin's. But you'll have to drive," Lowell said.

"You're serious?"

"My aunt just bought a pellet stove. She's got two cords of wood in her carport, but she doesn't need wood anymore. She wants it out. I need to do something nice for her 'cause even she hates me, and she'll put up with anybody."

"Thanks," Freddie said.

"There's no use in me beating around the bush about why I called you," Lowell said and lowered his voice. "I haven't called you in a long time, but I've always liked you, Freddie. I've always trusted you. Look I've got eighty-five pot plants growing in my house. The problem is my oldest sister wants to move back in there while I'm gone. It's her place as much as mine. I can't say no. She's been living in Colorado. She used to be alright but she's a Bible eater now, too. So I got to either burn the plants or give them to someone I can trust."

"I thought you'd quit that," Freddie whispered.

"I told you I did, but I didn't. I used to sell to a guy and he got busted. I thought he was going to turn on me so I told everyone I sold the plants. But I just moved them to a different place for a while and started selling to Indians only."

"But I don't know how to grow anything," Freddie said.

"My nephew goes to college in Ellensburg. He'll drive down and handle most of it. If you agree, we'll set it up in your basement. All you have to do is water them four times a week. He'll do the rest. The lights are on timers and I have heaters that will regulate the temperature. It ain't a lot of work."

Freddie rubbed his face with his hands.

"I can get you between five hundred and a grand a month," Lowell said. "My nephew will come by twice a week to do most of the maintenance. He'll sell it, but he won't sell out of your house, and no one but him will come by. There's a harvest in a month. You'll get a chunk of money then . . . Look, I know you're broke, and that's why I'm asking you. The risk ain't much, Freddie, but there's always risk. And a year and a half is not a lot of time, but it is a bit of time. I've been growing for almost twenty years and haven't had many problems. My nephew's a good kid and to be honest, cops don't care about weed like they used to."

"Can I think on it for a couple days?" Freddie asked.

"I would if I were you," Lowell said.

"You mind if we get another pitcher?" Freddie asked.

"We'll get a couple more."

"You really aren't coming back to the paint store?"

"Shit no," Lowell said and filled his glass.

*

They met on the reservation a week later on Freddie's day off. They borrowed Lowell's cousin's truck and took two trips loading and then unloading the firewood, leaving it in a pile on Freddie's front lawn. When they were done, Freddie took Lowell inside the house and down the stairs to a large basement. Rows and rows of old cardboard boxes lined the walls. There was furniture, kids' bikes, a weight set, old windows, two doll houses, a Soap Box Derby car, an old saddle, and tools. There was hardly enough room to walk.

"You sure have a lot of shit down here," Lowell said.

"It was my grandfather's house," Freddie told him. "It's been in my family for three generations. Every single one of them was a pack rat, and I guess I am, too, 'cause I can't throw any of their things out. But there's a back room." He led Lowell to a door and opened it and turned on the lights. Inside the large room were two rows of fluorescent lamps that hung over a sixteen-by-eight-foot diorama.

"It's Gettysburg during the Civil War," Freddie said. "I recreated the Battle of Gettysburg."

Miniature farms and trees and houses sat on the papier mâché hills. There were soldiers on horseback fighting and canons and wagon trains. There were half-destroyed buildings and tent hospitals and makeshift military camps. Hundreds of dead soldiers were strewn about.

Lowell picked one of them up and looked at it. "Did you paint all these?"

Freddie nodded.

"How?"

"I had a magnifying glass and used tiny brushes. It's not that hard."

"Serves them right to kill each other after killing the Indians for so long," Lowell said and put the soldier back down and pointed to a half-burned-out house. "And the houses, how did you build them?"

"Some from kits. Others I built on my own."

"It must have taken years."

"Yeah, it did."

"Does the train work?"

"It used to," Freddie said. "But I've taken it apart."

"I've never seen anything like it," Lowell said.

Freddie looked at the battlefield. "Fifty-seven thousand men got hurt or killed during this one battle. More people than live in our entire town. And it was summer and they were left in the sun to die. Can you imagine what that must have been like? And what did it get them? Most of them were kids, hadn't even kissed a girl. Most of them were dirt poor. All that death and destruction and I'm here a hundred and fifty years later painting fake blood on them like it's a game. Look, I'm broke. If you're serious about the money, you can use the room. If I go to jail, I go to jail. I don't have my kids and I'm going to lose the house if I don't do something soon. So what does it matter." He went to the diorama and pushed one of the tables over and half of it crashed to the floor. Soldiers and trees and houses and buildings spilled out on to the bare concrete, and tears welled in his eyes. He wanted to stomp on the buildings and papier mâché mountains, but he couldn't. He had worked so hard on them for so long. He went for the other table leg, but Lowell stopped him.

"Don't break the table, Freddie," he said. "We can use it to set the plants on."

71

9

Pauline stepped out of the elevator, clocked in, and was prepped by the day nurses. A CT scan had discovered a nick in Leroy Kervin's bowel and he was in surgery. Mr. Delgado, the alcoholic with the GI bleed, was back, and there was a new patient in room two, a middle-aged woman recovering from a ruptured appendix. The teenage girl, Jo, still hadn't eaten, and the old rancher, Mr. Flory, was going home the next day.

Pauline began with Jo. The TV and the main lights in her room were turned off and she could see the girl by the dim bedside light, closing her eyes as she walked in.

"You can't fool me," Pauline said. "I know that trick. I've used it a lot myself." Jo remained still, with her eyes shut, and Pauline took a tube of lip balm from her shirt pocket and set it on the bedside table. "I got you something. It's like Chapstick but better. This place always makes my lips chapped and this stuff really works, and it looks like you could use it." She waited for a moment but the girl remained motionless so she turned on the overhead lights and moved to the side of the bed where Jo's abscessed leg was. "Alright then, straight down to business. I have to check the packings. You don't have to talk if you don't want to. Just let me know if anything hurts. If it does, all you have to do is tap on my arm and I'll stop. Okay?" She waited for a moment but still Jo didn't respond. Pauline pulled back the white bed sheet and blanket, lifted the gown, and inspected the three packings.

"They're looking better, Jo," she said and covered up the girl again. "So how's it been going with the food? They say you haven't eaten yet." She again looked at her but still the girl lay with her eyes closed. "How about some TV, then?" She turned on the set and went through the channels until she came to a car race. She kept it there and turned up the sound. She charted in the corner of the room and left.

In the hallway she looked at her watch and went to room seven.

"How are you this evening, Mr. Flory?" she asked. The old man was awake and lying on his side.

"I'm going home tomorrow," he whispered.

"I heard they were cutting you loose."

His face looked pale and exhausted, and she thought he'd aged years in the short time he'd spent in the hospital.

"I'm going to miss you, Mr. Flory. You know I'd never met a real cowboy before you."

"I wasn't much of cowboy," he said.

"I bet that's just you being cowboy humble."

He smiled. "I'm going to miss you, too, Pauline."

"Good," she said. "I like to be missed. They told me your wife and daughters just left."

"They went home to get the house ready."

"I bet it'll be good to get home, huh?"

"I don't want to die here," he said.

"Don't talk like that, Mr. Flory. You'll make me cry."

"I'm just telling the truth," he said.

"Maybe."

"We both know."

"I bet your family will be glad to see you home."

The old man shook his head.

73

"Why wouldn't they be, Mr. Flory?"

"I've been a burden to them all for a long while now."

"I'm sure they don't think that. Probably just the opposite. But I know you'll all be happy to be out of here. Hospitals are depressing any way you look at it, Mr. Flory. That is unless you're having a baby and neither of us are." She laughed. "Anyway, make sure to tell your wife I'm going to miss her. She makes the best cookies I've ever eaten and she always looks so nice. She told me she dresses up hoping it'll make you feel better somehow."

"She's a good woman," he said faintly.

"I think she might like you, Mr. Flory."

He coughed again and tried to clear his throat. "She goes to church every week. It takes her an hour and a half each way to get there. Every week since I've known her, no matter what, she goes. Even if it's snowing and I tell her it's not safe, she'll go. There's no arguing with her about it, no arguing at all. When we were first married I'd go with her, but I didn't like the church. I didn't like the priest. In my heart . . . in my heart I just don't believe in it. I hate admitting that out loud but it's true. Lately I've been thinking a lot about it. You can't help it when you're in my situation. But even now when I know I'm dying, I still don't believe in it. I believe in something, but not that. I don't think about it like a club or a business run by a celibate man. It's hard to explain the way I feel. But now I start questioning things. I know you can't force yourself to believe in something, but now I'm trying to. 'Cause if there is a heaven, if there really is, my wife and daughters will be there someday, but I won't be there with them. 'Cause no matter how hard I try I still don't believe." The old man closed his eyes in exhaustion.

"If it is true . . . then I'm gonna be without them forever and there's nothing I can do to change it."

"You'll be with them, Mr. Flory. They make exceptions for good-looking old cowboys."

He opened his eyes to see her. He reached out his hand and she took it. "I sure like you, Pauline."

"Thank you, Mr. Flory. I feel the same way about you." She sat down across from him in the bedside chair and sighed. "But if you keep talking like this, buster, I'll need a drink and a good cry. So we have to get back to business. How's your pain tonight? They upped your dosage again, huh?"

"The pain's always the same no matter what they do," he whispered.

"I'm sure sorry about that. You got a rough deal. Hit the button anytime you want, Mr. Flory. I'll let you sleep now. If you need anything, you know how to get ahold of me." She placed her hand on his arm and squeezed it twice and left.

In room five Mr. Delgado was alone and asleep, recovering from emergency surgery. Pauline checked his IV and vitals, made notes on his chart, and left. In room two the woman recovering from surgery for a ruptured appendix was awake. Her husband sat in the chair next to her holding her hand.

"He's nervous because he's never been in a hospital before," his wife said.

"Not ever?" Pauline asked.

"No," he said.

"You weren't born in one?"

"No."

"Then you're lucky."

"That's what I keep telling him," his wife said. "But there's no talking with him when he gets upset. Anyway I'm the one in pain. I'm the one with stitches and the scar. What's he whining about?"

He laughed and stood up and kissed her. Pauline checked her vitals and the incision, and together they helped his wife to the toilet, and took her on a short walk up and down the hall.

At dinner break she went to the cafeteria and ate two bowls of tapioca pudding and drank a cup of coffee. When she came back to the sixth floor she went first to the girl's room. The TV was on, but the sound was down and the channel changed, and Jo watched it half-asleep.

"I knew you couldn't take NASCAR," Pauline said.

"I hate NASCAR," Jo whispered and turned her head to see her.

"I was betting you had some smarts. Alright, you know why I'm here. It's that time. We have to change the packings."

The girl's face fell.

"How's your pain right now? Do you think you can manage it?"

"It doesn't hurt too bad," she said. "I just don't like seeing what you're doing. Is it okay if I keep my eyes closed?"

"Of course," Pauline said and pulled the curtains around the bed. She took back the sheet and blanket. Jo pulled up her gown showing the three bandages on her left leg. Pauline washed her hands, put on a pair of sterile gloves, and went to work removing the old dressings from the open wounds.

The girl kept her eyes shut and clenched her fists tightly.

"My dad had the NASCAR station at home. He watched races every night after he got off work."

"Where was that?"

"Where I grew up."

"Where did you grow up?" Pauline asked. She had taken two of the dressings out and had one to go.

"Rainier, Oregon."

"But you don't live there now?"

"No," she said.

"Why not?"

"I hated it there, so I ran away."

"Where'd you go when you ran away?"

"Why do you want to know?"

"I'm just curious," Pauline said.

"Why?" she gasped.

"Are you okay?"

"I opened my eyes for a second and saw what you're doing. I have to remember to never open my eyes."

"When I was your age all I thought about day and night was running away. I just never knew where to run to." She finished removing the dressings. "That's why I'm asking. We're halfway done, how are you doing now?"

"I'm alright. It doesn't hurt that bad. It just feels weird."

Pauline pulled off her gloves, washed her hands again, and put on a fresh pair. She began cleaning and repacking the open wounds. "It won't take much longer, so just hang in there, and keep your eyes closed until I tell you . . . So when you ran away where did you go?"

"I went to Seattle. I met Bob and his friends there. Bob's the guy who stinks. After that they went to San Francisco, so I went with them. But we didn't stay long because they found out about the house."

"The house with no water?"

Jo nodded. "There's no electricity either, but there's a mini-mart a mile away. We go there almost every day. It's near Tampico."

"What's the house like?"

"It's old and white. It's a farmhouse. There's a huge yellow barn behind it. The barn's really nice."

"And nothing works out there?"

"Everything's shut off."

"Don't you get cold?"

"They have a fireplace, but you're right, it's always cold in there. I spend most of the time in my sleeping bag."

"Whose house is it?"

"It's Captain's grandparents', but I guess they're dead. So his parents own the house but they live in California somewhere. It's just sitting there empty."

"Who's Captain?"

"He's just one of the guys," she said and flinched. She grabbed part of the blanket and squeezed it.

"You alright?"

"I'm okay."

"You're pretty tough."

"No I'm not."

"Abscesses really hurt. I know that."

"I just wish they'd go away."

"They will soon enough. How did they start?"

"You know how they started."

"I don't. That's why I'm asking."

"From needles," she said softly. "You know they're from needles. They started to get bad a month ago. Captain said they'd go away but they didn't."

"What were you using?"

"Heroin," she admitted.

"Have you been using a long time?"

"No," she said. "To be honest, I don't even like it. I don't like the way it makes me feel. Bob and Captain say I'm just a chipper. I only do it once in a while. I don't like seeing blood, so they do it for me. I won't do it on my own. That's why they put the needle in my leg. Even seeing a bruise on my arm makes me queasy. They say it's too much of a waste to snort it. But they keep most of it to themselves anyway. When they do give me some, they just give me a little. And now I just feel sick all the time, so I don't know if it's from that or the abscesses."

"What about your parents? Aren't they worried about you?"

"I'm emancipated. Anyway, I'm not going back there."

"You're sure?"

"Why do you ask so many questions?"

"I don't know," Pauline said. "I've always been like that."

"I wish you'd stop. It's starting to really hurt now. You'll go faster if we don't talk."

"Of course," Pauline said. "We're almost done. Just a couple minutes more."

Jo winced and again squeezed her eyes shut.

Pauline did the rest of the work in silence. The girl's face became red and tears leaked down her cheeks, but she said nothing more and made no sound. Pauline finished bandaging the new packs, covered her again, charted, and then left the room.

When she next came back it was an hour later. She entered to find two teenage boys in the room: Bob, the kid she had met before, and another boy who was over six feet tall and looked to weigh more than two hundred and fifty pounds. He had stringy brown hair and a boy's beard that was spotty and untrimmed. He wore a duct-taped green parka with layers of shirts underneath. He stood in front of the bed eating Jo's dinner from the bedside tray.

"What do you think you're doing?" Pauline said to him.

"What's it look like I'm doing?" he said with a mouth full of food.

"I didn't know you were a patient here."

He took a drink from the soda on her tray. "Jo doesn't like to eat. You'd have just thrown it out."

"Did she say you could have her food?"

"She doesn't care," he said.

"Don't you want her to get better?"

"She won't eat this. The only thing I've ever seen her eat are candy bars."

Pauline pointed to the other boy. "I told Bob the last time he was here that I'd make him leave if he was this dirty and smelled this bad. What you guys don't seem to understand is that your friend is really, really sick."

"We don't have a shower," Bob said. "I told you that last time."

"Not everyone has running water," the other boy added and finished eating the dinner. He set the plate down hard on the bedside tray. There were bits of food on his face and in his beard. He was beginning to sweat in all his layers of clothes. Jo's head was turned facing the wall. She kept her eyes closed.

"What's your name?" Pauline asked.

"Captain," he said.

"Captain, I don't think you get it. Jo almost died."

"She's not that sick," Bob said. "I've seen people with worse ones."

Pauline turned to him. "You're a doctor?"

"I'm just saying," he said.

Pauline looked at her watch. "Visiting hours are over. If you care about her at all, at least clean up in the visitors' bathroom before coming here. Go to a thrift store and buy a shirt and a pair of pants."

"Fuck you," said Captain. "We don't have to do anything you tell us."

"Then I'm calling security," Pauline said.

There was an unopened soda can on the bedside table. Captain put it in his coat pocket. "We were leaving anyway," he said and looked to Bob and they both left the room.

*

When her shift ended, Pauline drove home. She didn't open a bottle of wine, she just drank tea and finished the application for the school nursing position. She changed the sheets on her bed and for the first time in a month tried to sleep in her bedroom. But her mind raced and sleep wouldn't come, so she went back to the living room and the TV.

The next day she dropped off the application at the school's administrative office, ate at a Mexican restaurant, and forced herself to walk for an hour. As she did, she passed through downtown, and the blocks of struggling and empty stores. She came to a group of high school girls sitting at a picnic table outside a coffee shop and thought of Jo. She had always struggled with bringing her work home with her. There were times, when she had first become a nurse, that her patients would overwhelm her. She would become engulfed by them and intertwined in their lives. It took her years to build a wall around herself, and still at times she struggled. Now she would allow herself only a moment to falter and then she would quickly pull herself together once again. But the girl reminded her too much of herself and the way she felt at her age. Alone and voiceless and unwanted and worthless.

*

Even though she had desperately wanted to, Pauline had never run away from home. Her mother had left them when she was seven, and she was forced to live alone with her father until she was eighteen. He had worked the graveyard shift at a warehouse driving a forklift. He would sleep during the day and he would yell at her if she was too loud or woke him. Even as a child she had to beg him to go to the grocery store and beg him for money for clothes and things she needed at school. There would be days when he would hardly speak to her, and weeks when he wouldn't shower. No one explained to her that her father was mentally ill. She had to learn it herself; she had to navigate it alone.

She had become friends with a girl across the street, Cheryl Wheeler. From age twelve to eighteen she ate most dinners there, at Cheryl's house, with her family. When she turned fifteen Cheryl's father hired her to work at his dental office cleaning on Friday nights and doing secretarial work on Saturdays. She saved what money she could and dreamed of escape.

As the years passed her father's moods seemed to grow worse. They became poisonous snakes she had to jump over daily. He would pick on her. He would say cruel things to her. He would make fun of her weight or her appearance or her intelligence. One day he would blame her for what he considered "his failure of a life" and then he'd wake her in the middle of the night and tell her how smart she was, how the whole world was meaningless except for her.

He would forget her birthdays, and for Christmas he would buy her a wrong-size Snoopy sweatshirt, or a Frisbee, or a board game: Candy Land, Monopoly, or Risk. He would be excessively miserly and then for no reason or occasion would buy her an expensive gift, once a watch and another time earrings. Both of which she liked. None of it made sense; it just exhausted her.

And then two weeks before she left for college in Spokane, she came home from a shift at Shari's restaurant to find a used Ford Focus in the driveway. Her father had saved two years for it. A car for her to drive to college. She would have student loans for seventeen years, but she had a car. Her whole life she felt both hatred and empathy for him, and in the end only an inescapable responsibility. A vague duty she couldn't quite understand.

The day she left in her new car with her all belongings packed inside, he stayed on the cot in front of the TV saying nothing. After that day she would visit him, but never again did she stay more than a night there, and never once did she let him see inside her apartment or anyplace she ever lived.

Pauline parked at the hospital that afternoon and walked up the six flights of stairs to her floor. She put her coat and purse away and clocked in. In report the charge nurse told her two things: the girl, Jo, had snuck out in the middle of the night, and the old man, Mr. Flory, had finally gone home.

10

Pauline entered room nine to find Leroy's mother, Darla, sitting in the chair next to his bed, reading a novel to him.

"I'm sorry to interrupt," Pauline told her.

Darla set the novel on her lap and took off her reading glasses. "You're not interrupting," she said tiredly. "I'd about had it anyway."

"They say the surgery went well."

Darla shrugged her shoulders. "That's what they said."

"What book are you reading him?"

"*The Light Seekers*." She held up the faded science-fiction paperback.

"What's it about?" Pauline asked and went to the computer and looked at Leroy's chart.

"Do you want the short or the long version?"

"The long," Pauline said and laughed. "I wouldn't mind being in a sci-fi book for a minute or two."

"Well, let me see. This one is set on a planet that has seven moons," Darla said and eased back in her chair. "There's a group of women, probably around twenty of them, who travel endlessly across their planet. They're nomads. They hold five golden spears called light wells, and the light wells can find water, which is nearly nonexistent on the planet. When they get close to a pocket of water the golden spears glow. In the water are power crystals. The women eat the power crystals; it's their only food. The problem is they're always getting shot at by these creatures called Zybons.

85

They're aliens with fancy guns, and their only food is the women. Oh, and I forgot, the women are always bathing each other in the water they find. They've done it five times in less than three chapters."

"Bathing women?"

"And all the women are gorgeous and are always kissing each other."

"I bet was it written by some dumpy, middle-aged man."

Darla laughed. "It was. I checked. At least it's funny that way. I don't even like science fiction, but Leroy loved it so much. This is an old book of his I found in a box of his things. Maybe it makes him happy somehow to hear it."

"And he has a personal reader."

"He does," she said.

"That's pretty lucky."

"I'm not his first one. His girlfriend, Jeanette, used to read to him. My brother got Leroy into science fiction, and then Leroy got to know her because of it. They met at some science fiction movie marathon when he was fifteen. He told me that all through high school she'd read novels to him at night, while they were on the phone together."

"Really?"

"Sounds so boring," Darla said.

"She must have really loved him," Pauline said and finished looking through Leroy's chart.

"They were crazy about each other. She'd come to our house for dinner three or four nights a week, and they'd have the weirdest conversations. All in science fiction, it was like they were from a different planet."

"That's funny."

"To tell you the truth, I loved it. Those dinners were the

best part of my day a lot of times. She'd help me cook, she'd cut out recipes and we'd make them together. Jeanette's a great girl. You know she and I lived in an apartment together when Leroy first got hurt. Imagine having to live with your boyfriend's mother. Leroy was in a military hospital in San Diego, and we moved down there together."

"Were you there a long time?" Pauline said and checked his oxygen level and adjusted his tubing. She looked at the chest tubes for air leaks, and measured the fluid level on the canister on the floor beside his bed.

"A couple years," Darla said. "We rented a one-bedroom apartment next to a freeway. It was an awful place, but the only place we could afford. I should never have brought her into that. Safeway transferred me to a store in Oceanside so at least I had work. She got a job, too. I worked nights and she worked days so someone could always be there with him. The whole time we just passed each other like zombies . . . I can start taking things pretty hard, but she always kept me from being like that. She always kept me from feeling sorry for myself."

"It's hard not to feel sorry for yourself when you spend all your time in a hospital worrying," said Pauline.

"It's been like one long nightmare really," Darla said quietly. "From that first phone call saying Leroy was in a coma in a hospital in Germany to when they transferred him to San Diego. It's all been awful . . . Then the doctors told us they thought Leroy would never make a full recovery. We didn't believe them at first, but it had been over a year by then and he could barely feed himself. He could hardly walk. He couldn't talk and could barely use the bathroom by himself . . . In the end I made Jeanette leave. I called her mother and told her to come get her. Was she supposed to spend the rest of her life taking care of a man who really didn't exist anymore? A mother's supposed to do that, but not a girlfriend. Her mother and I finally convinced her to leave. I guess maybe we forced her to. I was there another ten months, but nothing changed. I got homesick. It took a while but I was finally able to transfer him to the group home here."

"Where's Jeanette now?" asked Pauline.

"She lives outside of Seattle. She's not married. She won't tell me if she's dating, but I hope she is. I know she has a good job and I've seen pictures of her apartment and it's cute and in a nice neighborhood. She was mad at her mom and me for a while but she got over it. She calls me on Leroy's birthday. Calls on Christmas and Thanksgiving and Easter. Even on Fourth of July. But we don't see each other anymore. It's too hard when we do. But we have the phone."

"Does she know what's happened?"

"No," Darla whispered and looked at the floor. "I know I should call her but every time I try I can't. Maybe I don't have it in me to make those kind of calls anymore. Maybe I'm just worn out. She always wants me to call and tell her how Leroy is. Call if anything has changed either good or bad. But I never do. She doesn't need to be constantly reminded of it. Maybe I'm wrong but I don't think so. And if I tell her what's happened now, she'll just come here and spend all day and night with him and ruin her life again. I wish she'd just get married and have kids. She'd be free from it then. At least mostly. I worry about her like she's my own daughter. You know we only have one rule when we do talk, and it's that we can talk about everything except the military."

"You know I almost became an army nurse," Pauline said as she began charting on the computer. "They pay off your student loans, and your starting pay is better than what I make now. But when I got out of school they had an opening here, and here doesn't seem as bad as seeing all those soldiers get hurt."

"I don't even know how you do it here," Darla said. "I break out into a cold sweat every time I just see this place."

"Sometimes I do, too," said Pauline and laughed. "Alright, I guess I better get back to it."

"I'll see you later," Darla said and put on her reading glasses. She picked up the novel again, but was too tired and set it down. She leaned back in the chair, and closed her eyes.

*

The soldier with the painted face pulled the knife from Leroy's chest. He wiped the blood from it on Leroy's shirt and put it back in its sheath. He took a pistol from his holster. He cocked it and pressed it to Leroy's forehead, but as he did Jeanette grabbed a lamp and swung it at the soldier's head and hit him with all her strength. The soldier crashed to the ground unconscious. She rushed to Leroy and helped him to his feet as blood poured out of his chest. She led him to the kitchen. With a frying pan she broke out the large window above the sink, and glass spilled out onto the fire escape.

"I can't make it," he whispered.

"Of course you can make it."

He leaned against the kitchen table in such pain he could hardly stand. "Go without me."

"I'm not leaving without you," Jeanette said and grabbed his arm and helped him onto the counter. She got him out the broken window and onto the fire escape. They climbed down four floors on rusted metal stairs. Leroy could barely walk by the time they got to the street and blood leaked from his chest and poured out on to the ground. They stumbled toward the city. He leaned on Jeanette and she carried him along and dusk became night. They went until Leroy could no longer walk. Behind an abandoned car they hid and rested. For hours he slept on the dirt and asphalt. When he woke, Jeanette was holding him and running her hands through his hair and he felt no pain.

They began walking again, and he felt almost normal, like nothing was wrong or had ever been wrong. None of it made any sense. They passed a military shipyard where an aircraft carrier and a destroyer were being built. Beyond that was a large construction site where a series of military office buildings were being built. Beyond that was a new ten-story fitness and rehabilitation center. And then came block after block and story after story of new military housing.

*

They left the city along a two-lane road. Rain began to pour and caravans of military trucks passed them in long lines, their tail lights glowing red and disappearing into the night. Leroy held on to Jeanette's hand and for hours they continued along. They passed dozens of overturned cars on the side of the road and the remains of three derelict houses. They came to the top of a hill and saw, in the distance, a small coastal town.

They took a side road and the pavement turned to gravel and they headed toward the ocean. There were neither lights nor moon, but it was a road Leroy knew. They came to a log house set on the edge of the woods. Leroy unlocked the door and turned on the lights. The walls and floor inside were stained wood, rustic and plain. He lit a fire in the woodstove and went to the fridge and took two Rainier beers from it.

"I've always wanted a place like this," Jeanette said.

"It was my uncle's place," said Leroy. "When I was a kid I used to spend weekends here."

"And you even have beer," Jeanette said happily as she warmed herself next to the fire.

"My uncle said it was bad luck to leave a fridge with no beer in it. He said it was lonely enough being a fridge, that the least you could do was leave beer so it would have something to look at and admire all day."

Jeanette laughed and looked around the room. A loft was above them, and a bathroom in the corner. The main room was bare except for a couch, a desk, and an old table. The kitchen was plain and small, with shelves instead of cabinets. There was a sink, a stove, an oven, and a fridge. The walls were bare except for an old water-stained poster near the woodstove.

"Is that Norrin Radd?" she asked.

"You know the Silver Surfer?"

"I love Shalla-Bal."

"You know Shalla-Bal?!"

"Of course," she said. "I own the entire Silver Surfer collection."

"Man oh man," he said.

"Where did you get the poster?"

"One time my uncle and I drove to a comic book convention. He had an old Pontiac Le Mans and we drove it all the way to Vancouver, British Columbia, where the convention was. We spent three days there. On the last night we walked back from the convention to the motel, but when we got there his car wasn't parked in the space in front of our room. Turns out somebody had stolen it. It was a car he bought when he got back from Vietnam. He'd had it almost twenty-five years. We called the police and filed a report, and then we went out looking for it ourselves. We spent hours going up and down all the neighborhoods we could walk to. My uncle said he knew we would never find her, but that at least we were suffering for her, at least we were grieving and trying to help her at the same time. My uncle had ideas and theories and superstitions about everything.

"Anyway, by the time we got back to the motel it was dawn and we went to sleep. We were woken hours later by the police telephoning. They hadn't found the car but they had found a bunch of my uncle's things. Whoever stole the Le Mans threw everything from the car out on some guy's lawn, and the guy was so mad he called the cops. The funny thing is we put all the posters and comic books and souvenirs we'd bought from the convention in the trunk in case our room got robbed." Leroy laughed and took a drink off the beer. "But it rained during the night so most everything we'd bought from the convention was ruined. That's why the poster looks like it does. My uncle had an old suitcase with jumper cables and flares and spare belts in it. The suitcase had his name, phone number, and address on it. That was on the lawn, too, and that's what led the police to call us."

"Did they ever find his car?"

"No, we had to take a bus back home. After that he bought a Plymouth Valiant, but the head gasket blew after a couple months. Then he got a white Ford pickup, which I still have. But it's in storage."

"In storage because you were going to join?"

"Yeah," Leroy said.

"But you're not going to join now?"

"No."

"Are you sure? They'll come after you."

"I'm sure."

"I'm sorry I got you into this."

"You didn't. You were just gonna make me breakfast. Anyway, we can stay here," Leroy said. "They won't find this place."

"I've gotten you in serious trouble."

"It's alright. But can I ask you a question?"

"Of course."

"How long have you had it?"

"The mark?"

Leroy nodded.

"A few years. Like I told you, my father made my mother and I go. We had to strip down naked, both my mother and me together, with my father there. My father and I never got along, not even when I was small. It was hard being in a room with him like that. I know it doesn't sound like a big deal but it was. My mother and I both stood there for a long time and then a nurse and a soldier came in. The nurse gave us each the shot and then she left the room. The soldier stayed. We had to wait an hour and we couldn't dress and it was cold in the room. When our time was over neither of us showed any signs so they gave us our release papers and our new ID cards that said we were okay. I moved out of the house a year later when I was eighteen and worked as a waitress.

"I lived with three girls in the same apartment building you came to. But two of the girls got the mark, and disappeared one night. I don't know what happened to them or if they're even still alive. The other got married to a soldier and moved away. I rented a smaller apartment in the same building and kept working. I didn't do anything else, not really. All my friends were going away or vanishing. It was like the world was moving on but I wasn't. I was stuck. It's hard to explain. And then it happened. I have a hard time getting up in the morning so I always take a bath first. I'll be nearly asleep and I'll light a candle and take a bath and listen to the radio and try and wake up. I do that every morning. When it happened I remember lighting a candle and getting in the tub as usual. But then I went to turn off the water with my foot. I had my eyes closed and then I opened them just for a second and by the candlelight I saw that my big toe was bruised, that the entire toe was discolored. I panicked. I sat up and touched it but it didn't hurt. The fact that it didn't hurt was the worst feeling I've ever had. I scrubbed my toe raw, but the bruise didn't go away. I didn't know what to do. After that I quit talking to most everybody. At work I forced myself to be happy, to talk and joke around with the customers. I can't begin to tell you how hard that is to do day after day. Then one lunchtime I heard some soldiers talking. They were saying they'd heard that ice slowed the mark down. I didn't know if it was true, but I began icing my toe and then as the mark grew, my entire foot. I'd do it every day for hours at a time. I'd spend all night listening to the radio and icing *my foot and hoping that someday I'd get out of the country and that somehow I wouldn't be alone for the rest of my life . . . Now I don't know about anything and I'm just scared all the time."*

"We'll be okay here. Don't worry. They'll never find this place." Leroy went to her and held her in his arms. A wave of euphoria engulfed them both and Jeanette kissed him.

*

Darla turned on the TV and watched the news for a while and then turned it off again. She picked up the book, put on her glasses, and read for another half-hour before stopping for the night. She got up, put on her coat, bent down to kiss Leroy, and then left the hospital.

II

At five-thirty am Freddie McCall woke on the group home
couch. He silenced the alarm on his phone and sat up exhausted. He found the energy drink in his coat pocket,
drank it, and then washed his face in the kitchen sink and
made a pot of coffee. He turned on the TV and waited for
Dale, but again the day man arrived thirty minutes late.
Freddie ran out to the driveway and shouted at him as he
parked his car in the drive. Dale half-heartedly apologized
and went inside, and Freddie got in the Comet to find the
battery dead. The car wouldn't start, and he had to go back
in and ask Dale for a jump.

He drove home as fast as he could. He took his Logan
Paint Store uniform and went into the bathroom. He set the
clothes near the box heater, shaved, put on his uniform, and
left.

When he parked in front of Heaven's Door Donuts, Mora
waved both arms back and forth from inside. He flashed his
lights twice and she took the two boxes from the counter and
came out to the parking lot where Freddie rolled down the
window.

"You're late again," she yelled.

"Dale was late again."

"That Dale, I've never met him but I'm really starting to
hate him."

"Me too," Freddie said. He took both boxes and set them
on the seat beside him.

"Did you hear the game last night?"

"Parts of it," Freddie said.

"It was horrible, huh?"

"It seemed like one long power play against us."

"Jesus, you look tired, Freddie."

"I know."

"You shouldn't drink those energy drinks. At least take them off the backseat so I don't see them. Okay?"

"I will."

She put her hand on his arm. "I only put in a single donut hole for you 'cause that's all you deserve. This is the third time this week I've had to come out here and freeze my ass off."

"Thanks, Mora. I don't even deserve that."

"You're going to have to buy me a coat," she said and turned around. "I'll see you tomorrow, Freddie."

"I'll see you tomorrow," he said and left.

He opened the store four minutes late and drank coffee to get through the morning rush. At eleven-thirty, as he mopped the retail floor, Pat parked his wife's Pontiac Grand Prix in the front lot. He came through the glass doors carrying a frozen chicken-fried steak dinner and a liter of Dr Pepper.

"How was it this morning?"

"Jensen came through with seventy gallons of Aura."

"No kidding?"

"He cleaned us out. I knew he'd like Aura. There were a half-dozen other hundred-dollar sales. Plus Barney got that job redoing the apartment complex and bought twenty gallons of primer. He said he's coming back this afternoon for ten more. If he doesn't make it today, he'll be in tomorrow."

"Not a bad day, considering," Pat said and took off a brown leather aviator coat and hung it on a hook on the back wall. He put the frozen dinner and soda in the fridge, opened the remaining box of donuts, took out a chocolate bar, ate it, and then took another. "I'll be in my office," he said. "And look, unless someone comes in and asks for me specifically, tell them I'm out."

"Alright," Freddie said.

"And Freddie?"

"Yeah, Pat?"

"Inventory was dead-on except for a missing two gallons of Satin Impervo."

"Impervo?"

"You have any ideas where the two gallons went?"

"I remember you took two and gave them to your brother in-law. Do you think it could be those?"

Pat looked at him and took a bite of the second donut. "Maybe," he said and walked into his office and shut the door.

Freddie finished mopping. At ten minutes to noon Pat emerged from his office, went to the refrigerator and took the frozen dinner from it, and put it in the microwave.

"Freddie," he said.

"Yeah, Pat?"

"I'll be using line one with my wife."

"Alright, Pat," he said.

The microwave bell rang and he took his lunch and soda back to his office. James Dobson's voice came through the thin office walls into the retail space and Freddie could hear it for the next hour. When the program finished, Pat came out of his office. He dumped his lunch and his empty soda bottle in the retail trash can, put on his coat, and looked outside at the cold, gray day.

"These damn winters kill us."

"At least we're doing better than last year," Freddie said.

Pat nodded. "I have to meet with the company lawyer and then run some errands. I'll try and make it back but I'm not sure I'll be able to."

"Alright, Pat," Freddie said.

"And Freddie?"

"Yeah, Pat?"

"Make sure you keep the back gate locked. There's a bunch of kids around out there today."

"It's an administrative day. The kids have the day off. They won't bother anybody, and tomorrow they'll be gone."

"Administrative day?" Pat shook his head and left. Freddie watched him get into his wife's car and drive away. He waited ten minutes and heated a bowl of water in the microwave, opened a package of ramen noodles and set it in. He ate lunch and placed his restocking orders. Afterward he sat at the counter and leaned against the wall. He tried to stay awake until the afternoon rush began, but he was overcome with such exhaustion that he had to lie down on the floor behind the counter. He lay on his back and his thoughts spiraled toward blackness: the house, the plants, his kids, prison, sleep, Lowell, the group home, his ex-wife. They were all trying to suffocate him. And then the sound of the buzzer rang. A customer walked through the swinging glass doors. He pulled himself together and stood up.

*

He closed Logan Paint at five-thirty and drove home to find a U-Haul truck backed up to his garage door. The house inside was warm; a fire burned in the fireplace. In the basement he found Lowell and a boy hanging shop lights from the ceiling. There was a twenty-gallon tub of black-looking liquid sitting in the corner as well as a half-dozen gallon jugs set in wooden boxes. There were rolls of black plastic and lengths of two-by-four and a crate of tools. They had two electric heaters and a humidifier running.

"Hey, Freddie, good to see you," Lowell said and came down off the ladder and introduced him to his nephew.

The kid was standing on a stepstool putting in a three-foot-long fluorescent light fixture. He looked like Lowell but was very thin and young. He had long, dark hair that fell to his shoulders and he wore a faded Black Sabbath T-shirt and black jeans.

"Go shake his hand," Lowell said, and so the boy got down off the stool and went to Freddie and put out his hand. "Hi," he said.

"Nice to meet you," Freddie said and they shook hands.

"Ernie's going to come by two times a week to take care of the plants," Lowell said. "He'll trim them and move them around. He'll water them on the days he's here, and he'll tell you what to do on the days he ain't. The lights are on timers and the heaters all have thermostats so you won't have to worry about them."

"What's in the tub?" asked Freddie.

"Mystery magic water," Lowell said, grinning. "Ernie will mix it up when we run low. I swear by my nephew, so don't worry." He looked over and pointed his finger to him. "Just don't bring any of your friends around."

"I wouldn't," Ernie said.

"I'm serious."

"I told you I won't."

"What days do you think you'll come, Ernie?" asked Freddie.

"I don't have classes on Thursday. I'll come then for sure and then probably on Saturday. Uncle Lowell said not to bother you on Sunday 'cause it's your day off."

"We should have a harvest next couple weeks. You'll see some money off that. Ernie will be the guy to pay you. You alright, Freddie? You look pretty rough, man. You losing weight?"

"I am a little bit."

"And you're going gray."

"Yeah."

"I guess we all go gray if we get lucky."

"I have to admit I'm a little nervous, Lowell. I've never done anything illegal, not really."

"If you weren't nervous you'd be a dumb shit, and you ain't a dumb shit, Freddie. You're just broke. Look, when I get out, the first thing I'm going to do is get my ass over here and move these plants. I promise you that. Like I said, the risk ain't much, Freddie, but there's always a chance of something going wrong."

"I know," he said.

"We're going to finish the lights and load in the rest of the stuff and then get some Mexican food. You should come."

"I'd like to but I have to take a nap and then go to work."

"Hanging out with the retards, huh?" Lowell asked.

Freddie nodded and walked back up the stairs. He put more wood on the fire and sat down, worried. He stared at

101

the flames and looked at the fabric of the couch. He remembered when his parents bought it from a furniture store brand-new. His mother put a plastic slip over it and then a blanket. When she died, the first thing his father did was take all the plastic off the furniture and wear his shoes in the house.

The old couch had weathered him and his parents, a dog and two cats, and finally his youngest daughter, Ginnie. He thought of all the times she'd lain on the couch recovering from surgeries. How he'd light a fire and set the TV where she could see it. It would be weeks at a time she'd be there, nursed night and day by his wife and him.

"Now I'm gonna end up in prison," he said to himself, and he said it over and over until he almost believed it as truth. He set the alarm on his phone and lay down on the couch and put the sleeping bag over him. He woke two hours later to hear Lowell and Ernie's voices come up from the basement. He changed out of his paint store clothes and left for his shift at the group home.

*

The next evening when he got home, a beat-up white Volkswagen Bug was parked in the drive outside of his house. Inside he could hear Lowell's voice drifting up from the basement vent. Again the house was warm. There was a fire in the fireplace and on the kitchen table were containers of Chinese food. In the basement eighty-five marijuana plants sat on different tables. The large plants were three feet tall and set in rows; the smaller ones were less than a foot and put in a separate makeshift room made out of black plastic and two-by-fours. There were little blue flags sticking out of some plants, yellow flags out of others, and orange out of others. The humidifier, two space heaters, and four fans were all running. Ernie stood trimming the plants with a small pair of scissors while Lowell wrote out instructions in a binder.

"Off work, huh, Freddie?" Lowell said when he saw him.

Freddie nodded.

"How was the Bible eater today?"

"He put in his two hours."

Lowell shook his head and drank from a can of beer. "I got Chinese food upstairs and there's a case of beer on your back porch."

"It's his last night," Ernie said. "We're gonna celebrate."

"Ain't much of a celebration," Lowell said.

"At least you'll get to see Uncle John," Ernie said.

Lowell nodded. "I have an uncle, Ernie's great uncle, who was convicted of armed robbery ten years ago. He'd be out by now, but they won't let him 'cause he's an Indian."

"He used his dog as a getaway driver," Ernie said to Freddie. "He'd park down the street from the store he was going to rob, and he'd leave his truck running and his dog would guard it."

"That's true," Lowell said. "It wasn't much of a plan."

"What happened to the dog?" Freddie asked.

"That's a good question," Lowell said. "The white cops probably shot it."

"No," Ernie said and laughed. "My mom kept him. He would bark at shadows and at spots on the wall. And he would steal cubes of butter off the table. But he was a good dog except that he got hit by a car."

"Well," Freddie said. "I gotta take a nap before I go to work. Good luck, Lowell. I'm sure sorry you have to go."

"It's going to be okay, Freddie," he said. "Don't worry. Nothing will happen. You'll see. Ernie will take good care of things."

"Okay," Freddie said and went upstairs. He ate a plate of kung pao chicken from a container on the table, and went to the couch to take a nap before his shift. But as he lay there he could smell the plants leaking up through the vents. His mind raced with worry. He knew he wouldn't be able to sleep, so he changed his clothes, took another postcard from the stack he'd set on the kitchen table, and left.

He drove to the hospital and took the elevator to the sixth floor, and walked down the hall to Leroy's room. But even as he entered he could see that Leroy's condition had worsened. His face was more bloated. His skin was ashen.

Freddie took the postcard from his pocket. It was a 1960s vintage color illustration of a woman with wild blond hair standing on a cloud with a ray gun in her hand. Behind her, in the far distance, a rocket blasted toward the sky, and to the left of her a spaceship hovered. She was dressed in a skin-tight red-and-black jumpsuit. He put the card on the table next to the bed and left.

12

It was five pm when Pauline woke hung over on the couch to the phone ringing.

"I think I broke a tooth," her father said.

"Which one?"

"One of the back ones."

"Does it hurt?"

"Of course it hurts. It's broken," he said. "What should I do?"

"I don't know," she said and sat up. "Do you want me to come over?"

"You don't have to," he said.

"How much pain are you in?"

"Some," he said.

"I'll find a dentist and pick you up and we'll get it pulled tonight."

"I'm not going to a dentist tonight."

"If your tooth hurts that bad we have to get you to the dentist."

"I'm not sure if it hurts that bad."

"Are you able to eat?"

"Not really."

"How's your grill?"

"I don't think you can barbecue in the cold."

"You can," she said. She got up off the couch. She walked into her bedroom and began changing her clothes. "How about a steak dinner?"

"Tonight?" he asked.

"I have the night off. Steak is your favorite, isn't it?"

"It's been a long time since I've had a steak."

"I think since your birthday."

"You're right, it was then," he said. "That sounds good, a steak."

"But wait," she said. "I'm an idiot. I forgot about your tooth. Maybe steak would be too much." He paused for a long time and she brushed her teeth and went to the toilet.

"Are you alright?" she said finally.

"I was just checking my tooth. I don't think it's broken. Maybe I just have a cavity. I bet it'll be fine."

"Are you sure?"

"I think it was just a nerve or something but now it doesn't seem so bad."

"Good," she said. "I'll be there after I go to the store."

"Alright."

"But listen. I want you to clean the kitchen and the bathroom. You have exactly one hour before I get there with the bag of groceries. If you haven't cleaned both I'm walking right back out the door and going home."

"Jesus!" he cried.

"What does that mean?"

"Okay, I'll do it."

"Good," she said and hung up.

*

She arrived an hour later to the house dark and cold. The TV was on and her father was on the cot under the sleeping bag and electric blanket. She turned on the lights and

106

walked into the kitchen. The sink was filled with dirty bowls and spoons. The counter was littered with a dozen empty soup cans and an empty cracker box.

She set the groceries on the kitchen table, took a bottle of wine from the bag, and opened it. She took a milk glass from the cupboard and filled it half full, and went into the living room and turned on the heat. She took off her coat and set it on the couch and went back to the kitchen and began cleaning. When the dishes were done, she cleaned the counters and took out the trash. She put two potatoes in the oven, made a salad, and walked to the living room and sat down on the couch.

"Where are your glasses?"

"I can't find them," he said. "I can see the TV alright without them."

"What are you watching?"

"It's one with Lee Marvin."

"You still like old movies, huh?"

He nodded.

She sat with him until a commercial came on, and then went to his bedroom. She stripped the sheets and blanket from the bed and put them in the washing machine. The bathroom was as it always was. The toilet seat and the floor around it was covered in dried urine. There were empty toilet paper rolls and two moldy towels along with a can of shaving cream in the bathtub. An empty tube of toothpaste, a broken bar of soap, and a disposable razor sat in the sink.

She walked back to the kitchen and poured more wine in her glass, drank half of it, and went back to the bathroom and cleaned it. She took the vacuum from the closet and ran it over the bedroom and the hallway. She waited until there was a commercial on the TV, and then ran it around him and his cot. When she was finished, she filled her glass with more wine and sat down and looked at the TV.

"Okay, buster, is the movie over?"

"It just finished," he said.

"Then you're going to get up and take a shower. I put some clothes on the bed and I want you to wear them."

"Right now?"

"Of course right now," she said. "I'm getting hungry."

"I don't want to take a shower."

"Get up, old man," she said. "That's an order."

Slowly he hauled himself off the cot and shuffled down the hall to the bathroom.

Under the back porch awning she lit the propane barbecue, and then set the kitchen table and turned on the radio. When her father came out he was dressed in tan pants and a navy-blue sweater. His hair was combed and he was clean shaven.

"You look good," she said.

"I feel good," he said and sat down and looked at the bottle. "How about a glass of wine?"

"You know you're not supposed to drink with your medication."

"I know," he said. "Just a half of a glass."

"Alright," she said. She went to the cupboard and took a small glass and poured him a drink. She leaned against the counter.

"Here's the plan. The steaks are almost done, and then we're going to eat. I brought ice cream for dessert and then we're going to watch a movie I pick. Then I'm going to finish the laundry and make the bed and I'm going to spend the night."

108

"You're going to spend the night?"

"I feel like acting like a family tonight."

"I'm glad you're staying," he said.

"Good."

His wineglass was empty and he looked at it.

"No more," she said.

"Just one more. I'll be fine with one more."

"Don't fall apart on me, deal?"

"Okay," he said and she filled his glass.

They ate dinner at the kitchen table, and then she made the bed and folded his laundry. She opened another bottle of wine and he ate a bowl of ice cream before falling asleep as they watched TV.

When she woke the next morning it was snowing and her father was in the kitchen. He had made coffee and was cooking eggs. The radio was playing and the heat was still on. His hair was combed and he was dressed in the same tan pants and blue sweater.

"Thank you," she said and kissed him on the cheek.

There were tears welled in his eyes. His face began twitching and he coughed to clear his throat. "I love you so much," he said to her. He coughed again, poured her a cup of coffee, and tears streamed down his face. He dished out scrambled eggs onto a plate next to a half-dozen saltines and some chopped iceberg lettuce, and they sat down and ate.

*

It was past noon and snowing in flurries when she left his house. She was driving towards her apartment when she turned around and headed for the outskirts of town. She parked in front of a duplex in a subdivision near the town's only golf course and knocked on the door twice. When no one answered, she let herself in with a key. She called Cheryl's name as she walked through the house until she came to a bedroom and knocked on the door.

"Are you alone?" she asked and slowly opened it.

"What time is it?" Cheryl moaned.

The room was dark except for a line of light coming between the curtains. The air was stale with the smell of cigarettes and alcohol and sleep. Pauline went inside. She opened the curtains and the light of day fell in.

"Twelve-thirty," she said.

Cheryl rolled from the light. She moved her head underneath the comforter.

"Come on. Get up," Pauline said.

"It's my day off. I didn't get to sleep until five."

"At least move to the couch so we can watch TV."

Cheryl sighed but got out of bed. She stood naked in the middle of the room. On the floor she found a pair of sweats and put them on. She walked to the living room and fell on the couch and put a blanket over herself. In the kitchen, Pauline made a peanut butter and jelly sandwich, poured a glass of water, and took four ibuprofens from a bottle above the sink and walked back to the couch.

"Take a couple bites, then take these." Pauline put the pills in her hand. Cheryl took a bite, swallowed the pills, and turned on the TV.

"I need you to help me do something," Pauline said and sat next to her on the couch.

"What?"

"You're going to say no, but you shouldn't say no."

"Great," she sighed. "What is it?"

"There's a sixteen-year-old girl who was my patient. She ran away from the hospital. I'm pretty sure she's staying twenty miles from here in an abandoned house. She's the only girl there with a bunch of guys. They're runaways. Anyway, the guys have been taking advantage of her. I'm almost certain of that. She has abscesses on her leg from using heroin and she won't eat. The abscesses aren't healed enough for her to be on her own. She's really messed up but I like her. There's something about her. You'd like her, too. I know you would. She snuck out of the hospital a couple days ago. A graveyard nurse said she saw two boys come by her room around three am. We only allow one visitor late at night. The nurse remembers making one of them leave but when she came back again the girl was gone, too. I need you to come with me and help get her out of there."

Cheryl took another bite of the sandwich and turned the channel on the TV.

"Did you listen to what I said?"

"Kind of."

"What do you think?"

"What did you do last night?"

"Hung out with my dad."

"So he was nice last night, huh?"

"He was great," Pauline said. "He even made breakfast this morning."

"You have one good night with him and now we're going to get shot helping some girl who'd probably rob you if she could."

"Maybe."

"Remember he'll be an asshole for the rest of the month and next month and next year. It's always the same, and you always get suckered by it."

"I don't want to talk about him."

"You're serious about this girl?"

"It won't be that bad," Pauline said.

"But that's what you say about everything."

"I know," Pauline said. "But this time it's true."

*

The snow that had been falling all morning stopped as they headed away from town. They passed the warehouses and farm equipment stores and an old dilapidated trailer park until they were outside the city limits. Farms and ranches with snow-covered hayfields began to appear miles apart from each other.

"The girl, Jo, told me it was a white house with a yellow barn," Pauline said as she drove slowly along the empty country road. "She said it's a mile from the mini-mart we just passed but I don't know in which direction."

"And they don't have electricity?" Cheryl asked. She looked sick in the light of day. She nursed a bottle of Diet Coke and smoked a cigarette and stared out the window.

"I don't think so," Pauline said.

"Then we'll look for a place with no lights on anywhere," she said.

Wind blew fallen snow across the long stretches of fields. They drove up and down side roads for an hour until Cheryl saw an old yellow dairy barn next to a white house. The farm was surrounded by acres of empty fields. A mailbox and a gravel road came into sight, and Pauline turned on it and drove toward the home.

There were no cars and no sign of life as they came to it. They parked on a gravel turnaround and got out. It was a two-story 1930s farmhouse, its white paint faded and bubbled and cracked. It looked vacant but not derelict. A large snow-covered lawn surrounded the home and a fenced garden sat near the barn. In a pile in the driveway were an old dog-house that had been broken up and a picnic table lying on its side, half the wood planks gone. There were shoe prints in the snow everywhere. They walked up the steps to the front porch. There were two metal lawn chairs bent and broken and a pile of scrap wood in a large stack next to the front door. Cheryl stood behind Pauline holding on to the back of her coat. Pauline knocked on the door but there was no answer. They could hear no noise from inside. They waited for a minute then walked back to the large gravel lot between the house and the barn. It was there they saw a chimney and a thin line of smoke coming from it. They walked around the house to find a back porch with a windowed door. They looked inside and could see through the kitchen into the living room where a fire was burning. Pauline knocked again and a boy came into sight.

"Do you remember me?" Pauline called out through the glass. "I'm the nurse from the hospital. I'm one of Jo's nurses. You're Bob, right?"

"What do you want?" he yelled back. He stood, nervous, twenty feet away. He had on a coat that was too large for him. His jeans were the same—dirty, with holes, and his worn-out tennis shoes were covered in black electrical tape. His face was white and hollow. His nose and eyes were red

113

and his forehead was covered in acne.

"Is Jo here?" she asked.

"Why do you want her?"

"'Cause she's sick. I want to make sure she's okay."

Another boy came from the living room. She remembered him from hospital, Captain. He looked even older and larger than she had remembered. He had on a leather coat and underneath it five or six T-shirts. He wore ripped black jeans and a red ski cap.

"What are you doing out here?" he yelled in a man's voice.

"I want to help Jo," Pauline said. Cheryl moved closer to her as she saw the bigger boy move toward them.

"There's nothing wrong with her," said Captain.

"I know she's not alright and you know it too. Look, I don't care what you guys do out here, I just want to check on her. Her bandages need to be changed. I can do that, no big deal, and then I'll leave. But if you don't let me in I'll call the police. I swear to God I will."

The two boys talked, and then Bob came to the door, unlocked it, and let them into the kitchen. There were empty fast-food bags and crushed soda cans and frozen-pizza boxes on the old white-tiled counter. The sink was clogged and filled with brown water and mold. There were white painted wooden cabinets in the kitchen and a framed crochet picture that read *The Ranch Life Is the Good Life*. There was a five-year-old farm equipment calendar on the wall near a large window, and a small kitchen table with two metal chairs underneath it. The floors were worn red linoleum and amid the trash on it were broken dishes, cups, and bowls.

114

They followed the boys into living room where Jo lay on a couch in a sleeping bag. There was another boy in a sleeping bag on the floor near the fire. The room was dark, the only light coming from the kitchen and a single windowpane in the corner of the room. The rest of the windows were covered with garbage bags and cardboard held in place with tape. There was a small, dying fire in the fireplace and the room was cold. On the carpet near the front door were pallets and boards used for firewood and again there was trash: beer cans and pizza boxes and food wrappers.

Pauline went to a large window and pulled the cardboard off it and light streaked into the room. She went to the sleeping girl and called her name. She put her hand on Jo's forehead and then softly shook her until her eyes opened.

"Hey in there, are you okay?" Pauline whispered. But the girl didn't respond. Pauline drew back the sleeping bag. Jo wore flowered pajamas that smelled of urine. Gently she pulled the bottoms down the girl's legs. The bandages were intact but a smell came from them. She peeled the top bandages back showing the packed wounds. They were each dark with blood and pus.

Bob paced around the edge of the room while Captain put a piece of wood on the struggling fire and sat down in a chair.

"Jo's going to die if she stays here," Pauline said and put the bandages back in place. She pulled up the girl's pajamas. "We're going to take her back to the hospital."

Bob stayed at the edge of the living room. He looked at the two women standing over the girl. "You ain't taking her. We didn't say you could. That wasn't the deal."

"You'd rather have her die?" Pauline said.

Bob looked at Captain, but Captain just stared at the fire. The other boy in the sleeping bag finally sat up.

"I don't want her to die," he said. "I like Jo."

"Good," said Pauline.

"But could you help me, too?"

"What's wrong?"

The boy undid the zipper and with great difficulty got out of the bag and stood.

"Can I show you something?" he asked. He was scrawny with red hair and didn't even look fifteen. His teeth were brown and he had dried blood underneath his nose. "Could you help me take my shirt off, Bob? I can't do it on my own." His voice was soft and meek, almost a girl's voice. Bob went to him and helped take the sweatshirt off. The boy stood with his upper body bare and showed Pauline the inside of his right arm. It was bright red with an abscess the size of two silver dollars on it.

"I've been washing it," he said. "I've been putting rubbing alcohol on it, too, but it just keeps oozing this stuff out."

"You should come to the hospital with us," Pauline said. "You've seen Jo's legs. That's going to happen to your arm. You can't wash it away. If you don't get it taken care of, you could lose your arm."

"She's just trying to scare you," Captain said and then stood up and held a metal fire poker in his hand. He looked at the redheaded boy. "I've seen those things get better on their own a thousand times."

"Look," Pauline said and pointed at Captain. "You don't know what you're talking about. You know you don't, so just quit it." She looked at the redheaded boy again. "If you

116

want to lose your arm then stay. I deal with these things every week. I know how they get. I wouldn't lie to you."

The boy didn't say anything. He just looked to Bob but Bob wouldn't look at him.

Pauline went back to Jo, who was now awake and watching.

"We're going to get you out of here, okay?" Pauline said and helped her out of the sleeping bag.

"Don't move her," Captain said.

"She told you to quit talking," Cheryl said as she stood behind Pauline.

Captain began nervously pacing around. He held the metal poker in his hand. The redheaded boy couldn't stand anymore and sat back down on his sleeping bag exhausted.

"Jo is being treated for chlamydia. I'm sure one of you guys gave it to her. So get it taken care of."

"Can you get it from getting head?" said Captain.

Pauline lifted the girl in her arms. "I can't believe you guys would really treat Jo this bad. I just can't. I don't want any of you visiting her again. If you do, I'll call security. After I call security, I'll call the cops and have them come out here." She held Jo as tight as she could in her arms and looked at the redheaded boy who was trying to put his sweatshirt back on.

"What's your name?" Pauline asked.

"Cal," he said.

"Look, Cal," she pleaded. "There's a huge infection in your arm. They're going to have to take all the infected skin and muscle and carve it out like they've done to Jo. I'm not trying to scare you. I swear on my life I'm not, but you could really lose your arm. We have room in the car and I want

117

to take you to the hospital. That's where you need to get it fixed. You'll be alright if you come now. I'll take care of you. I give you my promise on that."

"I ain't got any money," the boy said.

"It doesn't matter. You won't have to pay for it," Pauline said. "The hospital will take anyone. They took Jo and she doesn't have any money. Please Cal, come with us. You can always come back here when you're fixed up."

He wiped his tear-streaked face with his good hand. "I'll go to jail if they find me," he admitted.

"Going to jail is better than losing your arm," Pauline said. But the boy didn't say anything more. He looked to Captain but Captain wouldn't look at him. So he turned away from everyone and got in his sleeping bag again.

Pauline's arms grew tired holding Jo, but still she begged the boy. "Please come with us, Cal. Bob and Captain, they don't know how bad your arm's going to get, but I do. It's not going to get better here, no matter how much you try to clean it."

Cal looked at her and tears welled in his eyes. "I ain't going," he said and lay back down. He turned his face away from them.

Pauline's arms were beginning to shake. She couldn't hold the girl much longer, so they left him there. They went out through the kitchen and Cheryl opened the back door and Pauline carried Jo to the car. She set her in the backseat and they left the old farmhouse.

"Are you alright back there, Jo?" Pauline asked as she drove.

"Yeah," she said faintly.

"Are you in much pain?"

"Not really," she said and closed her eyes. "Thanks for coming to get me."

"I couldn't leave you out there alone. This is my friend, Cheryl."

Cheryl turned in her seat and said hello.

"Hi," Jo said.

Pauline looked in the rearview. "Why would you go with them, Jo?"

"I don't know."

"Please tell me why?"

"They said they were going to leave town without me. They said they were going to go to Mexico and live on the beach, and I would never be able to find them in Mexico."

"But they don't care about you."

"I know."

"But you still wanted to go with them?"

"They're the only people I know," she said.

13

A soldier picked the lock on the cabin door and crept in. He found them inside, in the loft sleeping. He pushed the point of his rifle into Leroy's chest until it broke his skin and muscle and split his ribs apart.

Leroy woke screaming in agony. He tried to push the rifle out of him but his arms wouldn't work, they wouldn't move at all. With his spare hand the soldier threw off their blankets leaving them naked on the bed. He saw the mark on Jeanette's foot and leg and pulled the point of his rifle out of Leroy. He grabbed his radio, gave his location, and called them in. Jeanette tried to stop the blood leaking from Leroy's chest, but the soldier took Jeanette by the hair and threw her to the ground. He spoke with an accent Leroy couldn't make out, and sweat poured down his face as he ordered them to dress.

They were forced to leave the cabin. Leroy walked half dead and wheezing and Jeanette held him up as they went. Along a washed-out logging road they walked toward a military holding vehicle. The soldier was behind them when his radio called, and for a moment he was distracted. He stopped and set his gun down and took the radio from his holster.

"We have to run now, Leroy," Jeanette whispered. "We have to try now." As quick as they could they ran off the road into the forest. Blood soaked through Leroy's shirt and spilled down his pants and onto his shoes as they went. The soldier yelled at them to stop. He dropped the radio and grabbed

*his rifle and began shooting wildly in their direction. He
chased in pursuit and was nearly on them when he fell and
his gun went off. He'd shot himself in the leg. They heard
him screaming as they disappeared into the trees.*

*They didn't stop running until they came out the other
side of the forest, until they could see the ocean laid out
below. Patches of sun hit the water miles offshore. Clouds
and tankers were in the distance and the wind blew heavy. A
small town was below them, in a cove. Leroy felt his strength
suddenly come back. He lifted his shirt to see there was no
wound where the rifle entered. There wasn't even a scar.*

*They ran down the hill until they reached the town, and
Leroy led them through a maze of streets and alleys until they
came to a marina. He led them past dozens of cabin cruisers,
commercial fishing vessels, and sailboats. He stopped in front
of a dilapidated twenty-six-foot fishing boat, and jumped on
board.*

*"What are you doing?" Jeanette said worriedly from the
dock.*

*"It's alright," Leroy said. "You don't have to worry. I own
this boat."*

"You own it?"

"Yes, now come on. Hurry!"

*He grabbed her hand and brought her aboard and started
the engine. White-and-blue smoke billowed from the exhaust
pipes, and the motor idled rough and uneven. He untied from
the dock and backed out into the marina.*

"This is really your boat?" she asked.

*Leroy nodded. "We were fixing the body when my uncle
died. If you think it looks bad now, you should have seen it
before. My uncle got it off this old guy who lived next door to*

121

us. He had it in his backyard. It was covered with moss and algae and filled with rainwater. It had been sitting out of use for twenty years. The old man was a shut-in who never left his house except to go to the library and the grocery store. But he liked my uncle, so he gave the boat to him for free, as a present."

"Will it make it away from here?"

"I don't know," he said. "We hadn't really started working on the engine."

*

They headed north for hours and the engine sputtered and coughed but it didn't quit, and finally just past dusk they came to Kingston, a naval base town. They found a public harbor, paid two nights' moorage, and parked in a slip.

They went to the city center to find food and sleeping bags. Along the way they passed a wooden marquee that read, Welcome to Torpedo Town, USA. The downtown was desolate except for a rundown grocery store that was still open. They went inside to find it empty except for one cooler of beer and soda, a wall of military baseball hats, a glass case full of knives and glass pipes, and a back shelf with dozens of dusty and dented cans of food. They asked the cashier if there was a store where they could buy bedding, but the old man couldn't speak English. They bought beer and all the cans that weren't expired and went back to the boat.

There was no propane to run the stove so they ate the food cold, out of the can, and listened to the radio and drank Rainier beer. There were no blankets of any kind. They huddled together on a damp mattress and waited out the night.

*When morning came, Jeanette left to find bedding while
Leroy looked over the engine. The belts were frayed; there
were exhaust leaks and oil leaks. He could see gas leaking
from the fuel pump and from the carburetor.*

*He walked through the marina asking for a mechanic,
and was told of one whom he found sitting on a faraway
dock, smoking a cigarette and reading a magazine. Leroy
brought the boat over to him. The man looked anorexic with
bad skin and a small bent nose. His hands were caked in
grease and he wore stained coveralls and dirty white tennis
shoes.*

*He looked over the motor. "Well," he said. "You're right.
I'd change the belts. Your fuel pump and carburetor are pretty
shot, too. I can rebuild the carb, but it might be better to just
get a new one. The fuel pump is nothing, it's easy to put in
and cheap. If it was me, I'd change the belts and plugs and
wires and probably the distributor. The oil leaks aren't that
bad. You can leak a lot of oil and still get by. But you have
a couple exhaust leaks that'll hurt worse. I could try and get
those stopped. How soon do you need it?"*

"As soon as you can."

"You're not from here?"

"No."

"Where are you heading?"

"North," Leroy said.

"What's north?" the mechanic asked.

"I'm not sure," Leroy said.

*The mechanic looked at him and smiled a mouth full of
tiny, brown broken teeth. "Bring her back tomorrow and I'll
get it done." He quoted a price. Leroy agreed to it then took*

the boat to the marina gas station, filled the gas and propane tanks, and went back to the slip. An hour later Jeanette came carrying two used sleeping bags, three blankets, and some old sheets she'd bought from a makeshift store in the garage of an old woman's house.

"Nothing in this town's open anymore," she said. "The only place I came to that was open was this old crazy lady who sold stuff out of her garage. It wasn't cheap either. The sleeping bags were twenty dollars each and they smell moldy. She just sat there and talked, but I couldn't understand anything she said. On the way back I met an old man on the street and he told me of a Laundromat that's still open. I would have gone there but I'd spent all my money."

Leroy told her about the mechanic with the rotten teeth and took her below deck and drew the curtains shut. He turned on the overhead light, and lifted the mattress off the bunk where they had slept. He removed a loose board from the bunk's frame. In a small space below it a wooden box sat, and inside the box was seven thousand dollars wrapped in a plastic bag: his uncle's lifesavings. He took two hundred from the bundle, giving a hundred to Jeanette and putting a hundred in his wallet. On the galley table he emptied an old coffee can full of change. They picked out thirty-odd quarters and went back to find the Laundromat.

The whole town seemed even worse in the stark daylight. Everything was in a state of disrepair. Businesses were boarded over, cars were burned, and houses were vacant, their doors gone and their windows broken. Trash covered the streets: old bikes and grocery carts and rotten garbage. They walked nearly a mile and saw only three people, and the people they saw were old and frail. At the end of downtown

124

across from the railroad tracks they came to a brick building. On it was a marquee that read, *Lilly's Laundry and Dry Cleaning.*

Inside, the ceiling was falling off in chunks from water damage, and the walls were stained from it. A short, hefty, middle-aged woman stood on a chair, and was bent over a rusty washing machine, cleaning it out. She wore a long denim dress that came down to her feet and underneath it a long-sleeve white turtleneck. There was a black work glove on her left hand and her face was wrinkled and blotchy.

"You'll just make it," she said in a cheerful voice. "The last load was five minutes ago but that's okay. I just live in the back, and I got nowhere to go tonight. Put the sleeping bags in the big washers, four and five. Don't use number one, two, or three. The others just put in seven through ten. And only use the first two dryers. The others are broke." She smiled at them and got down off the chair. She stood barely four feet tall. She put the chair back against the wall, and disappeared into the back.

They put their things in the washers and sat down on a wooden bench and looked out the window toward the deserted street.

"You know, when I was kid," Jeanette said. "I had a friend whose parents had a cabin a hundred miles north of Vancouver, British Columbia. It was on the water and the only way you could get to it was by boat. It was in the middle of nowhere. My friend and her family would spend a month there each summer. They would swim every day and explore the inlets in a small boat that had an outboard motor. When she got back she'd show me pictures. Hundreds of pictures. On the back of each one she would write down where it was taken and what it was about. You can't believe how beautiful it was there. It seemed like the most beautiful place ever made, like the most beautiful place that ever existed. One summer they invited me and I'd never been anywhere. I mean I'd been to California, to Fresno once for a funeral, but that's it. I wanted to go to the cabin in Canada, more than anything I did, but my father didn't trust anybody. Even though he knew the family and thought they were decent people, he wouldn't let me go."

"What about your mother? What was she like? What did she say?"

"I've always liked my mother," Jeanette said. "But she just did whatever he said. She always did what he wanted even if she thought it was wrong. Her whole life with him was like that. She'd just bend. It's weird thinking about her. Sometimes I think I'm more ashamed of her than of him. At least he did what he wanted, what he thought was right even though so much of the time it wasn't right. But her . . . I don't know. It just makes me sad and sick to my stomach to think about her."

"Are they still together?"

"No, he left us when I was in high school. He met a woman and moved in with her. He told us one night and then he was gone. He left all his things except for his guns and clothes. We didn't know he had another life with a different woman. No one knew, but I guess he'd been with her for a long time. Maybe over a year. It's strange that someone who always talks about the importance of family runs off with a woman no one even knows about. Runs off with a woman and doesn't even help us pay our bills. Just abandons us."

"Maybe we should go where your friend's place was,"

Leroy said. "Maybe we could be like them."

"Do you think we could?" she said. "More than anywhere in the world, that's the place I've always wanted to go."

"I don't know if the boat can make it. But we can try."

"Then let's try," she said.

*

The mechanic was asleep in a chair when they parked the boat in the shop's slip the next day. On his lap sat a bag of mini candy bars, the wrappers scattered around his feet. When they jumped out and tied to the dock the mechanic woke and they talked of the repairs and the mechanic said he would have the boat done the next afternoon.

Again they walked to the city center and went aimlessly past streets of failed businesses. They passed a community center with an empty swimming pool. They passed a closed-down high school. On a flyer in the window of a liquor store, they saw a poster that said there was a daily shuttle to an Indian casino. The shuttle left every hour from the parking lot across the street. They stood under the awning of an old building and rain fell and they waited until a small bus appeared and stopped. The door opened and inside the seats were filled with old people. The bus drove twenty miles before it stopped in front of a brand-new casino called Warrior's Wind. They walked into the main lobby where a colored sign hung from the rafters: Welcome Navy Underwater Specialists!

Old people and soldiers milled about everywhere. The soldiers, some drunk and others half-drunk, were dressed in clean and new uniforms and Leroy and Jeanette nervously

127

walked through the casino, up and down rows of slot machines and past the table games and casino restaurants. They came to a lounge and sat at a table in the back and ordered two Rainier beers.

There was a band playing in the back corner of the room. A woman with bright-orange hair sang while an overweight man sat beside her playing guitar. There were people dancing near the bandstand. Three soldiers who sat across from them began yelling at a soldier who sat alone in front of them. The soldier wore a different kind of uniform. He stood and began arguing with them so the three soldiers got up as well. They pushed the lone soldier, and he fell back past his table and knocked into Jeanette, pushing her over in her chair. As she fell to the ground her pant leg and tights got caught on a table leg and ripped, exposing her bare leg. Even in that light they all noticed the mark.

Leroy grabbed her hand and they ran through the maze of the casino. They knocked over old people and weaved in and out of slot machines and gaming tables. Soldiers began chasing behind them. They found an exit and made it out to the parking lot. They could hear a growing pack behind them, all screaming, a sea of horrible noise. They couldn't escape. They could feel the soldiers breathing down their necks, they could feel their hands reaching for them. They began saying awful things to them, whispering it in their ears. And then they were caught. They threw Leroy to the ground and stabbed him in the chest with a bayonet and shoved a hose down his throat.

14

Freddie McCall walked down the sixth-floor hall to find Leroy moving his legs around in his bed. It was as though his whole body were twitching in pain. His eyes were wide open. A faint moan came from the tube in his throat. His face was pale and wet with sweat. One nurse was holding him still while another added restraints to his legs. They increased the pain medication on the drip and waited until he settled. Then one of the nurses left the room.

"It's okay, buster," he heard the other nurse say gently. Pauline looked up and saw Freddie in the room. "I know this looks scary. Leroy's tolerance to the pain meds is increasing again so he's waking up. He'll be okay. It's pretty normal for this to happen, but he moves around more than I've ever seen when someone's intubated. We restrained his arms but now we've had to restrain his legs."

She sat with him until his breathing settled and his movement stopped, and then she double-checked the ventilator and the chest tubes. "I think he'll be okay now," she said and began typing on the computer in the corner. "The doctor will be down in a couple minutes."

Freddie nodded and then she left the room. He looked in his coat and took out a postcard, an illustration of a woman riding a rocket. She wore gold goggles and had flame-colored hair. The bikini she was wearing was blue and white and the rocket was cherry red. On it, in white cursive letters, it read: *THIS IS THE SPACE RACE WE WANT TO WIN!*

He put the picture in front of Leroy's face. "Look at this," he said gently.

Leroy began to open his eyes.

"Don't worry. It's me, Freddie," he told him. "I brought you a present."

For a moment it looked as though Leroy saw the picture, but just as he seemed to realize it his eyes closed again. Freddie put the postcard on the bedside table and took off his coat and sat down in the chair next to him. The nurse came back with the doctor. They examined Leroy and talked about him and again left. Freddie turned on the TV and clicked through the stations until he found an episode of *Bonanza*. He had twenty minutes until he had to leave for work.

*

At six o'clock the next morning he left the group home and drove to his house. Even in the freezing cold the smell of the plants drifted up from the basement. Would the smell travel? Would his neighbors smell it? He'd been avoiding them for almost two years, since his wife and daughters left. What did they think of him now? And if they smelled the marijuana, would they know what it was? Mr. and Mrs. Hughes were old and they didn't worry him, but the Jacksons weren't. Richard Jackson worked for the fire department. Maybe he suspected something already.

He started the shower and turned on the box heater. He put his paint store clothes next to it, set the kitchen timer for ten minutes, and got in. As he stood under the hot water he looked at the old white shower tile and remembered his grandfather installing it. His grandfather smoking a cigarillo, with his greased-back hair, making sure each line was straight. He had been a perfectionist. It was his bathroom, it was his house, and now Freddie was losing it.

He dressed and drove to Heaven's Door Donuts and parked. He walked inside to see Mora leaning against the glass counter in red sweats and a white apron. She was watching the news on a portable TV that sat on a shelf in the corner of the room.

"You're ten minutes early," she said.

"Dale was on time for a change," Freddie said. Mora moved her large body back and bent down and sighed from the effort. She took five donut holes from the lowest shelf, put them in a plastic basket, and set it in front of him. She poured him a half a cup of coffee.

Freddie drank from it and took an old hockey puck from his coat pocket and set it on the counter. "I was looking through some boxes last night, and I found this. It's from the '82 season when the Winterhawks won the WHL championship. I'm not sure what game it's from, but there's writing on it. It's my dad's handwriting. It says 'Hawks '82'. It's my after-Christmas Christmas present to you."

Mora picked it up and flipped it over and read the writing. She grabbed his hand and squeezed it. "Thank you," she said. "Maybe it's from the championship game."

"Maybe," he said.

"Let's just say it is."

"Alright."

She took her purse from the shelf below the register, put the puck inside it, and leaned down on the counter again. "You look really beat this morning, Freddie."

"I know, but I'm okay," he said.

"Are you sure? Maybe you should go to a doctor."

"I'm okay, really." He ate a donut hole and washed it down with coffee.

"Did you get a chance to talk to Ginnie and Kathleen last night?"

"I did what you told me and wrote down a list of questions. That seemed to work better. We were on the phone twice as long that way, but you can tell they get bored."

"Kids have no attention spans. You know that."

Freddie picked up another donut hole but set it down. He looked at Mora and suddenly tears flooded his eyes. He couldn't explain why it happened right then, but he began to sob in front of her.

"What's wrong, Freddie?" she asked.

He stared at the rows of donuts below the glass counter. He leaned across to her and whispered. "I can't keep going on like this."

Mora reached over and put her hand on his arm. "I know," she said. "How could you?"

"I'm sorry," he whispered and wiped his eyes.

"Don't be sorry. It's okay," she told him. "Tell me what's going on, Freddie."

When he finally spoke, his voice was raw and so quiet it was barely audible.

He couldn't look at her when he spoke. "I keep making bad decisions. Why are all my decisions bad? I'm going to lose everything." He wiped his eyes on his coat sleeves. "And I've failed everybody."

"Ah Freddie, don't say that."

"But it's true."

132

"It's not . . . You've known me here for thirteen years, right?"

He nodded.

"Think of all the nice things you've done for me. When Raymond left me you'd come in here every morning and you could tell, just by looking at me, that I needed help. I didn't even have to say anything and you'd invite me over for dinner. Your family took care of me. And you listened to me, Freddie. No one listens to me . . . You made me want to keep going when I didn't want to. So don't say you're a failure. You've never failed me, Freddie."

She walked out from behind the counter and went to him and put her arms around him. She smelled of donuts and soap and she was soft and warm. He collapsed into her and closed his eyes as two white work vans pulled in front of the donut shop with their headlights shining in on them.

*

He opened Logan's Paint at a minute before seven. There was the early morning rush but by ten-thirty it had cleared out, and he sat down and nodded off until half past eleven, then got up, made another pot of coffee, and began placing restocking orders when Pat came in.

"How was it today?" he asked with a frozen spaghetti dinner and a bottle of Dr Pepper under his arm.

"Just over two thousand," Freddie said. "The good news is they got the electrical and plumbing done on the Eccles apartment job. I stopped by yesterday on my way home. Drywall is going up next week and they ordered a hundred gallons of primer. My guess is they'll probably do a hundred and fifty of primer, then take two hundred top coat by the time it's over. Also, Gary came in. He's starting a couple jobs on the reservation. He spent three hundred today and he says it's just the start of it."

"Not bad," Pat said and went to the refrigerator. He put the soda and frozen dinner inside and went into his office. Twenty minutes later he came out and heated the frozen dinner. "If anyone calls for me, tell them I'm in a meeting. I'll be on line one with my wife."

Freddie nodded and continued his restocking orders, and the voice of James Dobson leaked through the wall.

"This is no time for Christian people to throw up their hands in despair. The moral principles in scripture have guided this great nation since the days of its founding, and we must remain true to them. This is a moment for greater courage and wisdom than we have ever been called upon to exercise. If we now choose to stand by idly while our foundational social order is destroyed, the family, as it has been understood for millennia, will be gone. And with its demise will come chaos such as the world has never seen."

*

Freddie arrived at the group home that night in such a state of exhaustion he could hardly do his chores. He collapsed on the couch at midnight and fell asleep only to be woken an hour later by shrieking. He ran down the hall to find Donald naked and screaming at Hal, who was trying to hide in his bedroom closet. When Freddie entered the room, Donald panicked and began physically attacking Hal. He hit the middle-aged man a half-dozen times before Freddie was able to break it up. Hal collapsed in a ball on the closet floor, and Donald ran from the room. Freddie helped Hal to his feet and out of the closet but when he did, Hal suddenly became hysterical. He ran in circles and screamed and punched his hand through the bedroom window. The glass shattered and his hand came back wet with blood.

Freddie ran to the bathroom and got the first-aid kit. When he came back to the room Hal was motionless. He just stood staring vacantly at his blood-covered hand. Freddie took him to the kitchen and put his hand in the sink, and blood poured from it. He turned on the water and put Hal's hand underneath the faucet and cleaned the wounds. There were three large cuts that would need stitching. He'd have to go to the hospital. Freddie sat Hal at the kitchen table, opened the first-aid kit, wrapped the wounded hand in gauze, and then put a kitchen towel around it.

When he finished, he made a hot chocolate and went to Donald's room. The naked man sat on his bed, crying. Freddie gave him the drink, waited until he finished it, and then helped him into pajamas and got him back into bed. He turned off the light and shut the door and went back to the kitchen, and to Hal. He called the manager of the group home to let her know what had happened, and then he called Hal's parents who said they'd be right over. Freddie hung up and took Hal back to his room and dressed him and they waited at the kitchen table for his parents to arrive.

It was twenty minutes later when the sound of a truck was

heard and the headlights from it shone into the front room windows. Hal's parents were an old, gray-haired couple. The woman was dressed in a red coat that came down to her knees. Her husband was thin with a leathered smoker's face. He wore a baseball cap and a worn canvas work coat.

"Oh Hal," his mother said. "Why did you do it, baby?" She kneeled in front of him and put her arms around him.

"Donald attacked him," Freddie explained. "I broke it up but Hal got so upset he punched out the window in his room."

"Poor Hal has always been picked on," she said. "His whole life has been that way. Instead of fighting back he just gets mad and smashes things or puts his hands through things. Windows or walls. He punched his fist through a TV once, didn't you, honey?" She kissed Hal's forehead while Hal's father remained silent at the edge of the kitchen.

"I think he'll need stitches," Freddie said.

"You poor little boy," she said.

The man coughed and turned to her and said, "He ain't a little boy."

"I know, Pop," she said. "I know." She looked at Freddie and whispered, "He thinks I baby him too much but what are you going to do? He's our boy and he'll never be anything but a little boy."

"He was a good patient, though," Freddie said. "I think I got all the glass out, but the hospital will know for sure."

"That's the thing," she said. "Once the drama's over he becomes catatonic. It's the only plus side. It makes him easier to fix." She took his hand and unwrapped the towel. The gauze was soaked with blood and she lifted it to see the cuts. "Oh boy, looks like he really did it."

"How bad is it?" her husband asked.

"Hospital bad."

"Figures," he said.

"Well, Freddie, thanks for not calling an ambulance. Our insurance doesn't cover ambulance rides. It would have cost us a fortune and we just don't have that kind of money. Okay, Hal," she said to her son. "You just stay here and I'll be right back with a travel bag." She kissed him again and then walked down the hall and came back carrying a small suitcase.

"I'm sorry about the window," she said.

"It's okay," Freddie said. "I can replace it."

"Just send us the bill," she said.

"It won't be that much. I can do it myself," Freddie said.

She thanked him and put Hal's shoes on, draped a coat over his shoulders, and they left. Freddie went to the garage and found a piece of cardboard and cut it to size and taped it over the broken window. He picked up the glass he could find, vacuumed the carpet, and locked Hal's door. He checked on Rolly and Donald, who were both asleep, and then he went back to the couch and watched TV. Dale was twenty minutes late but it was Sunday, his day off from Logan's Paint.

*

He ate breakfast at a diner on the way home as he always did on Sundays, and it was just past dawn when he entered his freezing house. He left his jacket on and started a fire and sat on the couch and watched TV until he fell asleep. When he woke next it was dusk and the fire had died. He got up and re-lit it and then took a piece of paper from his wallet. A long list of questions was written out and he looked at them and called his kids and spoke to each of them. When he hung up, he tried to sleep some more. But as he watched the flames he thought of his mother sitting next to the fire, warming herself. His father had always gotten off work earlier than she did, and in the winter he'd start a fire so when she came home she could sit near it and drink tea. She drank a mug of tea and ate four Oreos every day after she worked as a present to herself.

As he lay there, he thought of them and of all the times they had stood by the mantel. His parents and grandparents, his children. They all had framed pictures sitting on it. He tried to sleep but he couldn't. He was breaking the law, and he'd never really broken the law, not like he was now. He hoped his parents and grandparents, wherever they were, weren't watching him.

15

Pauline came from the hospital cafeteria. She was trying to hold a cup of coffee and eat a piece of chocolate cake and walk at the same time. She came to the stairwell entrance, put the plate of cake on top of the cup of coffee, opened the door, disappeared into the stairwell, and walked up the six floors.

In room eight slept a middle-aged woman with complications from esophageal surgery for chronic acid reflux. She had developed severe back pain and her heart rate had steadily increased while her blood pressure had dropped. She was scheduled for a CT scan to see if there were any leaks that the X-rays couldn't find. Her husband and three teenage daughters nervously paced around the room. Pauline checked the woman's vital signs and talked with the family and charted.

In room five Mr. Delgado was watching TV and eating French fries his wife had brought in. She sat next to him drinking a McDonald's milkshake and eating a Big Mac. Both of them said nothing as the nurse worked, and although it was against hospital policy to bring outside food to a patient, she ignored it and left the room.

In room three was Mrs. Dawson, a woman recovering from bowel resection surgery, and in room four she saw Jo, who was back from surgery. The girl smiled when she saw Pauline come in.

"You're awake and you're back on my floor. All good

news for me. How are you feeling, Jo?"

"Alright, I guess."

"On a scale of one to ten how would you rate your pain?"

"Four," Jo said.

Pauline looked at her watch. "I have a couple minutes and my feet hurt. Do you mind if I sit?"

Jo shook her head.

Pauline sat in the bedside chair. "How was surgery?"

"It wasn't that bad 'cause they put me to sleep."

"I told you it would be alright."

"I'm glad you came and got me."

"Me too." Pauline took off her shoes, stretched her feet, and then put them back on. "Have you been eating?"

"Not really," the girl said.

"Hospital food isn't as bad as people say."

"I know."

"Can I tell you something? For as rough as you've had it, you have great skin. All the nurses talk about it."

Jo tried to smile but her face was sunken with worry.

"You're going to be okay," Pauline said.

"But what am I going to do now?"

"Get better," Pauline said.

"Where am I gonna go after that?"

"You can worry about that when you get a little stronger."

"But they're going to leave without me."

Pauline looked out into the hall, saw it empty, and then turned to the girl and whispered, "They were gonna let you get sicker until you died or lost your leg. You have to think about that, because it's true. As much as it hurts to hear, they don't care about you, Jo. They just don't . . . Look, I know you're alone but you have to learn how to be alright

140

alone. If you don't, you'll end up in situations like you're in, and you don't deserve that."

"But maybe I do deserve it," she said.

"You really think so?"

"Maybe."

"What have you done to deserve living in a freezing house with no water, with three junkie boys who use you, who'd rather get a blow job than help you get better?"

"I've been pregnant," Jo said quietly and covered her face with her hands.

"You have?"

She nodded.

"What happened?"

"I had an abortion," she whispered, in tears.

"Oh, hon," Pauline said and set her hand on the girl's arm.

Jo closed her eyes and turned her head away.

"What about your family?"

"I won't go back there."

"You don't have an aunt or an uncle or cousin you could stay with?"

The girl shook her head.

"Those boys aren't going to end up anywhere good. Believe me. I know. I've seen it. I see it here all the time . . . If you have to follow a man around, there's a lot better ones to try."

The girl wiped her eyes and turned back to the nurse. "Do you have a husband?"

"Me?" Pauline said and smiled. "No."

"Why not?"

"I don't want one. How about you? Do you want a husband?"

"Me? Why would you ask me?"

"We're having a conversation. If we're going to be friends, you ask me a question and I answer it and then I ask you one and you answer it. That's how it works."

"No one would want me 'cause I'm a freak."

"You're not a freak."

"I am."

"I've seen a lot of freaks and you're not one."

"But I am," she said.

"You're not. I win. End of discussion."

Jo paused then cleared her throat and wiped her eyes again. "Why aren't you married?"

"Why are you worried about me being married?"

"I'm not worried about it. I'm just asking."

"I wanted to be once," Pauline said and got back up. "Alright, let's take a look at those packings. I got to get back to work."

"Who did you want to marry?"

Pauline pulled the curtain around the bed and took back the blanket and sheet. "I lived with a guy when I got out of nursing school. I wanted to marry him."

"What was he like?"

"He was alright at first," she said.

"What happened?"

"Well . . . he was always telling me what to do. That's one thing against him. I'd work all day then go to my dad's house and make sure he was okay and he'd tell me what to do. Then I'd go home and take care of my boyfriend and he'd tell me what to do. And the only things my boyfriend liked were sports, hunting, and drinking beer. He couldn't boil water; he could barely hold a job. But I loved him. I was crazy about him."

"Really?"

"Yeah, I kept asking him to marry me."

"And he didn't want to marry you?"

"No."

"Where is he now?"

"He moved back to Spokane. He's been married and divorced twice and has kids from both women. He went bald and got fat and is always out of work. The last I heard he was living with his brother." Pauline pulled back the bandages and looked at the packings. "Hey, they look good. They did good work on you. I bet you'll be okay in no time if you start eating."

"Why did you want to marry him in the first place?"

She pulled Jo's gown back down and covered her again with the sheet and blanket. "Back then I wanted to be normal. That was my big dream. Some of the friends I made in nursing school were getting married and having kids. I wanted to be like them . . . And I wanted him to admit that he needed me, that he couldn't live without me. I was young. Anyway, I did everything for him. I did his laundry, cooked, made sure he got up in the morning. Made his lunch when he worked. I watched football with him and went to car and sports shows with him. And then I would spend days freaking out." She put her hand on Jo's arm and gently shook it. "'Do you need me? Do you need me? Do you want me forever?' 'Do you want me for all time?' I'd say the stupidest things. I was a mess and I put a lot of pressure on him. It drove him crazy. It would drive anybody crazy. So in the end he left me."

"He really left you?"

Pauline nodded and pushed the curtain back and out of the way.

"Was it awful when he left?"

"For a while I was so heartbroken I didn't know what to do. I just wanted to die. But after a while it was okay." Pauline washed her hands. "In the end I was lucky to get out. He wasn't much of a man. I was just so scared of being alone and unloved that I would have married a tire if it had asked me. Anyway, Jo, you don't have to do anything right now. Your only job is to start taking care of yourself, alright?"

"I wish I was like you," the girl said.

Pauline went to the computer and began entering notes. "That's the nicest thing anyone has ever said to me. Thank you." She looked at the girl and smiled. "Okay, I have to get back to my other patients. I can't sit around all night having a good time. They fire nurses for that. And if you really want to be like me, eat. That's something I'm good at. Even if they give you some sort of casserole, alright?"

"Alright," Jo said.

*

When her shift ended, Pauline went to the hospital cafeteria and bought a banana and a piece of carrot cake. She took it back to the sixth floor where she found Jo alone in her room watching TV.

"I'm off work now and not your nurse anymore tonight. So don't worry about me ordering you around and torturing your leg." Pauline sat down in the chair next to the girl. "I brought you a present. If you eat the banana, I'll give you the cake. The guy in the cafeteria makes pretty good cake.

I had a piece earlier."

"Alright," said Jo. Pauline set the banana and the cake on the bedside tray. The girl peeled the banana and began to eat it. "Is it hard to become a nurse?"

"It can be. You have to go to college and then nursing school."

"How long does it take?"

"I was in school six years plus a couple summer schools."

"Do you have to be good at math?"

"It makes it easier. But I've always liked math and science. That part wasn't hard. The school part was pretty fun."

"I've never been good at math."

"Sometimes all it takes is a good teacher or two."

"Why did you become a nurse?"

"A lot of reasons."

"Like what?"

"Remember Cheryl?"

"She's the woman who was with you when you got me."

Pauline nodded. "Her father was a dentist and her mother was a nurse. Her mother was really nice to me. I wanted to be like her. You should have seen her. She was beautiful and she'd come home in her nurse's uniform and swear like a sailor. She was really funny and surly, but also very kind. She worked at this exact same hospital. She was the nicest person I met when I was a kid and the most fun to be around. I wanted to be like her."

Jo slowly took pieces of the banana and ate them. "What do you do on your days off?"

"Not a lot."

"Do you go on dates?"

145

"Dates?"

"Do you?"

"Not lately."

"Maybe you should meet a doctor."

"Does he have to be a doctor?"

"Everybody likes doctors," the girl said and finished the banana. "They're smart and nice and rich."

"I don't want to ruin it for you, but I haven't met a doctor that is all three of those yet."

"You haven't?"

"Most doctors have big egos, they don't know half as much as they think they do, and the ones with any kind of personality are usually married or are having an affair with a woman much better looking than me."

"I think you're pretty."

"Ha, but you're not a doctor, are you?"

"Doctors aren't like that, are they?"

"Some are."

"Really?"

"I'm sure there's a few good ones out there, too."

"I bet you'll find one," Jo said.

"You think so?"

"Yeah," she said. "I know you will."

"Thanks."

Jo lay back and closed her eyes for a moment, and then looked back at Pauline. "Do you live in a house?"

"I live in an apartment," Pauline said.

"Does it have a pool?"

"No. I'm not a pool complex sort of girl."

"Why?"

"I hate wearing bathing suits."

146

"I just go in shorts and a T-shirt."

"That's what I do, too," said Pauline. She bent over and took off her shoes. She set her feet on top of them and leaned back in the chair. "I have to let my dogs out. They're tired."

"Why don't you have a house?"

"I don't have the money."

Jo took the tube of lip balm from the bedside table and put it on her lips. "Don't nurses make a lot of money?"

"Not a lot, but some. Anyway, I have bills. I still have student loans, and I take care of my dad."

"Is he sick?"

She sat up and leaned over. "He's crazy," she whispered. "He walked off his job nine years ago, and he won't get another one. So I pay his bills."

"He's really crazy?"

"Crazy enough."

"I'm sorry."

"Me too," Pauline said.

"You know, if you married a doctor you could have a big house that has a guest room and your dad could live there and your husband could fix your dad."

"I like this story."

"And you'd have a pool."

"I don't need a pool."

"But you should have one anyway," Jo said and scratched the hand the IV needle went into.

"Is the needle bothering you?"

"No, it just itches sometimes."

"How about the cake? Are you going to try it?"

"Oh, I forgot," Jo said. She picked up the fork and took a

bite of it and then another bite.

"What about you?" Pauline asked.

"What do you mean?"

"Do you want a house?"

"Maybe, but one out in the desert."

"And I bet you'd marry a doctor," Pauline joked.

"No," and for the first time that night Jo smiled. Her face lit up and her teeth showed. They were straight and white, like she'd worn braces. She took care of her teeth. That was a good sign, Pauline thought. "I'd marry an inventor and he'd work in a big yellow barn and make amazing inventions. Everyone would think he was a failure but he wouldn't be."

"Who knew that you were so nice to talk to."

The girl again grinned.

"Do you like the cake?"

Jo nodded. "My mom makes good cake, too."

"Really?"

"She worked in a bakery for a while."

"What luck, having a baker for a mom," said Pauline and leaned over and put her shoes back on her feet.

"She's not a baker anymore. She was only a baker when I was really little."

"What's she like?"

"She hates me," Jo said.

"That can't be true."

"It is," she declared.

"Why would she hate you?"

"I told you one reason already. Anyway, I don't want to talk about her."

"Alright," Pauline said. "Fair enough."

Jo finished the cake and lay back in her bed. Her face became serious and sullen. "Why are you really here?"

"'Cause I like you. That's why I'm here."

"If you really knew me you wouldn't like me."

"Why would you say that?"

"Because it's true."

"I don't think so. Anyway, let's just relax for a second. We were having a good time."

"But you don't understand anything," Jo said, trying not to cry.

"I understand some things," Pauline said. "You're not as bad as you think you are. I know that. I know you're probably just used to beating yourself up, and you've backed yourself into a corner. But I'll help you out. I really will."

Jo turned her head away and closed her eyes. "You probably just want to have sex with me," she said barely. "That's what everyone wants anyway."

"Don't say that," Pauline said gently and stood up. "You know that's not true. You're a good kid. No matter what happens to you, that's what I think. Anyway, we had a nice conversation tonight and you ate. You can cry as much as you need to, and hate me as much as you want, but sorry to say I'll still like you tomorrow."

16

Leroy Kervin woke in the middle of the night to see that he was in the hospital room. His arms and legs were restrained and there was a dim light behind him. He could hear people talking in the hall and he could feel the pain in his chest and the tube down his throat. He didn't panic, he just saw where he was and didn't want to be there.

*

The chasing soldiers vanished from the casino parking lot and the casino itself became a haze of distant lights left behind them. For miles they walked along a barren stretch of road. Nothing was on either side but rain-soaked hayfields and barbed-wire fences. But as soon as he realized he felt better he began wheezing again; he began gasping for air. They came to a convenience store set back from the road. They walked along the parking lot and rested, hidden behind a dented dumpster.

"Are you okay?" Jeanette whispered.

"I don't know," Leroy muttered. "I don't understand it . . . Sometimes I feel fine and other times I'm in so much pain I can hardly stand it."

"Your breathing sounds awful now," Jeanette said.

Leroy tried to answer but he was unable to. She held his hand and he closed his eyes in exhaustion. When he opened them again she was holding him.

"How about now? Are you okay now? Can you speak?"

"Maybe I'm better," he croaked and slowly he made himself stand. He swayed back and forth in front of her, punch drunk and unsteady. "I don't think I can walk all the way back to the marina. We'll have to get a ride somehow, and if we can't get a ride you'll have to go without me."

"I'm not going without you. We'll find a ride," she said and they began watching the parking lot. A truck pulled in and three men in fatigues got out, bought beer, and left. After that a woman in a uniform with two kids came in a minivan. She kept the engine running, but left the kids in the car. An hour had gone by when a kid on a motorcycle came. He left the bike running, put the kickstand down, and went inside.

"This one," Leroy said and they got up and went to it. The motorcycle had bald tires, a dented gas tank, and its seat was covered in silver duct tape. The engine idled roughly and gray smoke came from the exhaust pipe. Leroy got on the bike, pushed up the kickstand, and Jeanette got on the back.

He was backing the motorcycle out of the parking spot when the boy ran out from the store. "What are you doing?" he cried. He was holding a Drumstick ice-cream cone and a can of root beer. He was thin and small with brown hair. He wore a flannel shirt and jeans.

"We have to take it," Leroy said in a shaky, uneven voice. He was hunched over the bike, barely able to hold on to the bars.

"But it's my brother's," the boy said. "He left it to me."

"I'm sorry," Leroy said and began wheezing harder. The boy ran up to the bike.

"My brother was killed in the marines, in the desert over there. In the war. The only thing I have of his is this motorcycle. I'll give you a ride wherever you have to go. I can fit three on. I've done it before. But please don't take my bike."

Leroy looked at the boy. "But we're in trouble."

"Please," the boy said.

Leroy looked at him again and swore to himself but nodded. They moved back in the seat and the kid handed Leroy the can of soda and the ice cream. He sat in front of him, half on the seat and half on the gas tank, and revved the engine.

"Where are you going?" he asked.

"Kingston."

"Kingston," the boy exclaimed. "I've never gone that far on this bike."

Leroy wheezed but couldn't speak.

"Will it make it?" Jeanette asked the boy.

"I don't know. I just got it running again ten minutes ago. That's why I left the engine on when I went inside."

The bike strained under the weight as they left the convenience store. The motor lugged and the bike grounded out with every bump and pot hole. Jeanette held on to Leroy who held on to the seat. The boy wiped rain off his face and kept the bike going until a mile out of Kingston when the engine quit. He coasted to the side of the road, and Jeanette and Leroy got off.

"I think she ran out of gas," the boy said. "The gas gauge doesn't work, and I only put three dollars in the tank."

"Thank you," Leroy whispered and leaned into Jeanette, his breathing growing more shallow.

"Are you going to be able to get gas?" Jeanette asked the boy.

"There's a station over that hill, but I spent all my money at the store."

Leroy took a hundred dollars from his wallet and handed it to the kid.

"That's a lot of money," the boy said, looking at it.

Leroy tried to say something more, but nothing came out. He handed the boy back his ice cream and soda and they left.

They went up the road until Leroy could go no farther. They slept in a field of wet grass. When they woke, it was still dark and freezing but he could breathe easy. They began walking and at dawn came to Kingston and found the only coffee shop open. In a room full of soldiers they nervously ate. When they were finished they walked back to the marina, where the mechanic was at work on their boat.

"I'll have it done this afternoon," he told them as he hovered over the torn-apart engine. He had a bag of potato chips next to him and took a handful with his grease-and-gasoline-covered hands and put them in his mouth. He washed them down with a can of Coke. "But I have a question. I was hoping you could pay me now. My rent's due and I owe the parts store. If you give me the money I can deposit it when I take my lunch break."

Leroy nodded and the mechanic went to his office and came back with the bill and started on the engine again. They went to the cabin and drew the curtains and locked the door. They lifted the mattress and the loose board. They took fourteen hundred dollars from the box to pay the mechanic and three hundred more to buy groceries. They went topside, gave him the cash, and left.

Again they passed back through the deserted city center, but the grocery store they had gone to the day before was now closed. A toothless old man riding a bicycle passed them and they called out for him to stop. They asked him if he knew of another grocery store, and he told them of the military commissary and gave them directions. As they went toward it, they saw an old woman with a young girl who had Down's syndrome pushing a grocery cart full of firewood, and a young man with no legs driving an electric cart down the middle of the street.

They walked until they came to the edge of town. The Laundromat they had used the day before was also closed. On its front window in black spray paint were the words GREEN LOADER. They looked in the window to see the short plump woman they had met the day before hanging by a chain from a large cast-iron sewer pipe. She was naked, and her entire body except for one hand, her neck, and head, were dark green and black and purple with the mark. There was a bullet hole in her throat and one in her forehead and a huge pool of blood at her feet.

"Oh my God," Jeanette shuddered. "Please, Leroy, let's get out of here." She took his hand and pulled him across the street and away from the building.

"What are Green Loaders?" she whispered.

"I don't know," he said.

"We'll be okay, won't we?"

"We'll be okay," Leroy said but he knew then, in his heart, that they never would be okay. They walked across the railroad tracks and past a half-dozen empty warehouses and buildings. A mile from town they came to a military base. It was a five-mile-long complex surrounded by thirty-foot electric fences and manicured green lawns. No buildings were visible except a commissary that was butted next to the fence with a large parking lot outside of it. Above the building an enormous neon sign read, ALL CITIZENS WELCOME.

The store was as big as two football fields, and it was painted glossy white and lit with massive fluorescent lights that hung from the ceiling. Aisle after aisle held civilian clothing, camping gear, sinks, couches, water heaters, plumbing supplies, electrical supplies, auto parts, produce, canned foods, meat, fish, lawn mowers, power tools, sporting goods, hunting gear, TVs, computers, and jewelry. It was the largest store they'd ever seen. They took a shopping cart and bought as much food as they could carry and made the trek back to the marina, where the mechanic sat watching TV in his office.

"She's done and good to go," was all he said and leaned back in his chair and grinned. He reached on his desk for a piece of beef jerky and opened a can of Coke. He adjusted the antenna on the TV, turned up the sound, and resumed watching his program.

*

They traveled five hours north along the coastline on calm sea. The engine ran strong and quiet, and they anchored alone in a small, sheltered bay. They drank bottles of Rainier beer and rain fell on the cabin roof and spaghetti sauce simmered in a pan on the propane stove.

"I'll never get that woman's body out of my mind," Jeanette said as they sat across from each other at the galley table. Tears welled in her eyes.

"Me neither," said Leroy.

"When we were in the store, I went to the bathroom. In the hallway leading to it was a bulletin board. On it were dozens of flyers. Some of them were about Green Loaders. One said

something about how when you first get the mark it turns a light shade of green. If you're green you're a coward, and if you're a coward you'll get the mark. So in their opinion anyone with the mark is freeloading off the nation. That's how they came up with the name. That's what the name means."

"That's crazy."

"I think so, too."

Leroy took two more beers from the icebox and opened them. "You know my uncle said a person can only see so many bad things before it ruins him."

"I hope that's not true."

"I think about it all the time, and lately I think he might be right . . . I remember when I was a kid my uncle would buy the Sunday paper and he and I'd look for boats, 'cause he wanted to live by himself on one. He'd read off each ad and ask me what I thought. Well, I didn't know anything about boats, but even so I'd blurt things out. I'd make up crazy things and it would always make him laugh. Anyway, the problem was that he had no money and every boat he liked was at least five grand. Then finally the boat we found was right next to us in the back of our neighbor's yard. But I think I told you about that."

"You did."

"Anyway, the point is he came back from the war and he had a hard time sleeping. And when he did sleep, he had nightmares. He'd moan and cry and talk in his sleep. He hated sleeping anywhere anyone could hear him 'cause he never knew what he said or did. He just heard about it later on. For a while, when he first got back he had girlfriends, but then he didn't have them anymore. My mom hoped he would get better as more time passed but he didn't. He got worse.

My uncle told her he'd seen too many bad things and that the bad things would never leave him alone. Not even when he was sleeping."

"That's an awful way to live," said Jeanette.

"It is."

*

The next morning they traveled farther north. They saw military ships and oil tankers, a half-sunk sailboat and a capsized trawler. They passed a naval air base and two dying coastal towns. The weather turned and rain became snow and visibility was lost. They had no running lights or spotlight. Leroy slowed them to a crawl and they took turns on the bow looking for deadheads with a flashlight.

They arrived finally in the town of Friday Harbor. The winds were flurrying snow in a constant wash. They found a public mooring, rented a slip, and collapsed in exhaustion. The next morning rain pounded down on the small boat. Leroy sat at the galley table and wrote out a list of supplies he'd need to rewire the running lights. When he finished they lifted the mattress to take money out. He pulled back the board and Jeanette took out the box. She set it on the table and opened it to find all the money gone.

All that was left was a note.

I told the cops and the military police about you. They know the make, the year, and the number of this boat. All Green Loaders should be burned alive.

She handed it to Leroy. "The mechanic?"

He nodded.

"How would he know?"

"I don't know."

"What do you think we should do?"

Leroy sat down defeated in the galley booth. He took his wallet from his pants pocket and counted a hundred and fifteen dollars. "How much do you have?"

Jeanette checked her purse. "Fifty-five dollars and my credit card."

Leroy rubbed his face with his hands. "If we believe the note then maybe they're already looking for us. If that's the case then we should just get gas and go. Maybe use the card now and save the money for emergencies." He started to get up and then fell back into the booth. His breathing became difficult again. His voice faltered. "It took my uncle years to save that money. And you know the only reason he did it is 'cause he thought he was going crazy and he wanted to make sure my mom had enough money to take care of him. He wanted to make sure he didn't make her life even harder than it already was. I know it was only seven grand but he was trying."

*

For three days they traveled farther north. They changed their American dollars into Canadian, and used Jeanette's credit card twice to buy gas and once at a grocery store before it was finally maxed out. The weather grew colder and Leroy became more and more tired. There were constant shooting pains in his chest, and he'd spend hours just trying to catch his breath. He began to weave in and out of panic, and his moods grew dark. He began losing himself in visions of violence and chaos and destruction. It was as if he were constantly falling and the only things he could see were the things of hell.

*

At four in the morning the graveyard shift nurse made a routine check on Leroy to find him with a fever. His face was sweaty and pale and he opened his eyes in panic and looked at her. She hit the Call button for help. Leroy's eyes followed her. He could see her and could smell her perfume. He watched her and then watched as another nurse came into the room followed by a doctor. He could hear them talking and he could feel the pain in his chest growing. His eyes became so blurry from the sweat and tears that soon all he could see were distortions of motion and light.

17

In the basement Freddie McCall found an empty cardboard box and began wrapping toy train engines in newspaper. There were eight in total and he set those on the bottom of the box, and put all twenty boxcars on top of them. In another box he put his remaining track and switches, transformers, and various wagons and buildings. He packed them into his car and drove ten miles to a suburban subdivision and stopped in front of a nondescript white house. He carried the two boxes to the front door, knocked, and a frail, bent-backed eighty-three-year-old man in striped railroad overalls answered and let him inside.

"How have you been, Terrance?" Freddie asked.

"Oh, I'm fine," the old man said. "But I have to say I was pretty surprised by your call." He let Freddie in and shut the door behind him. His front room was clean and stark with just a couch and a coffee table. There were no pictures on the walls or shelves. The old man walked like he was looking for something on the ground. When he looked at Freddie he moved his neck back like he was looking at the sky.

Freddie set the boxes on the coffee table. "Before you get started, Terrance, I know what you're going to say. Regardless of what it is I want you to have them. I can't think of a better person to take them over."

Terrance cleared his throat and shook his head. "I just don't understand why you don't want them anymore. It doesn't make sense. You've spent years building your collection."

"I know I have, but I don't need them now. And I want you to have them. I don't want you to worry, Terrance, but I might have to move out of my house and get an apartment. I won't have enough room for them if I do and I don't want them sitting in a storage space rotting away."

The old man moved his head back and looked at him. "Are the bills that bad, Freddie?"

"I just can't afford the house anymore. That's all. But it's okay. I don't need that big of a house. I live by myself now. Anyway, can't a friend give another friend a gift?"

The old man nodded. "But you kept the Erie-Berkshire, didn't you?"

"No, it's in the box, too. I know you've always wanted one, and I don't need it anymore. That's the main one I want you to have. But there's also the four Civil War engines plus a couple of oddballs. I even put in the Southern Pacific. I know it's not the best engine, but it was my first one and probably still my favorite. And of course all the cars. I put them in there, too, along with the mule train. I don't know where it'll fit in on your set, but I wanted you to have it 'cause it was the first one I ever painted."

The old man put his hand on Leroy's shoulder. "I'm about to have a hot lemonade. Do you want one?"

Freddie nodded and followed Terrance to the kitchen. It was a small and clean room and although his wife had died ten years previously it still looked like a woman's kitchen. Four ceramic fawns sat on a shelf near the sink, and two framed pictures of flowers hung on the walls. He took two cups from a wood cupboard and filled them with lemonade.

He set them in the microwave. As he stood waiting, he stared out the kitchen window and his hands shook and his nose ran and he took a red bandanna from his overalls and wiped his nose. When the bell rang, he took the drinks and handed a cup to Freddie, and they walked down the stairs to the basement where the old man had a twenty-by-forty-foot layout of Denver, Colorado, in the 1920s. He put on a worn railroad engineering cap and sat down at a control panel and began moving trains around the various tracks.

"I won't own them," Terrance said finally. "But I'll take good care of them until you want them again. That's the best I can do. It's either that or you take the boxes back to your car."

"Fair enough," Freddie said and smiled. "Thank you."

The old man nodded as his eyes followed a Denver to Salt Lake engine pulling a dozen various-colored box cars. "You look tired, Freddie. Are you eating right?"

"I know I look pretty worn out, but it's nothing to worry about, Terrance. I'm doing alright. And I'm eating pretty good."

"Are you taking your vitamins?"

"I'm trying to."

"You should always take your vitamins."

"I try to."

"I'm old but I'm not completely dim," Terrance said.

"I know that," Freddie said.

"I can see it in your face. You're having a hard time."

"I'm okay. Really, I am. I'm having a bit of trouble sleeping. That's all."

"The hospital bills have got you, huh?"

"They're a lot but I'm working on them."

"You'll let me know if I can help?"

"Of course I will."

"Do you need money, Freddie? I have some money. I can help."

"No, I'm okay, Terrance. You should hang on to your money. You might need it."

"I'm not gonna need it."

"You might," Freddie said. "You showed me those brochures. Those homes cost a lot."

"I don't have to go there yet," he said.

"But you have to save your money in case you do. You're the one that told me that it costs a lot to get old. That I should save my money. I don't want you to stay in someplace where they don't take good care of you just 'cause you gave me money. The place you're looking at, it's a nice place. So if you have to, you should stay there. So please keep your money."

"Alright," he said. "Your kids okay?"

"They're fine."

"You must miss them quite a bit."

"That's true. I do."

"You'll get them back, Freddie. I have a feeling."

"I hope so," he said.

"I've had some hard times, too, Freddie. They go away, at least most of them do."

"Thanks for saying that, Terrance. I'll be fine."

"I hate to be a pest to you, Freddie, but you do look so tired."

"I know, but it'll pass. Please don't worry. Anyway, I like the new trestle."

"It was a lot of work, but I like it, too." Terrance picked

163

up his cup and tried to take a drink, but his hands shook violently as he did and he set the cup back down. A pack of straws sat near the control panel and he took one from the package and put it in the cup. He bent down and took a drink while an engine chugged past him and headed up the new trestle and into a tunnel.

*

When Freddie arrived back at his house the Volkswagen Bug was parked in his drive. A fire was burning in the fireplace, and there was a half-full Hostess donut box on the kitchen table next to two empty plastic chocolate milk bottles. He could hear music and the sound of two voices coming from the basement. He went down the stairs to the back room and opened the door, and as he did the smell of the plants and marijuana smoke poured out. The fluorescent lights shone down as Ernie trimmed the plant's branches with a pair of small scissors while another boy watered them.

"Hey, Freddie," Ernie said.

"I thought you said you weren't going to come on Sundays."

"I meant to come yesterday, but I got too busy. It won't happen again. We won't be long. We're almost done. I'm doing some trimming right now. You have to stay on top of these guys if you want them to succeed."

The other boy laughed. He was also Indian and was tall and heavy. He was dressed in jeans and a black T-shirt. He had short, dark hair and wore army boots and had a red scarf tied around his left arm. There was a bong and a sandwich bag full of weed sitting next to a portable CD player that was playing.

Ernie took his glasses off and cleaned them with his shirt. There was a pack of Life Savers near the baggie and he took five and put them in his mouth.

"You're gonna eat the whole pack again," the other kid said and laughed. "I ain't even had one yet."

"You better get on it, then," Ernie said and laughed.

Freddie looked at the other boy. "Who are you?" he asked.

"This is Angel," Ernie said.

Angel nodded.

"Can I talk to you upstairs, Ernie?"

"Sure thing, Freddie," he said and set down the scissors. He chewed the Life Savers and took a drink off a can of generic orange soda, and followed him up the stairs into the living room where they stood next to the fire.

"You said you wouldn't bring anyone else here," Freddie whispered nervously.

"It's just Angel," Ernie said. "Angel and me go everywhere together. He won't say anything."

"Lowell told you no other people. I was there when he said it."

"Angel would rather die than tell anyone about this. He's Indian. It's an Indian thing."

"Don't mess with me, Ernie. Lowell and I worked together for eight years. I know all about 'it's an Indian thing.'"

Ernie laughed. His eyes were bloodshot and they looked worse behind his glasses. "Lowell told me you'd say that. But see I've known Angel my whole life. His mom and my mom are best friends. He hates cops."

Freddie leaned against the mantel. His legs felt like they were going to give out. "Look, Ernie, I don't want you smoking in here. Lowell would be upset if he knew. You know he would. I'm worried enough about the smell as it is. I don't need you smoking it, too."

"There's nothing to worry about," Ernie said. "When it's cold out you can't smell anything."

Freddie sighed and sat down on a chair near the fireplace. He was beginning to have trouble breathing. He covered his face with his hands.

"You alright?" Ernie asked.

"I'll be okay in a minute."

"Do you want a glass of water?"

"No."

Ernie looked about the room and put another log on the fire. He went to the kitchen table, took a donut from the Hostess box, and ate it.

Freddie stood up and leaned against the mantel again. "Just no more smoking and no more Angel, alright? And no more coming on Sunday."

"Okay, Freddie," he said and finished the donut. He went to his wallet and took out an envelope from it and handed it to him. "It's a thousand dollars. Well, nine hundred and eighty, really. Angel and I had to get something to eat. Angel ate twelve bucks at Burger King. He eats a lot. I only spent seven."

"What's the money for?"

"Lowell said you aren't a criminal, and that you'd start having a hard time. I'm supposed to give you the money when you start freaking out. It seems to me like that's what's going on."

166

Freddie looked in the envelope and counted the money.

"We'll have a harvest in three weeks. You'll make more money then. White boys at my college buy a lot of weed. It'll be okay, Freddie. Don't worry." Ernie wiped his glasses once more, and then turned around and went back to the basement.

Freddie looked at his watch. He was taking the Sunday night shift at the group home. He had two and a half hours until it started. He stared at the nine hundred-dollar bills and four twenties in front of him. He put a hundred underneath the sink in an empty coffee container and put the rest in his wallet. He took a shower, changed, put two stamps in his coat pocket, grabbed the folder with his past-due bills in it, and left.

He drove to the grocery store and purchased money orders for his past-due water ($263) and electric bill ($556), leaving him with eighty dollars. He put the bills and money orders in envelopes and dropped them in a mail box and drove to the hospital. As he entered he noticed the sign for the cafeteria and went inside and bought dinner. He was looking for a seat when he noticed Leroy's mother in the back, at a small table sitting alone. She was dressed in her Safeway uniform and had black-framed reading glasses on top of her head. On the table in front of her was a half-eaten piece of pie and a cup of coffee.

"How's Leroy tonight?" he asked as he stood in front of her carrying his tray of food.

"Hello, Freddie," Darla said and shrugged her shoulders. "Not well, I suppose."

"Do you mind if I sit with you?"

"Of course I don't mind," she said.

He sat across from her and began eating his supper.

"Can I ask you a question, Freddie?"

"Of course," he said.

"I hate to bother you when you're eating but I can't help it."

"It's alright," he said and set down his fork.

She cleared her throat and looked at him. "Why do you keep visiting Leroy? You must have a family or people that need your time. I know you work two jobs. Did anything happen that night? Anything at all? You can tell me if it did. I won't get you in trouble, Freddie. I won't."

"It's nothing like that," he said. "I can see how you'd think it, but it's not why I'm here. When it happened I was asleep. I woke up 'cause I heard the sound of him falling down the stairs. I can only guess at why he did what he did."

"But still, you come here night after night."

Freddie looked at his food on the table, but he wasn't hungry anymore. He pushed the plate forward and set his elbows down. "I guess more than anything Leroy reminds me of my daughter," he said quietly.

"I didn't know you had a daughter."

"I have two daughters. The youngest, Ginnie, was born with hip dysplasia."

"What is that?"

"Both her hips had serious problems. As an infant we had her in different harnesses to correct the problems, but they didn't work. So eventually she had four different surgeries, but only one of those was successful. The doctors were always hopeful, but then she would never recover the way they wanted, the way they hoped. She was in a lower-body cast three different times, and she was in them for months each time. The doctors here couldn't do the operations. We had to go to Seattle and San Francisco. It was expensive to just get there and stay there, and then on top of that the medical procedure and medications were only partially covered. Medical bills began piling up. That's why I have two jobs."

"I'm sorry."

"Me too."

"What did your wife do for work?"

"She worked at a rental car agency, but she quit to take care of Ginnie. One of us had to quit, and I made more money. But obviously it hurt us losing her paycheck. We were going broke as it was. I've worked at a paint store since I was in high school. I've only had one real job. I never went to college." Freddie rubbed his face with his hands. "I used to lay awake for hours trying to think of a way out of our situation but I never could."

"I was like that when Leroy got hurt," Darla said. "I could never sleep."

"I started going down to the basement in the middle of the night and putting together a model train set," Freddie said and laughed in embarrassment.

"You have to do something," Darla said.

"I started building a train set that had a huge Civil War scene, the Battle of Gettysburg. I'd always read about the Civil War. Anyway, I'd pass half the night down there. It was the only thing I did that made my mind stop. It calmed me down. But I was spending money on it that we didn't have . . . I bought these little Civil War soldiers and I'd paint them. I'd put fake blood on them and have them stabbing and shooting each other. I painted them dead and on stretchers in field hospitals or walking down a road, wounded, with one leg or one arm. All that violence I re-created, and it comforted me . . . I'm sorry to go on like this, Darla. You must think I'm pretty awful."

"It's fine, Freddie. I know what you're saying. I under-stand. But please keep eating, I don't want to ruin your dinner."

"It's alright. I'm not hungry anymore."

"I'm sorry."

"It's not your fault."

"So what happened?"

"Our money got so bad we mortgaged the house twice, and I got the second job at the group home. A couple years went by and my wife started having an affair."

"That's horrible."

Freddie nodded. "I never would have thought of it hap-pening, but it makes sense. All I ever did was work, and to be honest by then I never really thought about how she was doing or how she was holding up. I was so worried about money and Ginnie that she'd become invisible to me. She left with my daughters almost two years ago. She'd fallen in love with someone else and they moved out of state together. It happened four years after Ginnie was born. So, four years of falling apart. By the end I didn't even have the energy to fight for them. To be honest I thought maybe they were bet-ter off without me. I thought maybe their new dad would be an improvement. At least he made more money. It was like waking up from one nightmare and falling into another." He paused for a minute, staring at his dinner. "I liked being a dad, more than anything else maybe."

"Not a lot of men say that," Darla said.

"I'm not telling you this to complain. I'm just telling you 'cause I don't want you to worry that something bad happened to Leroy 'cause of me."

"Thank you for telling me, Freddie."

"I owe you that . . . You know, when we first went into Afghanistan and then Iraq I was excited. I read about it like it was a sport, like an adventure story. All the different kinds of guns and helicopters and jets, and the strategies. And then Leroy came to the group home. I learned he was in the National Guard and got hurt in Iraq. I started realizing things. I started opening my eyes to things."

"I've never understood people's fascination with war," Darla said. "You know my brother went to Vietnam. It felt like I hardly breathed the whole time he was there. And what did it mean him being there? Why was he there? He made it back alive but he wasn't the same. He lost who he was, and for what?"

"Is he still alive now?"

"No."

"What happened to him?"

"He killed himself, Freddie. He shot himself in the head. He lived in the back of my house in a trailer. Leroy went to see him after school one day as he always did, but my brother was dead. He found him in the trailer like that, his head destroyed and all that blood. My Leroy had to see that. Just a week before my brother had gotten so down he went to the VA for help. They put him on some kind of medication, set up an appointment with a counselor, and sent him home."

"I'm sorry."

Darla nodded.

"Why after all that would Leroy join?"

171

Tears welled in Darla's eyes. "His boss was in the National Guard and that had a lot to do with it. This was before 9/11, before Afghanistan. There wasn't a lot to worry about and it was the National Guard. At the time I didn't know they sent the National Guard to foreign wars, and Leroy promised me he'd never have to go. Even so, I was sick about it. The only real fights we ever got in were over him joining. I begged him not to and his girlfriend begged him not to. I broke down crying and begged him because of my brother."

"But he joined anyway?"

She nodded. "I can blame his boss but Leroy was always impressionable, especially to men. In the end I think he just wanted to see."

"See what your brother saw?"

"Maybe," she said. "I hope that's not the reason but I think it might be."

18

Pauline walked down the sixth-floor hall and entered room three, Mrs. Dawson. She helped her from bed and walked her up and down the hall, and when she was finished she clocked out for dinner break. She went to the cafeteria, ordered two egg sandwiches, two orders of chocolate cake, and took them back to the sixth floor, to Jo's room.

"Hey, you're finally up," she said as she walked in.

"Hello," Jo said shyly.

"I'm glad you're getting some sleep."

The girl nodded.

"I'm on dinner break. I was thinking we could eat together." She set the food on the bed-tray. "I hope you like egg sandwiches. The cook makes them especially for me. It's a scrambled egg and cheese on a toasted sesame-seed bagel. It's my favorite. For dessert we have chocolate cake. What do you think? You want to eat with me?"

Jo nodded.

"Good," Pauline replied and took one of the sandwiches and sat down in the chair across from her.

"I'm sorry about last night," Jo said quietly. "I didn't mean to be like that. I didn't mean what I said. I know you're not like that."

"Good."

"I'm sorry I said it."

"I thought we did pretty good last night, considering. We're just getting to know each other. It takes a while for people to trust each other. So don't worry, okay?"

"You don't hate me?"

"Of course not. You were pretty normal if you ask me. Anyway, I can take it. So how was your day?"

"Nothing happened, really." She moved the sandwich in front of her and took a bite. "Linda repacked the bandages and I went for two walks."

"I'll have to do them again in an hour or so, okay? But I'll keep my mouth shut and go fast as I can, and then you'll have the whole night to sleep. Pretty soon you'll only have to change them once a day and then after that they'll be healed."

"Did you do anything before work?"

Pauline set her sandwich on the bedside table and bent down and took off her shoes and set her feet on top of them and moved her toes back and forth. "My dogs are tired again. Let me see. Today, well I went to the dentist. And after that I went grocery shopping, and then on the way home I stopped by my dad's and made him lunch. I guess that's about it."

"Do you always make him lunch?"

"A few times a week."

"Are you a good cook?"

"No, but my dad only eats a few things."

"What does he like?"

"Right now all he likes is chicken noodle soup, crackers, iceberg lettuce, and frozen burritos."

"That's it?" Jo said and smiled.

"He used to only eat TV dinners, but his cholesterol got so bad that I made him stop. After that everything had to be Taco Bell. He'd throw fits if it wasn't. But his cholesterol got

174

even worse. So now it's soup and frozen burritos and I try to
keep him away from candy unless I'm bribing him. Candy
is a sure way to get him to do something he doesn't want to
do. Anyway, more importantly, is there anything on TV?"

"I don't really like TV."

"You don't like TV?"

"No."

"I've never heard anyone your age say that."

"We could never watch it at home. I guess I got used to
it," she said and took another bite of the sandwich.

"Home where you grew up?"

The girl nodded.

"Why's that?"

"My mom thought it was a bad influence. We had to quit
watching it for real when she found God."

"She found God?"

"A born-again Christian."

"No TV after that?"

"No, just sports. My dad watches sports."

"Did your dad become a Christian, too?"

"Not at first," Jo said and set the sandwich down. She
pulled the sheet and blanket up over her chest and pursed
her lips together, and then relaxed and closed her eyes. "He
thought she was completely crazy for a while. All of a sudden the only thing she talked about was the Bible. It was the
weirdest thing in the world. She works at a meat-packing
plant. A lot of the people there are Christian. She started
going to church with them. At first my parents got in fights
about it. But my mom said it was just the devil and God
fighting inside my dad . . ." Jo opened her eyes and looked
at Pauline. "He left us for a few months. He moved in with a

guy we called Uncle Brian, but his wife got tired of my dad being there. She kicked him out and he didn't know what to do so he came back home. After a while he became sort of like her. Then we all had to go to church. But my brother was seventeen by then and he hated it."

"I didn't know you had a brother."

Jo nodded.

"Did you like going to church?"

"I didn't mind it, but my brother thought it was the worst. He ended up running away."

"Where did he go?"

"He went to Portland and lived there with some guys he knew. Then he got arrested for shoplifting. The police called my parents and they drove down to pick him up. They brought him home and made him go back to school. But he hated being home. They used to get in huge fights. One time he and my dad even got into a fistfight. After that he just quit saying anything. It was like he became a ghost. He never talked in front of them, not ever. Not even at dinner. It used to make my mom really mad. It used to drive her crazy. He only talked to me once in a while. One time, right before he left, he came into my room late at night and told me that if you quit talking, people forget you're there. They forget about you, and they leave you alone . . . He got a job for a logging company and quit school and moved into a trailer with one of the guys he worked with. He was there for a while but I don't know where he lives now. I think he works in Alaska somewhere, or at least he did last year."

"Do you like him?"

"I don't know him that well. He's four years older."

"Maybe you could find him. Maybe he could help."

176

"I don't know," Jo said. "To be honest, he never liked me."

"I'm sure that's not true."

"It is."

"What happened to you after he left the house?"

"I stayed for almost two years but I hated it there, so then I ran away."

"Where did you go?"

"Seattle," she said and reached for the lip balm.

"You must have been scared."

Jo nodded. "I'd never been anywhere by myself. Not anywhere at all. I took the bus. I wouldn't have stayed but I had a fake ID that my friend gave me. It said I was nineteen. And I had enough money. My parents kept their savings in cash in my dad's closet. There's a row of books on a shelf and one of them is fake. You open it and it's just a box inside and they put their money there. Over a thousand dollars and I took it. That's pretty bad, huh?"

"It's not the best thing," Pauline said. "But you had your reasons."

"I guess," she said.

"What did you do in Seattle?"

"The first day there I just walked around. I didn't like it. There's so many people and it's so big. And then night came and I didn't know what to do. I almost called home right then, but I would have gotten in so much trouble that I didn't. So I got a hotel room. It was called the Inn at Queen Anne. I'd never gotten a hotel room before that, but it was easy. It was just expensive, over sixty dollars a night. Once I was there I stayed. I shouldn't have, but I did. I was just too scared to find another place."

"What did you do during the day?"

Jo scratched the skin around her IV needle and looked out the window. "I tried to get a job. I knew I had to, but every time I filled out an application I'd lose my nerve. I've never had a real job before. I'd hand in an application but I'd never go back. I stayed in the room for almost two weeks. I didn't do anything but walk around and eat and look in shops. I even bought clothes. I bought two pairs of shorts and a pair of sandals 'cause it was winter and they were on the clearance rack."

"You're a smart shopper."

"Maybe, if you call buying sandals in the middle of winter smart." Jo giggled and covered her mouth.

"You have a cute laugh," Pauline said.

"I hate the way I laugh."

"You shouldn't. Believe me I've heard a lot of weird laughs and yours isn't . . . Anyway, when did you meet those guys?"

"There was a group of them sitting down by the water. Kind of by Pike Place. I'd seen them before. Bob started talking with me . . . It's weird when you don't talk to anybody for a long time and then you do. Anyone being nice to you feels so good. It doesn't matter who they are, or what kind of person they are. I started hanging out with them during the day, and then they stayed in my room until my money ran out."

"How long was that?"

"Maybe five days more."

"All the same guys that were in the house?"

"There was another guy there, too."

"Four guys and you?"

Jo's face suddenly fell. "I know what you're thinking."

"I'm not thinking anything," Pauline said.

"I know you are," she said.

"I'm not," Pauline said. "I just wanted to know the situation. What happened after you ran out of money?"

"I started staying with them," she said faintly.

"Where?"

"Most nights on the street. It wasn't that bad, really. They stole a sleeping bag and a coat and rain gear for me . . . But I got tired of it."

"Which part, having no money or sleeping outside?"

"I guess I got tired of them. Then I got pregnant." She stopped and covered her face with her hands and turned her head away and began crying. "You must think I'm disgusting."

"I don't think that at all. So what did you do when you got pregnant?"

"Nothing for a while."

"Did you know who the father was?"

"No." She began sobbing harder.

"Take a deep breath. It's okay," Pauline said.

"You don't understand what it was like. I was around them day and night and that's all they ever talked about. First they wanted to see my breasts. They'd go on for hours just begging me. Day after day after day just bugging me. So finally I showed them, but after I did it wasn't enough. It didn't stop. It got even worse. They wanted to see more . . . So one night it happened with Bob, and Bob told them all. So they all thought they could if they kept trying . . . They were always trying, always. They would get me drunk and stoned. They'd get me to pass out and then . . . I got so tired of it . . . Even when I was sleeping they'd try . . . It wasn't like they were my friends, really . . . When I told them I was pregnant they totally freaked out. It was scary how mad they were. They pushed me against a wall and yelled at me. Captain even pulled a knife on me. So I told them I wanted to get an abortion, but I didn't have any money . . . They were nicer after that. After that they left me alone. Then somehow a week later they got money and knew where to go. I think one of the guys, Monty, had money."

"I don't remember Monty at the house. Was he there?" Pauline asked.

"No, he left before that," she said and wiped her eyes with her hands. Pauline took Kleenex from the box on the bedside table, and handed some to Jo.

She wiped her eyes again and blew her nose. She looked out the window. "You don't know him," she said. "But he had a credit card. I saw him use it a couple times to get cash. I think he's from Arizona or somewhere like that. Once when we were alone he told me his family lived on a golf course and were rich. But I'm not sure if that's true. Sometimes he'd just disappear. When he'd come back you could tell he'd taken a shower and washed his clothes. He didn't ever use needles. Only Bob and Cal, the kid you met who had the abscess, and Captain did. Captain's the fat kid you saw. They all liked heroin. Monty was alright, really. He didn't even want to do it with me. Anyway he gave me the money so I got an abortion. But after that I never felt very good. I started feeling really sick a week later. One night I asked Monty for some more money, and he gave it to me. The next morning I got on a bus and went to Yakima and then hitchhiked home."

"Back to your parents?"

"Yeah," she said.

"How was that?"

"It was alright at first. They still had my room the same way, and my mom said she prayed for me to come back. But I kept feeling bad so she took me to a doctor. I wanted to be alone with him, you know? But she wanted to be in there with me, and there's no arguing with her. So she found out that I'd had an abortion. She found out that I had chlamydia, too, and that I had a really bad bladder infection. The doctor asked me if I did drugs. At that point I'd only smoked weed and drank, but I told him I didn't do anything. But it didn't matter to my mom. She hated me after that day. She really did . . . My dad would hardly speak to me after he found out." Jo reached to the Kleenex box and took a few more and wiped her eyes. She turned her head away from the nurse. "They made me start seeing the youth pastor from our church. He held meetings at night in his house. My mom made me tell everyone at the group that I'd had an abortion. She wanted me to talk about the pain it had caused my family and myself and God. She said it would help other people . . . I didn't mind doing it, though. I don't know why I didn't, but I didn't. And I didn't mind school either. I just hated when I was home alone with them . . . When I was, everything bad about me seemed ten times worse. Then one night my mom said she couldn't believe that she'd given birth to a girl who could kill a baby. She said the pain it caused her was almost unbearable. That only God gave her the strength to get up and go to work each morning. She told me that God would never forgive me because I killed a baby. The way she said all that, it's hard to explain but it was the worst thing that ever happened to me. 'Cause I believe in God."

"So then what happened?"

"I wanted to kill myself," she said in a near whisper. She closed her eyes and then opened them, still staring out the window. "But I just couldn't do it . . . I was going to cut my wrists but I don't like blood at all. My dad has a gun locker and I know the combination. He has a loaded pistol inside it. The locker is in the garage and I sat out there for a long time but I couldn't do that either. Once I almost pulled the trigger but then all I could see was blood everywhere. It just seemed so violent and awful . . . So a few days later I just left. This time I didn't have any money, but my best friend from school, she gave me enough to get back to Seattle."

"You went back to the guys?"

"Yes," she said.

19

With her shift over, Pauline sat in her car in the hospital
parking lot and waited for the defroster to warm the windshield. As she waited she called a twenty-four-hour diner
and ordered a cheeseburger, fries, and a strawberry milkshake to go.

At home she sat on the couch and ate and watched TV.
When she woke the next morning her throat was sore and
her head was congested. She was getting sick. She looked
through the grocery store ads and found two specials. She
dressed and drove to Safeway. She put twenty-four cans of
vegetable soup, an eighteen-pack of frozen burritos, five
Hershey bars, and a bottle of daytime cold medicine in
her cart and pushed it toward checkout. There were two
clerks working. She saw Leroy's mother behind one of the
registers, and went to it.

"I don't know if you'll recognize me," she said as she set
her items down on the belt. "But I'm Pauline, one of Leroy's
nurses. And you're Darla?"

She smiled. "Of course I recognize you."

"It's always strange seeing a person out of context."

"It is," Darla said and began checking the cans.

"You must think I'm crazy. Your son's nurse buying a case
of vegetable soup, a family pack of frozen burritos, Hershey
bars, and some cold medicine."

"Don't worry. I never pay attention to what people buy
anymore," she replied.

"The cold medicine is for me but the rest is for my dad. He only eats chicken noodle soup and frozen burritos. I'm trying to get him on salad but it's hard going. So now I'm thinking vegetable soup. Maybe he'll eat vegetables that way. Anyway, I'm coming with candy bars."

"A bribe?"

Pauline nodded.

"Are you working tonight?"

"I'm supposed to but I woke up with a cold. I'll try and get some sleep this morning. If I feel better I will. You get there around seven, right?"

She nodded.

Pauline took the coupons from her purse and said, "What are you reading to him now?"

"*The Caladriken Caves*," she said and laughed.

"What's this one about?"

Darla looked behind Pauline to see no customers coming. "This one's pretty good. It's set on a planet like Earth but it's not Earth. There's two tribes who live there. One has all men. Their tribe kills women and girls and steals their male children. They think women control the weather and that they intentionally ruin it. It's always storming there. Blizzards and floods and heat waves. There's volcanoes everywhere and hurricanes and tornados and earthquakes. The all-man tribe is crazy and really violent. The other tribe has men and women and kids. They're normal but they have to go underground and live in a series of caves to hide from the other tribe. They only come out once in a while to scavenge food, and they're always getting killed when they do. Their children, some of them, have never seen daylight. But the male tribe won't go into the caves because they think they're haunted."

"Are they haunted?"

"Yeah," Darla said and finished checking her groceries. "There are these huge worm bats that attack all the time. They come out of the dirt like a worm but they can fly and they have fangs." She laughed and put lotion on her hands from a bottle that sat next to the register. "Between you and me I can't put it down. It's all I've been thinking about. The main guy from the good tribe is named Luc, and he's really something."

"It sounds like a good one," Pauline said. She took out her purse and paid for the groceries. "If I'm feeling better I'll see you tonight, and if not I'll see you tomorrow."

"I hope you get some rest."

"Me too," said Pauline and she left. After her an arguing couple with three kids came pushing two full carts of food to Darla's register. They began stacking groceries on the belt and behind them a line slowly grew.

At eleven-thirty Darla received an emergency message to call the hospital. Leroy's doctor informed her that Leroy had been given a tracheostomy and moved to intensive care. He'd come down with pneumonia. When she hung up the phone she walked into her manager's office and asked for the rest of her vacation days, and put on her coat and left. She drove home and broke down crying at the kitchen table.

As she sat alone in her house she knew she had to make the call to Jeanette. A call she could no longer put off. She sat for a long time with the phone in her hand in a state of panic, and then slowly dialed Jeanette's work number and told her the news. She changed out of her work clothes and got in her car and drove to the hospital. On the third floor, in intensive care, a nurse led her to him. She could tell from the first moment she saw her son that afternoon that he was going to die. She went to him and kissed his forehead, each cheek, and his chin and sat down. She took the novel from her purse, put on her reading glasses, and read to him until her eyes grew weary.

*

At a marina in Bella Bella, British Columbia, they stopped with less than a quarter-tank of gas and rented a slip for seven days and with that they were flat broke. Each morning they walked through the small island town looking for jobs, and eventually Jeanette found work as a maid in a motel, and Leroy got on a construction crew building a vacation home on a nearby island.

They never went to the local restaurant or the local bar. They didn't socialize in any way. At night they would go to bed early and Jeanette would read to him from a stack of novels they'd collected from a paperback exchange. Months passed and winter set in and the sky never cleared. It grew darker until it was always either dawn, dusk, or night, and day disappeared completely.

One evening Leroy sat back in the cabin booth. He had just gotten off work. They had the radio playing and he drank Rainier beer and nursed a pint of whiskey that sat on the galley table while Jeanette made stew on the small propane stove.

"Last night," he said, "I woke up and I could hardly breathe. As I lay in the dark all I could think about was my mom. About how hard she worked for my uncle and me. I know I never talk about her, but that's not 'cause I don't love

her. I think it's just 'cause my whole life she's always been so solid and steady. There are so many other things in the world that are troubling or failing. The truth is I always think of those things, and not the things that keep me from failing. I know that's selfish and wrong, but it seems like that's the way I am. When I think of her I . . . I just feel easy. It's like she's my liver or arm or leg or heart. She's a part of me. When I finally shut my eyes I felt peace and it was easier to breathe. But then I woke an hour later and I'd had a nightmare about my uncle."

"Not much of a break, huh?"

"No," Leroy said. "I guess not."

"What happened in your nightmare?"

"My uncle went to the VA hospital one morning and told the staff there he was disappearing in depression. He was distraught. They sent him home with medication, antidepressants. I'm not sure why it was right then that he fell apart. Maybe people just get worn out. I never thought that was true, but now I think it is true. Maybe people can only take so much. Anyway, they gave him the pills and he came back to the trailer. He was there for a while longer. Then one day I came home from school and he'd written separate notes to my mom and me and left them on the kitchen table. And that was it."

"What happened?"

"I just remember in my nightmare I saw him and it was awful and full of blood. He was alone in his trailer and he wasn't breathing. He wasn't my uncle anymore."

*

A ship arrived from Seattle, Washington. There were eleven

men aboard and they docked at Bella Bella with engine trouble. They had to fly in parts and a mechanic from Vancouver to repair it. They were stuck there for weeks. A few of the men rented rooms at the local motel. Jeanette had heard through her boss that they were tracking down thousands of Green Loaders who were living illegally in Canada. The men on the boat were a part of a vigilante group called The Free, a collective who caught and killed people with the mark. There was a rumor that while they were there awaiting repairs, they'd found and killed two middle-aged women who were living alone in the forest. There was another rumor that they had gone thirty miles inland and found two couples hiding in tents near a lake and killed them and their dogs.

One morning Jeanette pushed her cleaning cart in front of a room and stopped. She knocked three times on the door and yelled, "Housekeeping!" When no one answered she unlocked the door and went inside to find one of the men from The Free ship lying on top of his bed, naked. She turned around and headed for the door, but as she did he told her he had been watching her for days. He told her he knew she had the mark, and that he just couldn't make up his mind if he was going to let her go or kill her.

She got out of the room and pushed her cart to the laundry where she locked herself inside and tried to think. She began crying. Leroy was at work for five more hours, and she wasn't even sure what island he was working on. Her boss wasn't there and if he were, what would she say? She was illegal and she had the mark. She'd be fired, and then what? She stayed in there for twenty minutes and, not knowing what else to do, she went back to work. She pushed her cart to the next room and knocked three times. She again called out *"housekeeping!" and went inside. But as she changed the sheets in the empty room the man from The Free came in dressed in muddy hiking boots and a camouflage uniform. He sat in a chair in the corner and stared at her.*

"I know why you're up here," he said. "And I know who you are and where you're from."

"You're not supposed to be in here," she said. "It's against the rules."

"I'm spending more money in this dump than they know what to do with. They don't care."

"Will you leave the room, please?"

"It's people like you who are ruining the country."

"But I'm not even in the country."

"You'll come back," he said.

"I won't."

"You will."

"Why are you here?" she cried.

"It's easier to find you. You stick out. Anyway, somebody's got to do it. You'll be back sooner or later and we don't need that. You'll be crawling under some fence or hiding in the back of some truck. What you don't understand is that at one time we had the greatest country in the world. The greatest country that had ever existed. Now it ain't shit and it's people like you who've ruined it. People who don't stand up for the flag. Who don't take their hat off when the anthem plays. Who won't sacrifice. For years the politicians gave everything to people who were too fucked up to hold a job or too lazy to do anything but lay on their backs and pump out kids who end up in prison or on welfare. But your turn is over. The test solves it and it'll save our country."

"How does the test solve it?"

"It gets rid of the weak and lazy. It gets rid of people like you."

"But you don't even know me."

"I know you," he said.

"How can you say that?"

"'Cause you're all the same." He stood up and walked over to her until their faces nearly touched. She could smell his breath. There was dried toothpaste on the corners of his mouth. She didn't run or push him away. She just sat down on the bed, defeated, and tears flowed from her eyes.

"See, you already gave up and I haven't even done anything yet."

*

She came back from work that evening so upset she could hardly speak. Once aboard she locked herself in the cabin and drew the curtains shut and waited. It was two hours before Leroy came down the galley steps. But when he did she just greeted him as she always had, and didn't mention the man from The Free at all. Through dinner she struggled not to break down and acted as cheerful and calm as she could. She read to him in bed as usual and he held her when he fell asleep. But the night passed slowly and she tossed and turned. She was wrecked with worry, and finally near dawn she woke Leroy and told him about the man and what had happened the day before.

They left Bella Bella that morning.

They headed farther into Canada, and hid inside the inlets of Princess Royal Island. Weeks passed until they came to the town of Kitimat and got a motel room for the night. The next morning they meandered through the shops of downtown, and in a sporting goods store they were drawn to a family shopping. The man and the woman both wore turtlenecks and the man wore gloves. They had two young children with them. Jeanette introduced herself to them and found out they were American. Recklessly she lifted the hem of her pants, showing them her marked leg. The man took off his right glove and showed her his marked hand.

In the back of the empty store the couple told them they had heard of a settlement a hundred miles inland. A settlement that the Canadian authorities left alone, where it was safe, where there was a school and a makeshift hospital. It was its own country inside of a country, they were told. The man wrote down the maps they'd need, and gave them the exact location of the settlement.

On the boat that evening, Leroy and Jeanette counted their money, and with less than four hundred dollars in savings, decided they would try to find it. The following morning they moved the boat to the bay and anchored. They took what they thought they would need and rowed the dinghy ashore. Jeanette went for supplies and Leroy looked for transportation. Three hours later he came back with a rusted-out red 1984 Ford Fiesta, which he'd hotwired and stolen from a hospital parking lot. They loaded it and left.

They drove a hundred and fifty miles on rough roads. They went farther into the wilderness, past clear cuts and dense forests, past rivers and lakes. As dusk approached they came to the mile marker they were looking for, and past it the logging road that led to the settlement. For ten miles they made their way on washed-out gravel until they came to a series of abandoned cars on the side of the road.

They continued on until they could see, in the distance, a series of pole barns and shacks: the settlement. They parked and got out. Farther along on the road they came to a dead woman in a green parka, her legs bent toward her head. She'd been shot in the stomach, and they could still see steam rising from her.

They passed more bodies, kids and old people, men and women. Some naked, others with no heads, some with no limbs. The Free was spray painted on every building, and vultures flew overhead by the dozen. Coyotes trotted in and out of the buildings, and in the distance gunshots rang out.

"Leroy, let's get out of here," Jeanette cried.

But Leroy couldn't move. He could hardly breathe, he fell to the ground wheezing. Jeanette struggled to get him up and back to the car. She drove them away from the destroyed settlement while Leroy fought for his breath, his eyes closed, his body huddled against the passenger-side door. When they came to Kitimat they abandoned the red car near the dinghy and Jeanette helped Leroy into it and she rowed them back to their boat.

*

In the middle of the night she woke to Leroy's arm over her, pulling her into him.

"How are you feeling?" she whispered.

"I'm better," he said. "But seeing all that was so horrible."

"It was the worst thing I've ever seen," Jeanette said. "Are you sure you're okay?"

"I'm sure."

Jeanette said, "You know I was just having a dream I'd

192

graduated from college. You and I were living in a one-bedroom house we'd bought together. You should have seen this place. The plumbing didn't work, the wood floors were spattered with paint, and everything was covered in grease. I don't know why there was so much grease on everything but there was. Anyway, we fixed it up until it was a really nice house. And the yard that had been all weeds and trash became a real yard. You poured concrete and built an awning so we could sit in the shade during the summer and barbecue. We planted trees . . . In my dream you had just come home from work and you were bleeding. You'd cut yourself on a job site. The cut was on your forearm. I tried to wash it out in the sink but it wouldn't stop bleeding. We decided to go to emergency. In the dream we didn't drive. It was like all of a sudden I was in the waiting room and you were gone. But you weren't in the doctor's office. You'd vanished. You were in the National Guard. You were deployed in Iraq. In the dream I panicked and when I panicked everything changed. All the walls turned gray and suddenly I was in an empty building that I couldn't get out of. I was alone and I couldn't find you, and I knew I'd be stuck in there forever."

"But that's not real," he said gently and kissed her neck and brought her closer to him.

"Maybe it is."

"I don't think so."

"In our house there were pictures of us all over. One photo had your uncle in it. He has long black hair and is wearing a corduroy coat. Your mother has short, brown hair and freckles. She's hugging your uncle and they look very happy. They're surrounded by snow and there's someone behind them that I can't quite make out. The image is blurry."

193

"I have that picture framed," Leroy said. "When I was thirteen my mom rented a cabin in the mountains and we spent the weekend there for my birthday. I'm the person behind her that you can't really see. My uncle took the picture on a timer, but I moved at the last moment. That's why it's blurry."

"How would I know that picture?"

"I don't know."

"You're going to join the army and get killed," she whispered. "That's what the dream means."

"It doesn't."

She moved her hands up and down his arms and stopped over a long scar. She turned on the bedside light and looked at it.

"See," she exclaimed. "You have a scar and before you didn't have a scar."

"No, I've had this scar for years."

"You haven't. I know. I feel your arms every night."

"I swear."

"How did you get it?"

"I cut it on a job," he said. "Like your dream said."

"I don't understand anything anymore," she said. "I don't understand what's real and what isn't real."

He kissed her neck again.

"In my dream I could see the couch we bought at the Salvation Army and the table and chairs we bought from a garage sale. I can remember us painting the walls and you wiring the basement so we could put in a washer and dryer. I remember buying towels and sheets and inviting your mom over for dinner. We had movie posters on our bedroom walls and a framed picture of Amália Rodrigues on our dresser.

194

We had a bathtub and a fireplace and we used to make love in every room 'cause you convinced me it was good luck. We had everything you could ever want . . . Why would I know all these things that aren't real? Why would I be dreaming about things like this if they weren't true?"

*

It was early morning and the woman who sat holding Leroy's arm couldn't stop weeping. Her name was Jeanette, and her thin fingers moved over a long scar on his arm while she spoke.

"A couple weeks ago I was going to the store and in the parking lot I saw an old red Fiesta like the one I had. Like the one you always had to work on. I just stood there and looked at it and I couldn't stop crying. I kept thinking about all the places we went in that car, of all the times you tried to fix it, of when we went camping in it or went to the beach or to the movies. I just stood there staring at that car, and I couldn't leave."

We had a bathtub and a driveway that we used to make dirty so every time we cleaned it up it seemed a real good trick. He and everything was clean every year. ... Why would I know all the things that used ... ? ... Who would I be dreaming about things the way they were sure I ...

20

Freddie McCall woke up on the couch to the alarm on his phone ringing. The fire had died out and the room was now cold. He rose and folded the sleeping bag, changed his clothes and washed his face, and drove to the group home and clocked in. He helped put everyone to bed, and then cleaned the kitchen and bathroom, did four loads of laundry, and fixed a cabinet door that was broken. It was past midnight when he finally gave out. He sat at the kitchen table and read the newspaper and fell asleep.

He woke up an hour later to his phone ringing and fumbled for it in his coat pocket and put it to his ear to hear his ex-wife's voice.

"Is that you, Freddie?" she asked.

"It's me," he said, trying to wake up. "Are the kids alright?"

"They're okay," she said quietly.

"What's going on? It's late."

"I'm not sure what's going on," she said.

"Where are you?"

"At home, in the basement. The girls are upstairs asleep."

"What's wrong? What's going on?"

She didn't speak for a moment and then she cleared her throat. "I have to tell you that I'm sorry I made such a mess of things."

"What are you talking about?"

196

"I'm talking about you and me."

"I made a mess of things, too," he said and sat up. "But we didn't get a lot of breaks."

"No, we didn't."

"So what's going on?"

"It was a mistake to move in with Rob. I knew that before I even did it. I guess I was just tired of living like we were living . . . I'm a fool, Freddie."

"You're not a fool. You were having a hard time."

"I always blamed you, and I'm sorry for that."

"Maybe you should blame me," he said.

"I can't blame you for Ginnie." She paused. "Do you ever think what it would have been like if she wasn't born?"

"No," he said.

"I do," she whispered. "I do all the time."

"You don't mean that."

"It's an awful thing to say but it's true. It would have been so much easier."

"Why are you calling?"

"I don't think Rob understood what having kids around would be like. I think it's too much for him. Tonight we started arguing during dinner. He's got a bad temper, and I can pick on him. I do pick on him. I can make things worse. I know that's true. Both the girls started crying so I yelled at him to stop scaring them. I said some nasty things to him and he got so mad he stood up and went to the fridge and pushed it over. It crashed to the ground and broke. It was really loud, and it scared everyone. I know he was shocked he did it. And then he stormed out and he hasn't come home."

"But the girls are okay?"

"They were upset but they're asleep now . . . Freddie, I

have to ask you a favor."

"What is it?"

"I want you to take the girls for a while."

"Of course I'll take them."

"I'm having a hard time right now, Freddie. In a lot of ways I am."

"I'm sorry to hear that," he said.

They didn't speak for nearly a minute after that. In the silence Freddie could hear Donald talking to himself in the back room. He knew that soon Donald would be coming from the darkness of the hall naked and screaming. "Why don't you just come home with them," he told her. "No pressure or anything like that, just temporarily. See how it goes. I can be better than I was. I will be better."

"I like that you say that, Freddie. I do. But I can't. You understand that, don't you?"

"I understand," he said.

"Can you buy plane tickets for the girls?"

Freddie sighed. "You know I'm broke and that I don't have a credit card anymore."

"I'm broke, too," she said.

He thought of all the money he sent her each month, month after month after month. He knew Rob made three times the money he made and owned his house outright, but he didn't mention any of that. All he said was, "I don't get paid for two weeks."

"I think they should come up sooner."

"Maybe once things calm down you can get Rob to buy the tickets and I'll pay him back."

"I'll see what I can do, but I have to go now, Freddie," she said and then hung up the phone.

*

The rest of the night he was sleepless. He started drinking coffee at four-thirty. He sat at the kitchen table and tried to think, but he was too tired to think. Dale arrived at six-thirty-five. Freddie, again late, rushed home, changed, and drove to Heaven's Door Donuts. He parked and flashed his lights twice and Mora met him in the parking lot with the donut boxes.

"You're even later than you were last week," she said. She wore her white apron and gray sweats and a red ski cap with a white cotton ball on top. She handed him the boxes and leaned down, resting her arms on the car.

"I have good news for a change, Mora. I'm going to get my girls back. Marie wants me to take them. She called a few hours ago. You were right. She can't handle it."

A large delivery truck pulled up next to them and four men got out and headed for the donut shop. She stood back up. "Geez, I'm happy for you, Freddie. You know I was praying you'd get a break and now you have one."

"I can't believe it either. But you better go," he said.

"I'll see you tomorrow."

"I'll see you tomorrow," he said and drove off.

He parked his car at Logan's to see three paint vans already in front, waiting. He apologized and opened eight minutes late. He handled the morning rush and drank cup after cup of coffee to stay awake. At eleven a semi-truck backed to the dock and delivered two pallets of paint. He checked them in and began restocking the retail floor. At twenty minutes to noon Pat parked his black Ford F-250 pickup in the lot and came in the front doors carrying a liter of Dr Pepper and a frozen turkey and mashed potato TV dinner.

"How was it this morning?" he asked.

"Jenson bought five hundred worth of Super Spec and I finally got the Oldham brothers out of Sherwin-Williams. They came in a half-hour ago."

"What did they buy?"

"Eight hundred dollars' worth of primer."

"That's good," he said. "Darn, that's really good."

"The margin wasn't the best, but I got them here. If I can get them to stay, I can start easing the margin back again."

Pat set his lunch in the refrigerator and took off his leather aviator coat and hung it on a hook by his office door. He cleared his throat. "If anyone calls for me tell them I'm in a meeting and I'll call them back."

"Alright, Pat, but before you go I was hoping to ask you something."

"What is it?" he said and went to the remaining box of donuts. He took out a maple bar and a twist and filled a cup with coffee.

"I was hoping I could get an advance on my paycheck. To tell you the truth, Pat, I'm in a serious jam. I might even need a loan for a couple months. Not much, maybe a thousand dollars? I'm getting my kids back but I don't have enough money to fly them up from Las Vegas. It's an emergency or I wouldn't ask."

Pat coughed but he didn't answer. He just took a bite of the maple bar and washed it down with coffee.

Freddie waited for him to speak, but when he didn't he continued. "You know I hate asking anything from you, and I haven't since your dad died, since you took over here. But now I'm afraid I need help."

Pat leaned against the counter and set the donuts and coffee down. "Darn it, I don't think I can do that right now, Freddie. Things are tight with me as well. I'd like to help, but it's hard all over. This economy is hitting everybody. That's for sure."

Freddie moved to the other side of the counter from him. His face haggard and pale under the bright store lights. He'd slept three hours the night before, and had already had four cups of coffee. He looked at Pat but Pat wouldn't look at him. "I know the store's slow," he said. "But winters are always slow and this year is better than the last two. I wouldn't ask if it wasn't a dire situation, but I'm afraid it's pretty bad for me right now."

Pat glanced past Freddie to the parking lot where a white painting van was pulling up. "I wish I could help, Freddie, but that's not the policy that this company has."

"The company is you and me, Pat. Everybody else is gone now. I've worked here for a lot of years. Your dad hired me out of high school. Your dad would always help a guy out. Always."

Two painters came into the store and walked toward the counter. Pat finally looked at Freddie and nodded his head to them, picked up his donuts and coffee, and went into his office. Twenty minutes later he came out and heated his lunch in the microwave. He then went back inside his office to call his wife, and Dr. James Dobson's voice began leaking through the walls.

*

Four days later, on Saturday, Freddie closed Logan's Paint Store at five-thirty. He sat in his car in the parking lot looking over a road map. He found a paper bag on the floor and wrote down the miles it would take to get to Coyote Ridge Corrections Center and divided them by the miles per gallon the Comet got. He counted the cash in his wallet and thought he had enough for gas and maybe dinner. He checked the oil and water, and got on the road heading east.

The Comet stayed in the right lane for three hours while tractor trailers grumbled past and passenger cars sped by. He saw miles of plains and barbed-wire fences and open hayfields and farms and ranches along the way. His car shook and rattled, the steering linkage worn and loose, making the old car sway in between the white lines of the interstate.

He stopped at a truck-stop twenty miles from the prison, exhausted. He could barely keep his eyes open as he ate dinner in the truck-stop restaurant. In the parking lot, in the backseat of his car, he spent the night in a sleeping bag. The next morning he washed up in the restaurant bathroom, got a coffee to go, and left.

The corrections center was a series of stark, colorless concrete buildings surrounded by tall cyclone fences, flood lights, and empty fields. He parked and went through the visitors' gate. He showed his ID, filled out the visitor form, and waited with dozens of other visitors until a guard brought them all to the cafeteria where they took seats and waited until the prisoners were brought in. He looked around at the other people waiting: Mexican, white, and black. There were babies crying and people whispering, and bored kids forced to sit still. The room smelled of Pine-

Sol and seemed like any cafeteria in any school Freddie had ever been in.

It was twenty minutes later when he saw Lowell come into the room in prison-issued clothes: khaki pants, a white sweatshirt, and tennis shoes.

"Hey Freddie," he said. He sat across from him. "It must not be good news if you're here."

"It's not," Freddie replied. He looked at Lowell. His hair was back in a single braid. He'd lost weight and looked worried and tired. "Marie wants me to take the kids back. The thing is I can't work two jobs and keep them so I have to sell the house. Anyway, I can't have them around the basement even if I could scrape by moneywise."

Lowell sighed and looked down at the table, but he didn't say anything.

"I'm sorry about this. You know I am. I just don't know what else to do."

"When is this happening?" he asked.

"I'm not sure. I don't have the money for airfare. Marie says she's broke, too. I even asked Pat for a loan."

"I bet that went great."

"I asked for a thousand but he wouldn't do it."

"You should quit on him," Lowell said and looked around the room. "You should just walk out. He'd be screwed; he doesn't know shit about the paint business."

"I know," Freddie said.

"But you won't?"

He shook his head. "I can keep Logan's going. I can get my kids through high school with that job."

"You want to work for Pat that long? You want to support him while he buys new cars and sits in his dad's office a couple hours a day?"

Freddie didn't answer.

"I'm sorry I'm in a bad mood, Freddie. I just didn't need to hear what you're telling me. My sister says she's going to stay in my house when I get out. So I either have to live with her or find a new place. And then another cousin of mine forgot to put oil in my motorcycle and burned the engine out. Shit ain't going my way. And now this . . . You've always been straight with me, Freddie, and we've been friends. But you're one of those guys who works his whole life and tries not to do the wrong thing, and all it gets you is guys like Pat. You make rich guys richer and all they do is ask for more, and you always give it to them. Let me just say this, if you work for Pat for ten more years, I don't want to know you, Freddie. 'Cause it'll say something about you that I don't want to see . . . Look, your basement is the only thing I got going for me when I get out. I don't have my truck. I won't have my house. I won't have shit."

"I'm sorry," Freddie said.

"You're sure?"

Freddie nodded.

"I'll make sure Ernie comes in a couple days to get rid of them," Lowell said and then stood up and walked back to the guards.

*

Outside in the parking lot Freddie sat in the Comet trying to get it to start. He'd flooded it, but even so he kept trying until the battery finally died. He got out of the car, took his jumper cables from the trunk, and opened the hood and waited for someone to come out.

A young Mexican woman with a baby and a toddler came through the last chain-link gate of the prison ten minutes later. She was a short, stout woman barely five feet tall. Her son, who was just able to walk, held her hand and she held a shopping bag and a baby in her other. They came to a white pick-up truck and she put the baby in a car seat and buckled the young boy in and shut the passenger-seat door.

Freddie walked over to her as she opened the driver's side. "Excuse me," he said. The woman seemed frightened at first, but then she smiled and said hello to him. She had two silver teeth that Freddie thought made her seem beautiful and exotic somehow.

"I'm sorry to bother you," he said. "But my car won't start."

"No gas?" she said.

"I have gas. Bad battery. I need a new battery," Freddie said. "Or maybe a new alternator. Maybe a new car." He grinned.

"A jump?" she said and smiled back.

"If you don't mind."

"I don't mind," she said and got up onto the bench seat. She shut the door and rolled down the window. "This truck is too big. I need a ladder." She smiled again. "Where is your car?"

"It's over there," he said. "The old black one with the hood up."

She started the truck and pulled up in front of the Comet. He opened her hood, placed the jumper cables on her battery, and then onto his and got in his car and started the engine. He got out again, took the jumper cables off, shut his hood and then the truck's, and walked over to her.

"Thank you," he said.

"You're welcome."

"Do you come every Sunday?" he asked.

"Every time we can, but I hate coming to this place."

"Have you been coming a long time?"

"Seems like it," she said and smiled. "And you?"

"It's my friend who's here. It's my first time coming to a prison."

"I wish it was mine," she said. "Today I tried to bring in tamales to him 'cause it's his birthday. He loves my tamales. They didn't let me give them to him, but at least I tried."

"Is he your husband?"

"Yes," she said. "But he's not much of a husband now."

"Well, thanks again," he said and began to walk back towards his car.

"Wait," she said.

He turned around.

"Do you want the tamales?"

"Of course," he said and smiled, and so again she smiled and her silver teeth seemed to shine. They looked at each other for a long while, both longing and desperate. He wanted to say something more to her. He didn't want the moment to end. But her boy, who was staring at her and bouncing his legs on the bench seat, said something in Spanish. She took her eyes off Freddie, shook her head, and answered him. The baby was in the car seat asleep. She looked in the grocery bag and took out a tinfoil package and handed it to him.

"Will you be here next Sunday?" she asked.

"No," he said. "I won't be here again."

"Then it was nice to meet you," she said and rolled up her window and drove away.

21

It was late into the night and near the end of Pauline's shift when she took her last break in the girl's room. Jo lay on her side in the dark and stared out into the hallway watching the hospital traffic pass by.

"So you're a volleyball player," Pauline said and sat across from her.

"How would you know that?" said Jo and turned on the bedside light.

"The shoes in the closet."

"How do you know what volleyball shoes look like?"

"I know a few things. I'm not as dumb as I look."

"I won those at a tournament when I used to play."

"You must have been pretty good."

"I wasn't really."

"I bet your parents were proud of you."

"It's the only thing my dad likes about me."

"I'm sure there are other things."

"No."

"I didn't think you'd be an athlete," Pauline said and sat back in the chair and stretched her arms.

"Why?"

"I don't know, but I like that you are."

"In a small town anyone can do sports. You don't have to be good."

"To win shoes you probably have to be pretty good."

"That's not true."

"If you say so," Pauline said. "Do you like chocolate?"

"Everybody likes chocolate," said Jo.

Pauline reached into her shirt pocket and took out a handful of miniature Hershey chocolate bars. She placed them in her palm in front of the girl. Jo took two and Pauline set the rest on her bedside table and looked at her watch.

"So how did you get them?"

"The shoes?"

Pauline nodded.

Jo opened the first chocolate and put it in her mouth. "Well, one time my mom drove me and this friend from school to a volleyball tournament. She made us all pray before we got out. It took a long time. She just sat there and went on about God and how he was going to help us win. It was really embarrassing, but at the end of the tournament we were both on the team that won. We each got a voucher for a pair of new volleyball shoes from Nike, a medal, and a ball."

"Maybe the praying worked."

"Maybe," Jo said.

"I'd like to watch you play volleyball sometime."

"I won't play anymore, but that's alright. I didn't like it that much and anyway I'm too short."

"Maybe you'll take it up again someday for fun."

"Maybe."

"I always liked playing," Pauline said. "I was even on a team for a while, but in the end I was always scared of the ball."

"The ball doesn't hurt that much when it hits you. That's what you have to remember."

Pauline laughed. "I knew that. At least in my mind I did,

but at the very last second I'd always turn away."

"You're not supposed to do that."

"I know. That's why I didn't last."

"Can I ask you a question?" said Jo.

"Sure," Pauline replied.

"I was wondering why your mom doesn't take care of your dad. Did she die?"

"No, she's alive but she left town a long time ago."

"Where did she go?"

"Phoenix, Arizona."

"Why did she go there?"

"She met a man at work and had an affair with him. He wanted to go there."

"How old were you?"

"Five," Pauline said and looked at her watch.

"Do you have to go?"

"I have four minutes left."

Jo opened another chocolate and put it in her mouth. "Were you upset when she left?"

"Sure, I used to hate her because of it." Pauline reached over and took one of the chocolates, opened it, and put it in her mouth. "But really, my dad . . . well all I can say is that I can't imagine being married to him. It must have been pretty awful."

"Why didn't you go with her?"

"Maybe you should be a detective. You sure ask a lot of questions."

"I don't like guns," Jo said. "Detectives have to carry guns. But I like trying to figure out things."

"Maybe you could be a detective that doesn't carry a gun. It could be your trademark."

"Maybe," she replied and looked at Pauline. "Why didn't you go with her?"

"Because she didn't want me to. I mean I didn't want to stay with my dad alone. I hated it there. My dad can be really crazy. And crazy is a tough one. 'Cause it always comes out different but then it's always the same, too. She knew all that but left me with him anyway. That says it all, I think."

"Did she ever tell you why she didn't take you?"

"Not really. I don't think about it anymore, but when I was your age I was obsessed with it. I used to get really depressed. But the truth is I never asked her why because I didn't want to know the answer. 'Cause really I already knew the answer. So in the end I just decided I would never talk to her again."

"Was it hard doing that?"

Pauline nodded. "And it wasn't the smartest decision. Being mad like that takes a lot of energy. It wears you out in a bad way, I think. As I got older I started seeing things differently, maybe from her side. She wasn't the most courageous woman. Maybe she thought she had to save her own skin, and maybe she thought that guy was her only shot. Or maybe she just didn't like me enough to take me. I don't know. It doesn't really matter why I guess. It took a long while but I learned to forgive her, 'cause I didn't want to spend my whole life angry. That doesn't mean I have to like her or that I have to keep in touch. It just means I've put her behind me more or less."

"Did you ever go to Phoenix to visit?"

"No," Pauline said and stood up. "I had to figure things out on my own. The first thing I learned is that you can be and do whatever you want. You just have to get up each morning and try to get there."

"Getting up is hard," Jo said.

"It's hard but not that hard. I'll help you."

"Why would you say that?"

"'Cause it's true."

"But why would you help me?"

"'Cause I like you. But now I have to get back to work."

"Do you have a lot of patients?"

"A few."

"Any nice ones?"

"Not as nice as you," Pauline said and began walking out of the room. She turned and looked at her watch. "You better be sleeping the next time I make the rounds or it's NASCAR for you, alright?"

"Alright," the girl said and smiled.

"Good-night."

"Good-night."

*

The next evening Pauline came on shift to find a dark-haired man in his twenties in Jo's room. He had a handlebar moustache and was seated in the chair across from her dressed in black jeans, a black leather coat, and motorcycle boots.

"I'm Randy," he told the nurse. He stood up tall and lanky, and put out his hand and Pauline shook it. "I'm the youth pastor at Carol's church."

"Carol?"

"I think you might know her as Jo. Her real name is Carol Coller."

Pauline said hello to the girl, checked her IV, and looked at the packings. "How are you feeling?" she asked.

"I'm okay," she said quietly.

"Are you sure?"

"I'm sure."

Pauline winked at her. "Then I'll leave you two alone," she said and charted on the computer in the corner of the room and left. When she came back an hour later the youth pastor was gone. The girl was alone and facing the wall and quietly crying to herself.

"Carol's a nice name," Pauline said. "Why didn't you tell me your real name?"

"I don't know," she murmured.

"Well it's a good name."

"The guys called me Jo," she said as she still faced the wall. "And when I got here I wasn't going tell them my real name . . . Do you want to know why they called me Jo?"

"Why?"

She squeezed her eyes closed and covered her face with her hands. "They called me Jo 'cause there was a crazy girl they knew named JoAnne. They called her Jo-blow 'cause she'd have sex with everyone. She'd blow anyone. All you had to do was ask her."

"But that's not your name, is it?"

"No," she said.

"You're not her, are you?"

"No."

"I like the name Carol," Pauline said. "May I call you that?"

"Okay."

"Was the pastor alright?"

213

Carol didn't answer.

"He likes motorcycles, huh?"

She smiled and opened her eyes. She turned to Pauline. "He thinks he's cool 'cause he rides a motorcycle around. But he's seriously not cool."

"How did he find you?"

"There was a child welfare lady that came by. She scared me so I told her my real name."

"I'm glad you did."

"I don't know," she said uncertainly.

"It was a good move," Pauline said and looked at her watch. "But now we're going to have to get to work 'cause I'm a little behind tonight. Are you up for me changing the packings?"

Carol nodded and Pauline left the room and came back with a cart of supplies. She set it next to the bed and pulled the curtain around. She washed her hands and put on a pair of sterile gloves.

"It's time for you to close your eyes, okay?"

"Okay," Carol said, and Pauline began removing the bandages and packings from her leg.

"Have your parents come yet?"

"Pastor Randy said my mom's so heartbroken she missed two days of work. They don't want to see me until I get better."

"She'll change her mind. She's probably just scared."

"They want me to go away."

"Go away where?"

"A Christian rehabilitation camp."

"They have those?"

"Yeah, and they cost a lot of money. They want me to go

214

there until I'm eighteen." Carol suddenly cried out in pain.

"Are you alright?"

"I just started thinking about what you're doing, and I opened my eyes. I know I should never do that, but I can't help it sometimes."

"It's gonna get easier and easier," Pauline said. "They're healing so fast now that pretty soon we won't have to do it at all. So where is this rehabilitation place?"

"In Idaho somewhere."

"Maybe it won't be so bad."

"They'll all hate me there. I know they will."

"You're a good kid. You're not any worse than anyone else. Maybe you'll meet nice people there."

"You don't understand anything."

"Maybe not, but the place could be alright. You never know."

"You hate me, too. I can tell. I can tell by your voice. You think I'm a freak and you want me to go to some camp for freaks so you'll never have think of me again."

"You know that's not true," Pauline said. "So lay off saying stuff like that, alright? Nothing's changed. I'm just trying to understand what's going on . . . Okay, we're half done." Pauline stood up, took off her gloves, and threw them in the basket along with the used packings and bandages. She washed her hands again, put on new gloves, and began repacking the abscesses.

"How's the pain? You holding up alright?" she asked, but this time Carol wouldn't answer. The girl kept her eyes squeezed shut, and turned her face to the wall and didn't speak again. Pauline finished her work and left the room. When she came by again for the last time during the night she knew Carol was faking sleep.

*

The next shift Pauline came on to find that the girl had disappeared in the middle of the night. The graveyard shift nurses had seen a boy in her room. They'd told him to leave and he had. They hadn't seen him again and didn't see anything out of the ordinary after that. She was just there one moment and then the next she wasn't.

The hospital called her parents and the youth pastor but no one had seen her. They called the police and filed a missing persons report, but her whereabouts were unknown.

Pauline worked the rest of her shift that night but when she got home she couldn't eat or sleep. The next morning she walked across her apartment complex and climbed the stairs to the second floor. She knocked on a front door until a naked man answered.

"Are you trying to scare me to death, Gary?"

The man was heavyset and in his late fifties and bald. His body was covered in black hair, and his penis was nearly hidden under his sagging belly.

"It's six o'clock in the morning," he grumbled.

"I called you three times last night."

"My phone doesn't work."

"Your phone works. I called from outside the door once and heard it ringing. Can you put some clothes on? I have to talk to you, and I can't do it this way."

Gary turned around and waddled down the hallway toward his bedroom. Pauline went inside, turned the heat up on the thermostat, and stood in the kitchen and waited.

216

"I thought nurses were used to seeing naked men," he yelled from the bedroom.

"I get paid to see people naked. That's the only thing that makes it bearable."

"Thanks a lot."

"I'm taking you out to breakfast."

"Why, what do you want?" He came from the bedroom in threadbare white jockey shorts and sat down on his couch.

"I told you to get dressed."

"I have underwear on. What do you want?"

"I checked the janitor's schedule last night and you have today off. I need your help."

"I don't want to help."

"You don't even know what it is."

"It can't be good if you're here this early."

"How's the job I got you?"

Gary coughed for a long time and shook his head. He got up and spit in the kitchen sink and then sat back down on the couch again. "You're going to hold that over me forever and that's bullshit."

"I was just asking. You don't need to get ugly. Seriously, how is it going?"

"Alright I guess," he said. He put his feet up on a plywood coffee table.

She pointed to an ashtray full of butts and half-finished cigarettes on the table next to his feet. "You know you're supposed to quit smoking."

"I have quit," he cried. He rubbed his face with his hands and sighed.

"There's more than twenty butts in there."

"They've been there a long time."

Pauline took the ashtray and emptied it in a trash basket in the kitchen. "If I see more than five in here the next time I'm over, I'm going to show up every morning at six and take you running."

"I'd like to see you go running," he said and laughed.

"Well if you make me, I'll start. Anyway, come on. Get dressed."

"First tell me why."

"'Cause I'm taking you to breakfast."

"Then what?"

"Come on," Pauline said.

He coughed again but got up and went back to his room. He came out five minutes later wearing jeans and a worn flannel coat.

"I thought you quit drinking," said Pauline.

"I have, mostly." He sat on the couch and put on his shoes.

"There are four paper sacks full of empty beer cans."

"They've been there a long time. I recycle now."

"I bet you recycle. Do you have a gun?"

"Jesus, Pauline," he cried. "You're getting me into something where I need a gun?" He walked to the kitchen table where a new pack of cigarettes and a lighter sat. He opened the cigarettes, took one out, and lit it.

"I'm glad you quit."

"Get off my back. Jesus, you could drive a man nuts. So why do I need a gun?"

"It's for just in case," Pauline said.

"I hate guns. Why would you think I'd have a gun?"

"What about a baseball bat?"

"Christ, can't we go eat first?" he said. "And if you tell

me I have diabetes one time while we're there I'll get a gun and shoot myself."

"Don't worry," Pauline said and opened the front door. "I want you to eat a lot. You might need your strength."

*

The morning was clear and the sun was rising into a dark blue sky when they arrived at the white farmhouse with the yellow barn. The fields surrounding it were still half-covered in snow, and they could see their breath as they got out of the car. In the early sunlight the house looked even more desolate and tired than Pauline remembered. She opened the trunk, took out a tire iron, and handed it to Gary. They walked past the gravel driveway and up the steps to the back door. Pauline knocked and looked inside, but this time she didn't see any movement or any sign of a fire. She knocked again and checked the door handle to find it unlocked.

Inside, the kitchen's cabinet doors were gone as was the wood trim on the baseboards, the doorway, and the windows. The pictures that hung on the walls had disappeared, and there was more trash everywhere. Old wrappers and food containers, fast-food bags, dirty clothes, and soda and beer cans. She walked to the living room where the windows were still covered and called out the girl's name in the darkness. Gary used his cigarette lighter to see his way to the blacked-out windows. He pulled the garbage bags down and light filled the room.

"Whose house is this?" he asked.

"I don't really know," Pauline said. They walked down

a hallway into the first bedroom. There were holes in the walls showing old lath and plaster and on the floor was a broken-up wooden dresser and a door they had tried to bust apart. All the baseboard and window trim was gone. The next bedroom was empty except for a pair of stained men's underwear and a frozen pool of vomit. All the trim on the baseboards and windows was gone. In the bathroom, the toilet and tub were full of shit and piss, and Gary gagged at the sight of it and went to the living room and lit a cigarette.

It was there that he called for Pauline.

In a sleeping bag behind the couch was the outline of a body. Pauline entered the room and went to the bag. She pulled it back to see the redheaded boy, frozen and dead. His young face pale and blue, his eyes still open. Around him on the ground were bloody rags, a box cutter, an empty bottle of rubbing alcohol, and two nails. She could see that he'd been lancing the abscess himself. He wore no shirt and his arms were covered in frozen pus and blood.

"Is there someone in there?" Gary said from the edge of the room.

"Yeah," Pauline said. "Don't come over here. You don't need to see it. It's not Carol. It's a boy that I've seen here before."

"Is he dead?"

She looked at Gary and nodded. She walked to the corner of the room where another sleeping bag lay with something inside it. She pulled it back to see an orange suitcase. On the tag it said the girl's name, Carol. Inside were clothes, two empty notebooks, and a small photo album. There were pictures of her holding a cat, of her standing next to a horse in the middle of a stream, her with a volleyball team, and another of her sitting on a couch with a boy who looked like her brother. She rummaged through the girl's clothes to find clean socks, folded underwear, and T-shirts. There was a volleyball jersey and a baggie full of medals. There was a plastic sack full of dirty clothes and a pair of sandals. She took a photo of the girl from the album, put it in her coat pocket, and turned to Gary. "Does your phone work out here?"

He looked at it. "Yeah," he said.

"Will you call the police?"

He nodded and called them and gave them the location, and they went outside, to the porch, and waited.

"Why would they just leave him out here?" Gary asked.

"He was probably too sick to travel and they didn't care about him." Pauline sat down on the porch steps. She tried to remember the redheaded boy's name but couldn't. "It's my fault," she said finally.

"How is it your fault?"

"I'd seen that boy out here before. I knew he was sick. I tried to get him to come to the hospital with me but he wouldn't. I should have called the police that day. I knew he was in trouble." Tears began falling down her cheeks and she wiped her face on her coat. "I knew he was in real trouble, but I blocked it out . . . I was so mad at them for being cruel to Carol, for taking advantage of her, that I didn't care what happened to them. She was safe so I blocked them out. But what does that make me?"

"He could have gone with you. He chose not to."

"Maybe," she said.

"Where do you think the girl is now?"

"I don't know."

221

22

It was just a blur of light when he opened his eyes. He could hear the TV. He wasn't in pain. The tube was out of his mouth, but he could just see that there was now a tube coming out of his windpipe. He could feel someone's hand holding his, and he knew instantly it was his mother's hand. It was warm and soft and he could feel the only ring she wore on her left middle finger.

And then for a moment he could see her clearly. She was sitting next to his bed watching the news. A wave of emotion overcame him. He tried to grip her hand to let her know he was there but his fingers wouldn't move when he asked them. He tried to make a noise, but no noise would come. He tried to move his feet and when that failed he again tried to move his fingers. But all the effort was exhausting him, and his eyes grew heavy and closed.

As she held his hand he remembered years before, her sitting at a high-school football game on a cold fall night. Her shift manager had let her leave work early and she sat in her uniform, in a winter coat, and drank coffee and watched him play. Every time he looked at the stands he saw her sitting by herself. He knew she didn't understand the rules of the game, and that she had never liked sports. Not any of them. There were groups of families in front of her and cheerleaders on the track in front of them. Around her were various other people: high-school kids, the occasional single parent, and then rows of empty bench seats.

Snow began drifting down as the clock neared the end of the game. He was sure she was probably freezing, but he knew she wouldn't leave. And then finally he caught a pass. It was a good catch but he got hit hard right afterward and the ball sprang loose. He'd fumbled. The opposing team picked it up and ran it into the end zone for a touchdown. The score was now 27–10; his team was behind. The game ended as dusk set into night. The next game began and she went to her car and waited.

He appeared forty minutes later and got into the passenger-side seat with a swollen nose and wet hair.

"Are you freezing?" she asked.

"I'm okay," he said.

"They don't have blow-dryers in the locker rooms?"

He laughed. "No, Mom."

"What happened to your nose?" Under the dome light she could see it was swollen with dried blood around the nostrils. She took a pack of Kleenex from her purse and handed them to him. "You might need these."

"I don't think it's broke, but it sure hurts," he said.

"Do you think we should go to the doctor?"

"The coach looked at it and thought it was fine. He said he knew about broken noses."

"Good. Then are you hungry?"

"Not really," he said and put his book bag in the backseat and they began driving home. "How much did you see?"

"I got off early and saw the second part."

"The second half," he said and laughed.

"I saw the second half," she said and smiled.

"Did you see me fumble the ball?"

"That guy hit you pretty hard."

"Not that hard, I just dropped it. I don't know why. I try so hard not to make mistakes but I make a lot of them. He stuck his hand through my face mask and hit my nose, too. You should see my uniform. It's all covered in blood."

"Did you bring the uniform with you?"

"Yeah," he said. "It's in my bag."

"I'll get the blood out."

"I'm sorry."

"Don't be sorry. That's just the game. I feel bad for your nose though."

"You're not disappointed in me?"

"Why would I be disappointed?"

"'Cause I fumbled the ball and got blood all over my uniform. Plus I missed two blocks and then when I played defense I missed a tackle. I bet I won't start next week."

"Everyone has bad games," she said.

"I hate that you have to sit out there in the cold just to watch me screw up. I know you don't like football. I don't think you should come anymore."

"I like coming," she said. "I like watching you. Don't worry about me. You did some good things out there, too. And sad to say your fumbling didn't change the fact that you guys aren't very good."

"Thanks," he said.

"You know what I mean."

"I know."

They drove through downtown and came to a stoplight. Across the street the marquee for the movie theater shone down.

"Look, *Blade* is finally here!" Leroy said.

"What's *Blade*?"

"It's a movie based on a comic book. *Blade* is a vampire but he's a good vampire. He doesn't drink blood. He has this friend who knows how to build guns and they have a hideout and a bunch of cool cars. *Blade* doesn't want to drink blood; he wants to be a good guy. It has Wesley Snipes and a guy named Kris Kristofferson in it."

"Kris Kristofferson's in it?"

"I guess so. That's what it says on the sign."

His mother took her glasses from her purse and put them on. She looked at the marquee.

"I like Kris Kristofferson. Maybe we should see it," she said.

"Tonight?" he said and suddenly his face lifted in excitement.

"Tonight." She drove through the intersection and pulled the car over and parked. She looked at Leroy. "When I first started working I was an assistant secretary for a big accounting firm. I was eighteen and I tried really hard. I wanted to do good, just like you want to do good. Like how you tried to do good tonight. Anyway, I filed all these papers wrong. Stacks and stacks of them. I had misunderstood how to do it, but it was two days of work I ruined and my boss was really upset with me. He said he was going to fire me. He even called me an idiot. In front of maybe twenty people he did. I had just moved out on my own. I had bills. I was in over my head as it was. To be honest I was flat broke. I couldn't lose the job. So I just started crying and I begged him not to fire me. In front of everyone I did."

"Did he fire you?"

"No, he didn't. He was just mad and not a very good boss. It won't help you, but here and there if you're a woman,

225

crying can get you out of a jam." She laughed and put her glasses back in her purse. "Anyway, I kept that job for a year until I found a better one. That filing mistake I made was no big deal. It was only a big deal that day. And that first night after it happened, even though I was broke, I went to a restaurant I'd always wanted to go to. I had chicken parmigiana and drank a glass of wine. Sometimes you have to treat yourself when you get beat up. When someone gives you a hard time sometimes you have to give yourself an easy time so that's what we're going to do. We're going to see *Blade*."

"Are you sure? You hate these kind of movies."

"I'm sure," she said. "If we missed the early show then we'll go eat and see the later one."

"Maybe we can get chicken parmigiana," Leroy said and smiled.

"I'd like that," she told him.

23

Ernie backed the U-Haul truck into Freddie's driveway but panicked. He couldn't find the brake and ran into the garage. He crushed the gutter and fascia board and dented the corner of the truck. It all made a booming crash and Freddie ran up from the basement to see Ernie staring at the damage by the glow of the porch light.

"Are you alright?"

Ernie shook his head nervously. "I'm sorry."

Freddie looked at his garage and the dent in the U-Haul. "Don't worry," he said. "It's not too bad."

"You think we can bang the dent out of the truck with a hammer?"

"It looks pretty bad, but we can try."

"And I ruined your gutter and broke a bunch of boards, too."

"I can fix those."

"Are you sure?"

"I'm sure."

"Uncle Lowell thinks it's all my fault, and now I did this." Ernie took off his glasses, cleaned them, and again looked at the damage he'd caused. He pulled the hair off his face, found a rubber band in his coat pocket, and tied his hair back into a ponytail.

"It's not your fault," said Freddie and rolled up the U-Haul's cargo door. "I have to sell my house. That's the problem." He pulled the ramp from underneath the bed and set it on the garage floor and then led them inside the house and down to the basement.

"I guess we have to start, huh?" Ernie asked.

"Yeah," Freddie said, and then the two men slowly took the eighty-five plants up the stairs and into the back of the truck. They put in the lights, the fan, the extra tables, the space heaters, and the gallons of Lowell's special plant food mixtures. When they'd finished, Ernie handed Freddie the truck keys.

"I don't think I should drive anymore, alright?"

"Okay," Freddie said and took the keys.

They headed north on the highway and drove nearly two hours without talking. The radio played and they drank generic orange soda that Ernie had brought in a paper sack that sat between them. They came to a mountain range lined with trees and covered with snow, and the U-Haul crawled slowly along. Ernie read out the directions he had written down, and as they neared the summit they exited and took a series of two-lane roads until they came to a gravel logging road. A mile down it they turned into a driveway and stopped in front of a derelict log cabin.

A middle-aged man opened the front door and came out and met them. He was thin with a pushed-in face and was the size of a jockey. Next to him stood an old German shepherd with bad hips that had trouble walking. The man's fingers were bent from arthritis and he pointed them in the general direction of a barn on the other side of the property. Freddie moved the truck to it and the man opened the barn door. Inside there was nothing but a large vacant room and three card tables.

"They're gonna freeze to death in there," Ernie

whispered to Freddie as they walked into the barn. He stopped in front of the man. "Didn't Lowell tell you they need to be warm?"

"I got a kerosene heater," the man said.

Ernie grew more upset. He paced the room back and forth. Freddie looked at the man and said, "Do you have Lowell's money?"

"Three thousand," the man said and took a wad of worn bills from his coat pocket. He handed the money to Freddie. Freddie counted it and gave it to Ernie who put it in his pants pocket. They opened the back of the U-Haul, pulled down the ramp, and began unloading. The man chain-smoked cigarettes and watched from the edge of the barn, but he didn't help. They put the lights and the plant food on the concrete floor. Ernie found an outlet and plugged in the two space heaters, and they unloaded the plants and set them on the tables.

When they finished, the man inspected each plant. He walked up and down the long tables. He stopped at a set of four that carried more dead leaves than the others. He took them off the table and set them on the floor.

"I ain't gonna pay for these."

Ernie walked over to the plants. "But those are healthy. They're just a little small. All plants have a few dead leaves, but I swear they'll give you good buds."

"I don't want 'em," the man said. He took another cigarette from a pack in his coat pocket and lit it. His dog stood alone on the other side of the barn and began barking at the wall. "Give me back a hundred of that money I gave you."

Ernie stood silent and motionless.

"Give him the hundred, Ernie," Freddie said finally.

Ernie took off his glasses and cleaned them with his shirt. He began to say something then stuttered, stopped, and took a hundred from his pocket and gave it to the man. They loaded the four plants back in the U-Haul and drove away from the cabin.

They kept silent until they got back on the highway. Freddie got the U-Haul up to fifty and Ernie turned on the radio. Only four more plants, Freddie thought, and it was over.

"Do you mind if we talk?" asked Ernie as he sat hunched over, leaning against the door and window glass.

"I don't mind," Freddie said.

"I didn't like that guy at all."

"There wasn't much about him to like."

"You know Lowell said that guy went to prison for raping his wife. How does a guy rape his own wife?"

"Just 'cause you're married doesn't mean your wife wants to sleep with you," Freddie said.

"I wouldn't want to sleep with him."

"Me neither."

"To be honest, Freddie, I thought if you got married your wife would automatically want to. And want to all the time."

Freddie laughed. "You're younger than I thought."

"I'm not that young," Ernie stated, but he sunk down in the seat even more. "Is it okay if I change the station? I hate this song."

"Pick whatever station you want," Freddie said.

Ernie moved the dial up and down on the radio and then looked out the window. "Did you see the guy's hands?"

"He's got pretty bad arthritis," Freddie said.

"And his dog was blind, wasn't it?"

"I think so."

"Why would he bark at the wall?"

"Maybe he was crazy, too. So what do you want to do with the last four?"

"I don't know," Ernie said. "What do you want to do?"

"Drop them off somewhere."

"Kill them?" Ernie asked.

"I guess," Freddie answered. "Or you could take them. I don't care as long as they don't come back to my house."

"I guess we could drown them in the river," Ernie said.

"Okay," Freddie replied. He drove until they came to the edge of town. He led them off the highway until they came to the river and parked on a dirt turnout. They got out of the truck and rolled up the back door and Ernie jumped inside and carried out the four plants. One by one he took them from their plastic pots, shook the dirt off the roots, and carried them down to the river and threw them in. When he was finished, they got back in the U-Haul and left. As Freddie drove them to the International House of Pancakes, he was so elated and relieved that he nearly began weeping.

*

Three days later a blond real estate agent sat in a car in front of Freddie McCall's home. She took pictures from the driver's seat, and then got out and walked up to the house and knocked on the front door. Freddie let her inside and showed her around. He took her to the kitchen and told her how he had remodeled it for his mother. How he had built the cabinets himself in a neighbor's garage, and while his parents were on a cruise he did the tile work and painted.

231

He installed the new cabinets, a new counter top, and a new stove and dishwasher. She took more pictures and then he led her to the dining and living rooms and told her how he'd refinished the fir trim and oak floors. He took her to the office that he had made for his wife out of a walk-in pantry. He showed her how he'd put in a window and built cabinets and shelves and a custom desk from wood his grandfather had left in the garage.

The agent looked in the cupboards and the closets, the basement and the bathroom. When she finished, she stood near the heat of the fireplace. The housing market had fallen out, she told him. The money wouldn't be great, not like it would have been a year earlier, but she was confident she could sell it. As she spoke, Freddie was unable to look at her. And then finally she asked him if he was certain he wanted to go through with it. "Yes," was all he told her and then they moved to the kitchen table, came up with a plan, and did the necessary paperwork.

*

When he arrived at the group home that night he could hardly do his chores. He collapsed on the couch at midnight and fell asleep watching reruns of *Wagon Train*. He slept uninterrupted for six and a half hours and dreamt that he had gotten lost in a blizzard and was stuck up to his chest in snow. He'd given up hope and was certain of his death when he was found by Flint McCullough, the scout from *Wagon Train*. Flint pulled him from the snow and threw him over his horse. He led them into the pure-white freezing hell of the storm. Flint laughed easy as they went. He wasn't worried. He told Freddie and his horse, Little One, the story of a three-day game of checkers he once saw that ended when one of the men suddenly stood up and shot himself. But the storm worsened and Flint quit talking and then he just stopped and turned around. His face grew frantic and blood spewed from his mouth and he screamed, "Freddie!"

Freddie gasped for air and woke up from sleep, startled. He opened his eyes to Dale standing over him, shaking him, telling him he was going to be late. It was six-forty-two.

24

Pauline called in sick and e-mailed the photo of Carol and her own contact information to every runaway shelter she could find in the Northwest, and then got in her car and drove to Seattle. It was night and raining when she arrived downtown and parked and began looking for the girl. There were thousands of people living on the streets there: staying under overpasses or sleeping in cars or worn-down old Winnebagos and camper vans, covered in tarps outside of closed businesses or sleeping in vacant lots or squatting in empty buildings. Old and young, men and women, kids and dogs. There were alcoholics and drug addicts, schizophrenics and sociopaths, ex-cons and war veterans, prostitutes and hustlers, runaways, and street kids.

She stopped every homeless person she could but no one had ever seen Carol. She went to the bus station and the train station, but most people there seemed threatened or uninterested when she'd show the picture of her to them. Everywhere there were buildings and alleys and people. Miles of concrete with endless places to hide. Hours passed and a cold rain fell in a constant downpour. She saw four street kids with backpacks, one of whom she thought might be a girl, passing on the other side of the avenue. She chased them down only to find they were all boys. They wore newer packs and black leather coats with white writing on them. Two of them had huge ear piercings and they all had tattoos and one boy carried a puppy in his arms. She took the photo of Carol from her purse and showed it to them, but none of them had seen the girl, and in the end they just asked for money.

Through Pioneer Square she asked along the bars where drunk people stood outside, under awnings, smoking cigarettes. But no one seemed to really look at the picture, and of course no one had ever seen her. She walked farther on until only the main streets were lit, and then she began walking down the darkened alleys, searching.

She came to two men standing under an alley doorway.

"I don't mean to bother you," she said. "But have you seen this girl?" She took a lighter from her purse and put it next to the photo. The men, both over thirty, looked at it but shook their heads. One was dressed in tattered raingear, and the other had cut two plastic garbage bags and taped them together in a makeshift poncho. Two grocery carts covered in a blue tarp stood in the rain, and at the end of a rope a pit bull slept underneath the door well. A third man came from between two buildings.

"I about fell in my own shit," he coughed. "I slipped and nearly went flying into my own mess. And still my guts ain't right and it's been, what, a week now?"

He came upon the two men and then saw Pauline.

"Who are you?" he said.

"I'm searching for this girl. Have you seen her?" Pauline again lit the cigarette lighter and put it near the photo.

"I ain't seen her. What are you, her mother?"

"I'm her friend."

The man had long, gray hair and an olive-drab rain poncho on. There were tattoos on his neck and one on the side of his face. He grabbed a bottle of malt liquor from the

235

man in the tattered poncho and drank from it as Pauline put the photo back in her purse.

"What else you got in there?" he said.

"Nothing," she replied nervously and began to retreat, but the man with the garbage sack poncho went after her. He grabbed for her purse but missed, and then the gray-haired man went after her. He took her arm and stopped her. His grip was strong and he pulled her into him. The dog woke and began to bark.

"Please," Pauline said. "I'm just trying to find this girl."

The man didn't answer. He grabbed her hair with his other hand. He pulled her head down as hard as he could but she kicked him at the same time and momentarily he let go and she ran down the alley toward the lights of a main street.

It was four in the morning when she finally returned to her car. She got inside and locked the doors. Carol was lost out there, in that, alone. She looked at her watch. For five minutes she let herself cry, and then she forced herself to stop. She started the car, turned on the radio, but she couldn't help it and began crying again. She shut the engine off and broke down.

*

Eagle Lanes bowling alley was also the home of the town's only Fraternal Order of Eagles. It was a weather-worn brick building in the industrial section of town. There were three trucks parked in front when Pauline got out of her car and headed for the front doors. Inside was just one old man bowling, his ball hitting the pins making the only noise in the place. In a back room was a small bar with a handful of people drinking and watching TV. Among them was Ford Wrenn. He was the same tall and skinny man with a baseball hat that she remembered. She went to him and said hello. He ordered a pitcher of beer, and they rented bowling shoes and a lane.

"I've never been good at bowling," Pauline said as they sat next to each other on a bright orange plastic bench seat, putting on their shoes.

"I've never been very good at it either. And now my fingers are too bent up to fit in the holes. Truth is I couldn't think of anything else to do," he said and laughed. "I haven't been on a date in a long time. But we don't have to do it if you don't want to."

"We're here, so let's stay. But don't laugh at me."

"I won't."

"At least we can get drunk, huh? It's the only good thing about bowling."

Ford laughed. "I'm glad you called. I didn't think you would."

"I didn't think you'd drive seven hours to get here."

"I don't mind," he said. "It gave me something to do on my weekend."

"But I'm going to be honest with you, okay?"

"Okay."

"I know we just met, but I don't want a boyfriend. I don't ever want one. That's the truth."

"Fair enough. You already told me that on the phone. I'm not the smartest, but I do remember you saying that."

"And I don't want your stuff at my place, and I won't give you a key."

"That's alright," he said. "You're jumping the gun

anyway."

"I just want you to know that."

"Okay."

"And we'll have sex only when I want to have sex."

"Okay."

"I don't like being pressured."

Ford sat back in the bench seat and took a drink off his glass of beer. He smiled. "Anything else?"

"I just want you to know I won't depend on you. Not ever."

"You don't have to if you don't want to."

"And we're not going to do it at my place."

"That's okay, too. I have money. I like the Red Lion."

"I'll pay half."

"I'm not worried," he said. "Relax, this is our first date."

"I know."

"We don't have to be like everybody else," said Ford.

"I wish that were true."

"It is true, if we want it to be. I'm on the road all time. The truth is I like thinking about you, and it's easier to think about you if we spend time together. Is that alright?"

Pauline nodded.

"Anything else?"

"I'm not gonna end up doing your laundry and calling you to see where you are. I'm not . . . I'm not going to fix you dinner to hear you say you hate it, or for you to not say anything at all. I'm not going to do any of that. If you say I'm too fat or if you start being mean to me or make me feel bad about myself, I won't ever see you again."

"Look," he said. "I might upset you sometimes. That's the way people are. They upset each other, but I won't do any of the stuff you said. I don't want to own you. I just want to be friends with you. Truth is I'm lonely and I'm getting older, and I like you. I think I know what you're talking about, but I don't get like that. I've never been like that."

"I just want to be clear."

"Fair enough. I think you're pretty clear."

"And I don't want you to say I'm your girlfriend. I'm not anybody's girlfriend."

"It's our first date," he said. "You have to relax a bit."

"Don't fuck with me," she said, her voice beginning to tremble.

"We're just bowling," Ford said. "You got to lighten up, chief."

"I need a drink."

"Me too," he said.

"Are you scared of me yet?"

"Not really," he said and smiled. "We both got some miles underneath us."

"Good. Do you like Mexican food?"

"Sure."

"Maybe we can get Mexican food and margaritas after this."

"Sounds good to me," he said and stood up.

"You're not married or got a girl somewhere else?"

"I was engaged once but I was just twenty-three. I was gone all the time and she met someone else. I've had a few girlfriends here and there, but I don't have kids and I'm not seeing anyone now."

Pauline stood up and smiled. "Well, alright then, I guess I said what I had to say."

25

A nurse came into Leroy Kervin's ICU room followed by two men in military uniforms.

"I don't know if you'll remember me," one of the men said to Jeanette and Darla, who both sat in chairs near Leroy's bed. "But I'm Harvey Lowery. I was Leroy's boss at Lowery Electric and his platoon leader in the National Guard. This is John Barr, a chaplain with the Guard."

Harvey Lowery was heavy-set and bald. The chaplain was a gawky young man in his mid-twenties. He was wearing a new uniform and carrying a Bible underneath his arm.

"I know this must be an extremely difficult time for you both," the chaplain said. "We are here to support you in any way we can."

Darla kept her eyes on Leroy as they spoke while Jeanette just stared at them with a look of terror across her face. Nearly a minute passed in silence and then Jeanette cleared her throat. "How can you think we want you here?" she said quietly. "Either of you? . . . Mr. Lowery, you're the one who convinced him to join. I was there. I remember. One weekend a month and two weeks a year. How the money would help, how it would help us with retirement. How it would help our country if there was a disaster like in New Orleans . . . I know Leroy was naïve and I know he signed the papers himself, but you didn't say anything about him being shipped to Iraq. You didn't say anything about him being sent to a foreign war. The National Guard never advertises that on TV or on their billboards. And where were you when we were in San Diego? I didn't see you quit your job and sit by his bed and take care of him. Praying every day and night that he'd get better . . . Both of you got him here so you don't get to say good-bye to him. We get to say good-bye to him."

Harvey Lowery stepped back. He began to sweat and he looked as if he were going to be sick. "I didn't know we were going to war," he said softly. "I didn't know they'd take us. I'm almost fifty years old and they took me. I don't know what to say except I'm sorry. A day doesn't go by that I don't feel awful about what happened to Leroy and the other men I lost."

Harvey Lowery looked at the chaplain and the chaplain looked back at him but didn't say anything. Darla stood up. "I'm sure you're both decent men," she said. "And I don't blame you personally for what happened, but still I don't want you here either. My life stopped when Leroy got hurt. I've done nothing but fight the military and the hospitals. For seven years I've had to advocate for his care and look after him, so I think it's my right . . . Harvey, I work at the Safeway on Fifth Street. I see you in there once in a while with your family. All I ask is that you shop somewhere else from now on. I just don't want to see you again."

*

Hours later Jeanette woke in the chair across from Leroy's bed to rain beating against the hospital window. She moved her chair closer to him and held his hand.

241

"Are you awake? Do you hear it?"

Leroy opened his eyes and put his hand on her leg.

"I've never heard it rain so hard," she said. "It's like they're hammering on the roof."

"I should get up and make sure everything's alright," he said.

"Please, don't get up."

Leroy turned on his side and moved closer to her and held her.

"What happened to your underwear?"

"Somebody stole them last night."

"Somebody stole them?"

"Every time I'm sleeping this man says it's too hot and he makes me take my underwear off."

"What does him being hot have to do with your underwear?"

"That's the question I ask every night," she said.

Leroy pulled back the blankets.

"What are you doing?"

He ran his hand over her. Her body up past her breasts was covered in the mark. Her arms had it to the elbows and it covered her entire back.

"Hey, it's freezing," she cried and pulled the covers back over them.

"I was just looking at you," he said.

"Well don't. I hate when you see me like this. You promised."

"But I like the way you look."

"How could you? I look awful."

"To be honest I like you better this way," Leroy said and pulled her into him.

"You're so full of it."

"I'm serious," he whispered and kissed her.

*

When they woke next it was almost noon. The weather had cleared and they could start moving again. They made breakfast and looked over their maps. They had decided on a route when they heard a series of blasts come from a ship's horn. They rushed topside to see the ship from Seattle entering the cove a half mile away.

"How could they have found us?" Jeanette cried.

"Maybe they don't know it's us," Leroy said. He pulled the anchor while Jeanette started the engine, and slowly they hugged the opposite coastline and headed toward open water. Through binoculars Leroy could see three men at the stern of the Seattle ship observing them with field glasses. They watched but didn't follow.

As night came they ran the boat blindly with only a single spotlight guiding the way. They headed north. They kept a lookout for the ship from Seattle but they saw no signs of it. The weather worsened and the wind blew sheets of rain sideways and the boat's engine lugged as it worked against the rough waters. It took them an hour and a half to go less than three miles and the boat took on water. It was four in the morning when they finally found a small bay, but as they moved into it they spotted, in the distance, a group of boats strung together. No lights came from inside them, not even running lights were visible. They anchored a hundred yards *from the cluster and collapsed.*

At dawn Leroy went topside again and began observing the group of boats with binoculars: three sailboats, two smaller fishing vessels, four cabin cruisers, and a large commercial fishing boat. They were all tied together. He could see no movement, no people, no lights, and no smoke from generator engines. He was pale with worry when he went below and woke Jeanette.

"We're almost out of gas," he told her. "I'm not sure we'll have enough to get to the next town. That weather last night might have ruined us. I think we're gonna have to see if they have any gas on that group of boats. Maybe if anyone's still there they'll let us buy some, but the thing is I haven't seen any people. There's been no sign of anyone, no movement at all and I've watched them for hours."

"Maybe they're all dead," Jeanette said.

"Maybe," he said.

Under the galley sink he took out a .22 pistol that was hidden in an empty soap box and loaded it with bullets while Jeanette steered toward the gathered boats. As they came closer they saw THE FREE written in black spray paint on the side of the nearest sailboat. Next to it they saw a man hanging by his neck from a rope off the side of the commercial fishing boat. He wore no shoes and was in his underwear, his hands bound behind him. His entire body was covered with the mark. His neck had stretched under his own weight. They saw more bodies, two men with the mark hanging the same way off the opposite side and four more leaned against the cabin of a sailboat with their heads blown apart.

Jeanette moved the boat alongside a partially sunk cabin cruiser and idled.

"The second I get onboard I want you to move back fifty yards from here, okay? I'll wave to you when I'm ready to get picked up. If anything goes wrong, head north as fast you can."

"I won't leave you," Jeanette said.

"You'll have to," he said and put the pistol in his coat pocket and jumped aboard the cabin cruiser and waved her off.

There was a tent on the stern made of tarps and two-by-fours. Under it were two propane stoves set on a tin table, but the propane tanks were empty. In the main cabin he found two young children, dead, in a bunk. He went to the controls but the battery was gone and he couldn't read the gas gauge without it. He looked toward the bow and saw five red-plastic gas cans, but when he lifted them, each was empty.

He moved on. He jumped to a twenty-eight-foot fishing boat. Inside its cabin there were two half-burned bodies lying on the floor, their faces hidden underneath a fallen table. The smell was burnt and rotten and damp. In the cockpit he found a dead woman. She was young, maybe thirty, with blond hair. Both her legs had the mark and she was handcuffed to a cleat with black plastic ties. He stared at her bloody face and thought of Jeanette, and no longer could he block out what he was seeing. He was suddenly overcome with the horror and his breathing became shallow and strained.

He boarded the fifty-two-foot commercial fishing boat and went toward the main cabin, but the door was blocked by a man with a bullet hole in his forehead. Both of his marked hands were nailed to the deck of the boat and a pool of blood surrounded him.

Why was he seeing what he was seeing?

He went to the opposite side of the cabin and entered from there. Below deck was a galley and a larger area that looked like a makeshift schoolroom. There was a blackboard and chairs and tables; there were children's drawings on the walls and Halloween decorations. Behind a desk were a dead man and woman. They were face down, their hands tied behind them. The man's wallet lay on his back. Leroy went through it for money but there was none.

He began to feel sick. He ran topside and tried to catch his breath, but he no longer could. He looked out into the inlet to see Jeanette watching him. He put one arm up, which meant he was okay, and then went to the next vessel, another twenty-eight-foot fishing boat. There were two dead dogs chained to a concrete weight in the middle of the deck. Blood was everywhere.

In the main cabin there was a naked old man dead on the floor nearly covered in the mark. Leroy moved past him to a see a broken door leading below deck. He went down the stairs to a galley that smelled of gasoline and found a half-full five-gallon can sitting on top of the galley stove. They had doused the main cabin in fuel, but for some reason hadn't set the boat alight. He searched the galley cupboards but found nothing. He began heading topside again when he heard a noise, a faint scratching sound.

He took the pistol from his coat pocket, as his chest seized in pain. He stood for nearly a minute in complete terror. He tried to listen. The scratching came from the forward cabin door. He moved toward it. He held the gun and opened it nervously to find a half-dead kitten on the floor.

He picked up the tiny black cat and held it in his hand.

He looked at the small room. It was stocked with boxes of restaurant-size canned food. He put the kitten on the ground and found a cardboard box, put it inside, and went topside and signaled Jeanette.

She moved the boat alongside the fishing vessel. Leroy tied their boat to it and put the kitten onboard. He loaded box after box of food and then untied them and Jeanette started the motor and moved them fifty yards away and cut the engine.

"Was it bad?" she asked.

"It was like the other place," he said, barely able to speak.

"What's wrong?" she cried.

"I can't breathe."

"Keep trying."

"Why do I see such horrible things?"

"I don't know."

"I don't want to see things like that anymore."

"They'll go away."

"I don't think they will."

"Was there any gas?"

"Just the one can and it was only half full."

"What are we going to do?" Jeanette asked.

"I don't know," Leroy said and then remembered the kitten. He went to the box and opened it, but there was nothing inside. It was empty.

*

Jeanette turned on a CD player. She set it on the table next to Leroy's bed. Amália Rodrigues's voice came quietly through the small speakers. She went into the bathroom with a washcloth, put it under the faucet, and came back and washed Leroy's face and arms and hands.

*

"What are you doing?" he asked.

"You were having a nightmare and I didn't know what else to do. In the movies when someone has a fever they always put a cold washcloth on them. Does it make you feel better?"

"Yes," he said.

"Are you okay now?"

"No. I swing from drowning in you to drowning into these violent thoughts . . . I want to die inside you but I'm scared I'll die inside one of those ships. I don't think my mind knows what to do and I can't control it anymore."

"You're just having bad dreams," she said. "They're just dreams. So shape up, alright? No more nightmares for you, okay?"

"I've never had a girl wash my face while I was sleeping."

"Now you have."

"I like it."

"I'll do it every day if you like," she said and laughed. "Well maybe not every day, but a lot of days. You'll be lucky if you keep trying. I swear you will."

Jeanette turned on the stereo and Amália Rodrigues began playing.

"I love her voice."

"I know."

"It makes me think of my uncle."

"I know that, too."

"Maybe we can just stay here and listen to her and rest."

"We'll rest for a while," Jeanette said. "But we have to keep going."

"But I'm so tired."

"Don't think about how tired you are."

"Last night I dreamt, and in my dream we were at Home Depot. We saw a dog wandering around in the parking lot. It was late, almost nine at night. I was buying something for work and you went with me. In my dream you'd always go with me, but for payment I'd have to take you to Dairy Queen."

"I love Dairy Queen," she said.

"I know you do . . . So we see this dog. He's a mutt and he's missing part of his ear. He looks like he's been sleeping under cars but he's young and pretty healthy, considering. Across the street from the Home Depot is Dairy Queen, so afterward we're in line at the drive-through and we see the dog cross the street coming toward us. He almost gets hit by a car, but he doesn't. Then we see a man on a bike nearly run him over. The guy starts yelling at the dog. But the dog keeps on moving. A happy-go-lucky dog, a dog about town. He didn't seem worried about anything. We have two cars in front of us and a few behind so we have to wait, but after we get the ice cream we decide to look for him. We spend half the night trying. We talk about where we'll keep him, what we'll name him, and that we'll have to buy him a collar and put our phone number on it. How we'll have to find a good vet to take care of him and we'll make sure to keep him up on his shots. We have his whole life planned, and it's an easy life. Will he sleep on our bed or won't he? What will his name be? Will he like camping? Will he like swimming in the lake? We're *already in love with him. And then finally after searching up and down street after street, we find him. He's lying on the side of the road, shot. Somebody had shot him. He was still breathing when we got to him, but his eyes were closed. We pet him and talked to him. We told him not to worry. We tried to comfort him. Why would anyone shoot him? Why would anyone shoot a dog walking by? How would someone have a gun at the exact time he passed them? Not everybody carries guns, do they?*

"When he opened his eyes and saw us, he relaxed. Somehow he knew who we were. I know it sounds crazy but he told us he had waited his whole life to meet us so he could die in peace. So he could die being loved. He told us he spent so many nights on his own just barely scraping by. Hiding out and hungry and lonely. We were right. He did live under cars, and in vacant fields and in culverts. He got food wherever he could. Trash cans and under bleachers and on the side of the road. As hard as all that was he said he knew if he could hang on long enough he would meet us, and then he would be able to disappear into us when he died. That if he could just make it until then he would never be lonely again . . . Maybe that's how things work. Who knows. In my dream we buried him in our backyard. And guess what music we had playing while we did it?"

"Amália Rodrigues," Jeanette said.

"Right," he said.

*

When dawn appeared The Free ship stopped a hundred yards from their boat and began blowing a horn. Soon after, an

250

anchor splashed and disappeared into the black water and a dinghy was lowered and two men boarded it. Leroy dressed and ran to the bow and began pulling the anchor, but the men aboard The Free ship began firing rifles at him.

It was the third shot that hit Leroy in the chest. He fell to the ground and Jeanette rushed to him and dragged him back to the cabin. She pressed a towel over the bleeding while the two men from the dinghy boarded the boat. They came to the cabin and forced them to the dinghy and blood poured out of Leroy as they took them back to The Free ship. They were put in a small, dark room, a porthole giving off the only light. Jeanette put her hands over the wound, desperately trying to stop the blood, but Leroy grabbed her arms.

"Don't," he murmured.

"You have to keep trying."

"I can't anymore."

"Please," she cried.

"It'll be okay this way. I want to be with you when I die and you're here. I think all along that's what I've been waiting for . . . See, for years my mind was in a fog, a fog that was all blurs of emotion. There was so much darkness. It was a horrible way to live. But then one night, for no reason, I woke up and I could see things clearly. I could think again. My brain wasn't injured. I was like I was before. I don't know why it happened like that, or why it happened that night, but it did. And when it did all I wanted to do was die."

"I don't understand why you'd want to die then. That doesn't make sense."

"It's because I wasn't sure it would last. I thought maybe it was just another emotion that would pass, that the clarity would disappear and I'd be stuck again. I can't begin to tell you how awful my mind was, how my emotions just bounced around day after day. I tried to kill myself so I could die with clarity, inside clarity. But of course I failed. I didn't know for a long time why I failed, but now I realize I wasn't meant to die until I saw you again. Until I was with you again. Because maybe when I die I'll disappear into you. I'll be inside you. I'm almost certain now that that's how it works."

"But you can't leave me."

"It'll be okay. You'll have a family someday. You'll have a lot of things. I know you will."

"But we're going to have a family together."

"We can't now."

"Yes we can."

"I'm sorry," he said.

"Don't talk like this," she said. "We just have to get out of here."

"We'll get out of here as soon as I die. Then you'll be free from them. You'll be free from every story about it, from every memory, and someday you won't hyperventilate when you see someone dressed as a soldier. And you won't cry when you pass a hospital or see an old red car or hear Amália Rodrigues. Those things will go away."

"No they won't."

"They will."

"But my memories of us don't stop. It's like they're always playing. Do you remember when my dad broke in on us? Do you remember that?"

"Of course," he said. "We were in high school and it was our big trip. You told your parents you were staying with a friend and I told my mom the same thing and we took my mom's car and drove to the mountains. It was in the middle

252

of winter and we rented a room in this little town. The place was above a pizza parlor. When we first got there we walked around in the snow. It was near Christmas. Everyone had lights up. Snow always looks nice reflecting off streetlights and Christmas lights. It was the first time I'd ever been any-where on my own, where it wasn't a part of school or where my mom or uncle weren't with me. I can't even begin to ex-plain how nice it was there with you. It's one of the best memories I have.

"I remember we walked through the town for hours and everyone we passed was nice to us; everyone was kind and said hello. When we went back to the room we got in the bathtub to warm up. I remember us just sitting there in the hot water talking. Talking about what kind of place we'd get when we could move out on our own. We were really in love. The funny thing is you had a notepad with you and you took notes about what we liked and what we didn't like. Which neighborhoods we thought were okay and which weren't. You sat back in the soapy water writing like a secretary. I remem-ber the bathtub was one of those old big ones and the water spigot came out on the side so we were facing each other from opposite sides of the tub. Then you began reading a Star Trek novel to me. I can't remember which one but I remember that it was a Star Trek one and that Khan was in it. I had a bag of M&Ms and I'd give you one every time you said, 'union break.'"

"Union break," Jeanette whispered. "I remember union break."

"I don't know why we didn't hear it, but the owner of the hotel opened our door and your dad came in. He found us like that in the bathtub. He grabbed you by the arm and *pulled you out. You were standing there naked and sobbing. He was so mad he was shaking and his face went so red I thought he would explode or have a heart attack. He pulled me out of the tub and shoved me into the main room, naked. He yelled at me so hard I thought he would kill me. Every time I tried to move away he would grab me and throw me against the wall. I had never been that scared in my whole life. You came out of the bathroom crying and holding my clothes. You begged him to leave me alone. 'Don't hurt him. Please don't hurt him,' you cried. He looked at you and grabbed you by the arm so hard that you fell to the ground. He called you awful things. He said he was going to get the police and have me thrown in jail. He was sure I was raping you. He said I'd spend my whole life in prison. There were veins on his face bulging, and he was spitting as he yelled. 'But I love him,' you said. 'We're in love. We're really in love.' And then he stopped. He just grabbed you by the arm again and made you dress, and then dragged you down to his car.*

"I remember the worst part of that night was that we didn't get to say good-bye to each other. He just drove you away. I didn't know what to do after that. I was scared that maybe he would come back so I took our things out of the room and left the key inside and shut the door. I got in my mom's car but it had snowed since we'd gotten there, and my mom had an old Buick and those things are horrible in the snow. I couldn't get it out of the parking spot. The wheels just spun and she didn't have chains. I couldn't get back in the room because I'd left the key in there so I just spent all night freezing in her car. When I finally got back home the next day, my mom was really upset with me. They had called my house to confirm the reservation, and that's how she found out. But the thing is, even when my mom was upset with me, all I could think about was you. I was just hoping you were alright, that your dad didn't hurt you. That he didn't drive too fast in the snow."

"See," Jeanette said. "We'll never be free . . . What you don't understand is all those years I was away from you, that I tried to forget about you, I never did. I was always certain you'd come back to me. That somehow, during our time apart, you had miraculously recovered, that you'd become my Leroy again. Sometimes at work I'd sit at my desk and I'd hear someone behind me and I'd be certain it was you. You were coming back to save me. At home, late at night when I'd hear a noise, I wasn't scared 'cause I thought the noise was you trying to find my apartment. When the phone would ring . . . You know what I'm saying?"

"Your memory will fade. You'll start a new life. That's the way it works."

"That's not fair. You're going to leave me all alone."

"I'll be a part of you. Like the dog, me and the dog."

"You don't know that for sure."

"I don't. But we were lucky."

"How can you say we were lucky?"

"We know what it's like to be in love."

"Really in love."

"Right."

"But please don't leave me, Leroy."

26

At nine am Freddie McCall parked at a gas station in Redding, California. He had driven for nearly eleven hours straight. He cleaned up in their bathroom, got a cup of coffee, and called his ex-wife. She gave him directions to her aunt Muriel's apartment two miles away and he wrote them down with a ballpoint pen on his palm.

"But Freddie, don't hang up yet," she told him. "I won't be here when you arrive. I'm leaving right after I hang up."

"Why?"

"I just can't see you right now."

"Tell me what's going on with you."

Her voice fell apart. "I don't want them back, Freddie."

He looked out of the windshield. He saw a group of hunters in camouflage get out of a black truck and go inside the gas station mini-mart. "You won't always feel that way," he said.

"I'm gonna go now, Freddie, but I'll call you," she said and hung up.

He got lost twice but finally parked in front of a rundown apartment complex. When he knocked on the door an old woman answered. She wore green shorts and a red Christmas sweater with a reindeer on it. Her feet were bare and looked blue, and her toenails were long and bent and discolored. She was a heavy woman in her seventies and smelled of urine and perfume.

"Hello, Muriel, it's me, Freddie," he said. "Do you remember me?"

"I remember you," she said stone-faced. Her eyes looked infected, red and sore and bloodshot.

His oldest daughter, Kathleen screamed when she heard her father's voice. She ran toward the front door through the clutter of the cramped apartment and pushed her great aunt to the side to get through. His youngest daughter, Virginia, moved behind her dragging her left leg. Freddie kneeled down and both of them fell into his arms.

*

An hour later he crammed the girls' suitcases into the Comet and they piled into the front seat and he drove them to a pawnshop.

"Why is there all that stuff in the back?" Kathleen asked.

"We're taking it to a pawnshop," Freddie said.

"What's a pawnshop?" Virginia asked.

"It's when you sell your stuff to a store. They give you money for it. You can have them hold it for you, and they give you money in return, and then if you pay them back you get your stuff back. Like a loan. But I'm just going to sell this stuff."

"Why?"

"I don't have enough money to get us home. Your mom called out of the blue. I wasn't ready. I almost have money, but it's a couple weeks away. So I have to sell this stuff instead. What did your mom tell you?"

"She just said to get in the car and that we were staying with you," Kathleen said. "She woke us up in the middle of the night and told us."

"That's true," Freddie said. "You are staying with me. It

happened pretty quick, and I know that's hard. But I think your mom thought it was the best thing to do it right then. Anyway, we're going to have a good time together, but first we need money."

He drove through the streets of downtown Redding until he found the pawnshop. They all carried in the things he'd brought with him: a table saw, chop saw, stereo, phone, CDs, TV, DVD player, air compressor, paint sprayer, Sawzall, two cordless drills, electric sander, router, and his mother's acoustic guitar.

He left with seven hundred and thirty dollars and they got back on the road. He drank two cups of coffee and an energy drink. He took seven calls from Pat, who was struggling to fill in for him, until he finally lost him in the mountains and turned off his phone. When night came he stopped in a small town off the highway. They checked into a motel and then walked down the street to a Chinese restaurant.

His daughters sat across from him in a booth as they ate. When they finished, Freddie set his elbows on the table and leaned over to them. "Are you both okay living with me?"

The girls nodded.

"You know your mom still loves you though, right?"

They looked at each other, but they didn't say anything.

"She does," Freddie said. "Sometimes people need to be alone to figure things out. Sometimes people just need a break for a while. It doesn't mean she's not always thinking about you."

"Is she going to come live with us at our house?" Virginia asked.

"I don't think so. I think she might stay in Las Vegas.

But let's not think about that, okay? Let's just let her have a break. Alright?"

His daughters nodded uncertainly.

"The only other news is that we've moved. I've got us an apartment. It's a nice place right by the school."

"We're not living in our house anymore?" Kathleen asked.

"No," he said.

"Why not?"

"I couldn't afford it, but the new place is good. It's really nice. You guys will like it. It's smaller, a one bedroom, but you guys will have bunk beds and I'll sleep in the living room. We'll paint your room a bunch of good colors. It'll be cramped but it'll be a lot of fun. The best news is that you can walk to school now. You won't have to take the bus, which means you can sleep in a bit longer. Plus in two weeks I'll get money from the house so we'll be in good shape."

"I don't understand," Kathleen said.

"You'll see. It'll be fine," he said.

When they left the restaurant, Freddie carried Virginia in his arms, and they walked down the sidewalk toward the motel. The night was dark and no stars shone, and a cold wind off the mountains hit them as they went.

"I think you're getting too big to carry," he told her and sighed.

"I'm not too big," she said and hugged him harder.

"Maybe you're right," he said. "Maybe I'm just out of shape."

"If you don't carry her, it'll take us forever," Kathleen said.

"I'll go another block and then my arms might need a break," Freddie said. "Is that okay?"

"It's okay," Virginia said. "I can walk."

"But she's so slow!" Kathleen said. "And it's freezing."

"We'll be okay," Freddie told her. "It's not her fault she can't walk as fast as you. She's on our team. You have to remember that, alright?"

"Alright," Kathleen said.

"Who's team is she on?" Freddie asked.

"Our team," she said.

"We have to stick together. There's no point if we're not nice to each other. Okay?"

"Okay."

"Good," he said.

Inside the motel room they watched TV until his daughters fell asleep. The girls in one bed and Freddie in the other. And finally, after being awake for twenty-six hours, he collapsed only to be woken up two hours later by his daughters' giggling.

"What are you guys doing?" he said softly. "It's really late."

"Ginnie's been hearing noises," Kathleen whispered.

"You have, too," she replied.

"I have, too," she said and they both began giggling again.

"What did it sound like?" Freddie asked.

"A mountain lion," Virginia said.

"Don't worry, a mountain lion could never get in here." He rolled over on his side and began to drift off when his daughters again laughed.

"What's so funny now?" he asked.

"You're the mountain lion!" Virginia said.

"You snore louder than anyone ever!" Kathleen said. "Louder than a mountain lion probably."

"Oh, so that's it."

They erupted in laughter.

"I know I snore like a mountain lion," he said. "I'm sorry about that. I'll try to stay awake until you guys fall asleep, okay?"

"Okay," they both said.

"It's hard to sleep in motels but we have a long day tomorrow so no more giggling, alright?"

"Alright," they said.

Freddie tried his best to stay awake. He could hear them rustling in their bed and whispering. But he didn't say anything more. He slept soundly, and the next thing he knew it was late morning and his girls were crawling on top of him, begging him to get up.

*

They ate breakfast at a diner and got on the highway. They had traveled for three hours when the Comet began to shake violently. It was followed by a loud hammering from below the trunk, and then something began dragging on the pavement. The engine revved to a whine, but the power was gone. He moved the car to the side of the highway and turned off the motor.

"What's wrong?" Kathleen asked.

"I'm not sure," Freddie said.

"Where are we?"

"I'm not sure," he said and looked around. There were

261

no houses or ranches that he could see. Just miles of sagebrush, gullies, and hills surrounded them. In the far distance there were mountain ranges and clouds that were slowly engulfing them. "Alright," he said. "You guys sit tight. I'll be right back." He got out of the car and kneeled on the gravel to see the end of the drive shaft lying on the ground. He got up and leaned against the trunk. He called for a tow truck and then he got back in the car and turned on the hazard lights.

"So what do we do now?" Kathleen asked.

"We wait for help," Freddie said.

"Then what do we do?"

"We have the tow truck take us to town. We'll drop the car off to be worked on then we'll get lunch or maybe dinner depending how long it takes them to get here. After that we'll get a room and wait until she's fixed."

"The Comet's really old," Virginia said.

"That's right. She is old, but she made it to you guys. That's the main thing. That's why she's the best car ever. She waited until we were together to get sick. Anyway, she'll be alright. She tried as hard as she could and now she's tired."

"If we get cold we could light a fire!" Virginia said.

"That's a good idea," Freddie said. "But there's a blanket in the back if you guys get cold. Let's start with that."

"Do you think we'll have to stay here all night?" Kathleen asked.

"No, but maybe."

"Rob had a brand-new truck," Virginia said.

"I bet it was nice," Freddie said.

"I like Candy the Comet better," Kathleen said.

"You remembered her name," Freddie said.

"She's the best car ever. She only gets sick after she does her job."

"That's right."

"What will we do if no one ever comes?" Virginia asked.

"Someone will come," Freddie said and turned on the radio. "Don't worry about that. Let's just sit back and relax. We'll listen to the radio and wait. It won't be long. Are you guys tired?"

"No," they both said.

"Then you guys get the first watch. I'm going to shut my eyes, alright?"

"Alright," they said and he leaned back in the seat.

He was woken up when a flatbed tow truck pulled in front of them and stopped. A short, chunky man came from the cab in worn canvas coveralls and walked toward the car. Freddie got out and the two men spoke briefly, and then he and his daughters waited on the shoulder of the two-lane highway while the man loaded the Comet onto the back of the tow truck. When he was done, Freddie helped the girls up into the cab. His daughters in the backseat, him in the passenger seat, and then the driver got in and took them down the highway.

"For as small as that car is," he said, "she sure is heavy, made of pure steel. They don't make them like that anymore." The man was in his sixties and had thin, short gray hair. He had a gut so large that it sat on the bottom of the steering wheel and rubbed against it. His left eyelid hung lazily over his eye and when he spoke he had a slight lisp.

"She's all metal," Freddie said.

"Made in America."

Freddie nodded. "I've been driving that Comet since I

was sixteen."

"It was your first car?"

"Yeah."

"My first car was a Chevy."

"Both made in Detroit," Freddie said.

"Now Detroit's gone to hell," the man said. There were no cars in front of them or behind them, and his breath filled the cab of the truck: Fritos and cigarettes and coffee. "You know at one time Detroit was called the city of the future, and for a while no one in the US would buy a car made anywhere else. Now it's the opposite. All the cars people seem to want are Asian cars and no one wants to live in Detroit. I heard they give away buildings there if you can pay the taxes on them." He shifted the truck into fifth gear. "I guess the only downside is that you have to live in Detroit," he added and laughed.

"My ex-wife has a Toyota. I bet that thing has two hundred and fifty thousand miles on it now, and it still runs pretty good," Freddie said.

"My wife has one, too. What are you going to do? To me, Detroit is like rich people. You always hear stories where the dad comes up the rough way, struggles and works harder than everyone else. He builds something, something of value. He spends his whole life doing it. Then his kids come along and take over. They're so well off that they don't understand how hard it is to create something good. They just see the money and run with that until it quits. Then everything is lost and even the good idea gives out . . . Are you guys warm enough?"

The girls said they were and Freddie nodded. "How much farther to town?" he asked.

"Ninety miles," the man said.

"You lived there long?"

"Twenty-five years this spring. But my wife was born there. She works at Molly's restaurant."

"The town's grown a lot, huh? I passed through it on the way down."

"It's grown alright, but it's all Mexicans now," the man said.

"It's starting to snow," Kathleen said from the backseat.

"It is," Freddie said and looked out the window. "Do you know of a motel near where you're taking the car?"

The man took a drink from a mug that sat in a cup-holder on the dash. "There's two just down the block from the shop, but I'm afraid you don't have much luck. There's an up-coming deployment and they're having the ceremony for it tonight. I'd be surprised if there are rooms anywhere."

"I forgot there's an army base near there."

"A big one," he said. "Of course now, with the wars, it's as full as a tick."

"I bet it is," Freddie said.

"All the construction outfits around here are booming."

Freddie looked out the passenger side window again. Snow was falling steadily. The man took another drink from his mug, and then put his hand in his coverall pocket, took a jelly bean from it, and put it in his mouth.

"It's all the stuff in the Middle East," he began to say. "If it was up to me I'd level the whole area, but you know they won't . . . Anyway in the end it sure has been good for the town. My wife says the restaurant's been so busy that one day they ran out of syrup."

"They ran out of syrup?" Freddie asked.

"Yeah, imagine that. A breakfast restaurant running out of syrup."

*

The tow truck arrived in town just after six pm. The driver backed the Comet in front of a closed auto-repair shop. He set it down and left. Freddie and his daughters walked to the two motels the man had mentioned but both were full. The second front-desk clerk called the remaining motels in town but none had a room. They walked to a Mexican restaurant and ate dinner. Afterward they went back to the last motel and Freddie left a deposit of one hundred dollars and rented two blankets. They began the walk back to the Comet to spend the night in the car.

"See, I told you," Kathleen said as they went along the sidewalk. "She's so slow."

"It's not Ginnie's fault," Freddie said. "Let's not talk like that anymore."

"And it's snowing and it's freezing, too."

"I'm going as fast as I can," Virginia cried.

"I know we're all tired," Freddie said. "But the main thing to do when you're tired is to remember to be nice. Remember to be kind. So let's make it that we are, understood?"

Solemnly his daughters both said, "Okay."

"I think I can start the car if I leave it in park. That way we can heat it up so it won't be so freezing. It won't be that bad. Candy's got a great heater and I'll tuck you guys in and tomorrow they'll have rooms and we'll be fine."

"And then Candy will get fixed."

266

"And then Candy will get fixed."

They came to the mechanic's shop and Freddie put the car in park and started the engine. Blue smoke engulfed them briefly, but soon the engine idled quietly. He turned the heater on full. He put Kathleen in the backseat and put a blanket over her. Virginia slept in the front, covered in a blanket with her head on his lap. Every hour he'd start the car and warm them.

The night wore on. He tried not to think of his ex-wife or the people who were going to live in his house or of the paint store and how mad Pat would be when he got back to work. He tried not to think of Leroy Kervin and the soldiers like him who would come home maimed and wrecked. He tried not to think of his daughter's leg and the bills that still loomed over his head. Would he even be able to continue to afford insurance for her? Would the insurance company drop her? Hardest of all, he tried not think if he'd be a good father on his own. Whether his daughters would suffer without a mother around. Would he, just being who he was, somehow ruin them? But all these problems would be, they would always be in the shadows, and every person has their shadows. He'd keep his job and with his daughters back he had a home again and a purpose. His life wasn't a nightmare anymore. He was free. His mind finally stopped racing and he grew tired. He could hear Kathleen softly snoring in the backseat and he closed his eyes.

At eight am a car pulled into the lot and a middle-aged woman and a small dog got out.

Virginia opened her eyes and said, "Is someone here?"

"Yeah, somebody just drove up," Freddie said and looked down at her head resting on his lap. He gently

267

brushed her hair from her face. "Are you ready to get up?"

"I think so," she said.

The woman saw the Comet and walked over to it, noticing Freddie in the driver's seat. He rolled down the window. "Good morning," he said. "We broke down on the highway and the tow truck dropped us off here last night. There weren't any motel rooms so we slept here." Kathleen sat up and then so did Virginia.

"You poor things," the woman said, looking at the girls. "I'll get the woodstove going and make coffee, so come on in. My husband will be in at nine. He'll love your car. He's a MOPAR man, but he loves all the classics."

"You think you guys will have time to get to it today?"

"Once I tell him you had to sleep in your car, he'll get working on it."

"She has a dog," Kathleen said from the backseat.

"I can't see it," Virginia said excitedly and tried to stand on the seat.

"Her name is Lollipop," the woman said happily. "She'll be excited to meet you girls."

"Thank you," Freddie said to the woman. He opened the car door and he and his daughters got out.

27

Pauline was seated at her desk in the middle school nurse's office. In the back were three green cots, and a twelve-year-old boy lay sleeping in the middle one recovering from an epileptic seizure. The lunch bell rang, but the boy didn't stir. Minutes later an eleven-year-old girl walked into the room. She was small and frail and wore a red eye patch over the empty cavity that was supposed to hold her right eye. She set her book bag down on the floor and opened it. She took a paper sack from it and went to Pauline, and sat down in the chair next to the desk.

"Hi, Colleen," Pauline whispered and pointed to the sleeping boy. "I like that shirt."

"Thanks," she whispered back.

"What did she make for you today?"

"Looks like hummus and tomato and red pepper and lettuce."

"Your mom sure knows how to make a sandwich."

"I also have carrot sticks and she made chocolate chip cookies. She put four extra in for you."

"Maybe I'll have just one. I'm on a diet."

"For how long are you on a diet?"

"Depends," Pauline said.

"You were on a diet last month."

"I know."

"You're not fat."

"You don't think so?"

"No."

"Then maybe I'll have two."

The girl reached into her bag and took out the cookies and set them on the desk.

The door opened and a young, black-haired boy with cerebral palsy walked in. He wore braces on both legs and walked with a metal cane. He was thirteen but looked much younger. He set his book bag down, opened it, and took out a paper sack. He went to the desk and sat in the other chair facing the nurse.

Pauline pointed to the sleeping boy and put her finger in front of her mouth.

"I brought lettuce for Donna," he whispered.

"Thanks, Gene," Pauline whispered.

"Can I feed her?"

"Of course you can. You don't have to ask. You feed her everyday. Let's just say it's your job."

"I'm going to eat first. Is that okay?" the boy said.

Pauline nodded and took a cookie from the plastic baggie.

"My mom made you a sandwich," Colleen said to Gene and handed it to him.

"Then do you want my peanut butter and jam?" Gene said to Pauline.

"What kind of jam?"

"Apricot."

"That's my favorite," she said. She straightened her paperwork, put it on top of the computer, and took the sandwich. The three of them ate, and when the boy finished he took the rabbit from her cage. He put her on his lap and fed her lettuce and carrot sticks until the lunch bell rang again.

"I'm afraid it's time for you guys to get back to it."

"Okay," the boy said and put the rabbit back in its cage.

"Tomorrow's Friday. I'm going to get us a pizza tomorrow," Pauline said.

"Really?" Colleen asked.

"It's a three-day weekend coming up and I'll miss you guys," she said. "So remember to tell your parents you won't need a lunch tomorrow. Colleen, make sure to tell your mom I'll get vegetarian on half of it. Now hurry up or you'll be late."

"Okay," they both said and left the room. Pauline ate the last cookie, checked on the sleeping boy, and went back to her paperwork.

*

On Sunday morning the Safeway parking lot was nearly empty. Pauline pushed her cart through the aisles, picked out what she needed, and headed toward checkout. Only one checker was working and it was Leroy's mother, Darla. She stood reading a magazine behind the register. She put it down when she saw she had a customer, and when she saw who it was, she smiled and said hello.

"How are you doing?" Pauline said and began putting cans of soup on the belt.

"I'm fine," Darla said. "I haven't seen you in a long time."

"I work days now. Monday through Friday. I usually shop on my way home from work."

"I always hated working nights. I bet you're glad you're off that."

"I am," Pauline said and finished emptying the cart. She stood across from her. "You know something, Darla? You look great. You cut your hair, didn't you?"

"You think it looks okay?"

"It looks amazing."

"I even started painting my nails." She put her hands out showing glossy red fingernails.

"And you've gained a little weight, too, haven't you?"

"You think it's alright?"

"It really looks good on you," Pauline said.

"How are things at the hospital?"

"I left. I'm a school nurse now."

"Is that good or bad?"

"It's good. I've been trying for years to get the job and finally I got it. It's a lucky break for me. I'm glad to be out of the hospital."

"I don't know how you could have done it every day. But now it's kids every day."

"Yeah," she said and beamed. "But that's good."

"My big news is I have a boyfriend," Darla said and began ringing up the items. "Not that you would care, but I can't believe it. It's ridiculous."

"Maybe that's why you look so happy."

"Stupid, huh? An old lady like me."

"It's great. What's he like?"

"He's one of the managers here. He'd been asking me out for years but I never had it in me. I was always too tired and felt too guilty. It's hard to let yourself have a good time when someone you love is in pain. He waited a couple months after Leroy died, and then he asked me to a baseball game. I hate sports, but instead of saying no like I always did, I

272

said yes. I don't know why I said it but I did. The next day I went to the mall and bought a hundred dollars' worth of new underwear. I'm fifty-three years old and it's like I'm in high school until I look in the mirror." She laughed and rang up twenty-four cans of chicken noodle soup, a twelve-pack of frozen burritos, and a jumbo-size bottle of chewable multi-vitamins.

"I have two coupons for these," Pauline said and handed them to her.

"Back to chicken noodle," Darla said.

Pauline nodded. "You have a good memory. My dad's stubborn. He won't eat vegetable soup. So now I'm all about vitamins, but the only kind he likes are chewable. We'll see how it goes."

Darla put the groceries in the cart. "It's good to see you, Pauline."

"It's good to see you, too," she said and pushed her cart toward the exit. She loaded her groceries into her trunk and then drove to her father's house.

Acknowledgements

This book couldn't have been written without the help of my gal, Lee, and Amy Baker, Angus Cargill, Cal Morgan, Jane Palfreyman, Jen Pooley, Sally Riley, Anna Stein, and Lesley Thorne. All have been too good to me, and all deserve a brand new Cadillac for their effort. I'd also like to send my gratitude to everyone at Faber & Faber. What luck to have such a great publisher. I would also like to thank Jessica Robertson for sharing her nursing knowledge. If you ever find yourself down and out in a hospital in Portland, Oregon and you get her as your nurse, you're one lucky sick person. Cheers also to Dr. Jason Bell for his medical expertise. Finally, I'd like to thank Chuck Holt for always helping a guy out when he trips up and hits the wall.

Also by WILLY VLAUTIN

ff

THE MOTEL LIFE

Narrated by Frank Flannigan, *The Motel Life* tells the story of how he and his brother Jerry Lee take to the road when bad luck catches up with them. Written with huge compassion, and an eye for the small details in life, it has become one of the most talked-about debuts of recent years.

'Courageous, powerful and wonderfully compassionate, this is a very fine novel.' John Burnside

'That rare beast: a book with the cadence of an old, well-loved song. Sad, haunting and strangely beautiful.' John Connolly

'A future classic.' *Dazed and Confused*

ff

NORTHLINE

At twenty-two, Allison Johnson is a lost young woman in need of a new start. Down among the lowlifes in Las Vegas, clinging to drink and to Jimmy, the abusive boyfriend whose child she is expecting, she has hit rock bottom. So when the opportunity arises to escape, Allison knows she must take it. She reaches Reno with just a few dollars and her ever-present best friend – Paul Newman. And as she struggles to start a better life it is imaginary conversations with the movie star's greatest characters and real acts of kindness from people she barely knows that might just rescue her from the difficult world she has found herself in.

'Resonant and full of compassion.' *Daily Telegraph*

'Exceptional.' *Independent*

'A novel that has the spare, devastating clarity and profund-ity of Raymond Carver.' *Metro*

ff

LEAN ON PETE

Lean on Pete tells the story of fifteen-year-old Charley Thompson, a kid who yearns for stability as his single-parent father moves them from job to job across the Pacific Northwest. Desperation brings Charley to a run-down horse track where he gets work of his own as a groom to a bitter, ageing trainer. It's there that he finds kinship with the horse Lean on Pete, and ultimately sets off on a journey to try and save them both. In prose marked by a haunting kindness, Willy Vlautin paints an extraordinary picture of life on the margins of contemporary American society.

'How good is contemporary U.S. fiction? This good; catch-your-breath good.' Eileen Battersby, *Irish Times*

'This guy is a real discovery.' Colm Tóibín, *Daily Telegraph*

'Brilliant. I hated finishing it.' Roddy Doyle, *Guardian* Books of the Year